Dead Weight

I heard a voice cry out from somewhere over near the stage where Levi, Danny, and two other men had a brightly painted wooden coffin with the word *Summer* written on it in large yellow letters up on their shoulders.

"It's heavy!" Danny called out. He was shorter than Levi and not nearly as broad, and even as I watched, he lost his grip. Since I'm even shorter than Danny, I wasn't at all sure what I thought I was going to do, but I darted forward to lend a hand.

"The stupid thing's just made of plywood!" one of the other men cried out, trying to adjust his stance when his feet slid. "There's no way it should be this heavy." He stepped forward, shifting his weight, then stepped back again just as I arrived on the scene, my hands out.

"Better not," Levi called and, with a look, urged me to keep my distance. "We're off balance. We're going to—"

The coffin slipped off Danny's shoulder, and after that, it was impossible for the others to hold on.

It hit the ground with more of a thump than plywood should make, and when one side of the coffin broke away and fell to the ground, it was easy to see why.

"Holy Toledo!" Like the rest of us, Danny saw the arm that flopped out of the casket, but unlike the rest of us, he apparently didn't watch the police shows on TV and remember that things like bodies in fake coffins should be left undisturbed. He darted forward and flipped open the lid.

Noreen Turner looked up at us, dressed in her camouflage, eyes wide open, the left side of her skull smashed in.

It didn't take a ghost getter to see that she was very, very dead . . .

The Legend of Sleepy Harlow

Kylie Logan

BERKLEY PRIME CRIME, NEW YORK

THE BERKLEY PUBLISHING GROUP
Published by the Penguin Group
Penguin Group (USA) LLC
375 Hudson Street, New York, New York 10014

USA • Canada • UK • Ireland • Australia • New Zealand • India • South Africa • China

penguin.com

A Penguin Random House Company

THE LEGEND OF SLEEPY HARLOW

A Berkley Prime Crime Book / published by arrangement with the author

For information, address: The Berkley Publishing Group,
a division of Penguin Group (USA) LLC,
375 Hudson Street, New York, New York 10014.

ISBN: 978-0-425-25777-7

PUBLISHING HISTORY
Berkley Prime Crime mass-market edition / October 2014

PRINTED IN THE UNITED STATES OF AMERICA

10 9 8 7 6 5 4 3 2 1

Cover art by Dan Craig.
Cover design by George Long.

For Oscar, who couldn't care less,
and Ernie, who couldn't care more.

ACKNOWLEDGMENTS

Anybody who knows me knows that Halloween is my favorite day of the year. I love the swirling mixtures of orange and black and purple. I love the idea of dressing up in costumes and decorating the house with everything from lights that look like pumpkins to my purple Halloween tree complete with spooky ornaments. Even the chill in the air doesn't bother me on Halloween, though it certainly will by the next day when I realize that the fine weather is over and winter is close at hand.

Writing about Halloween has made creating *The Legend of Sleepy Harlow* extra special. Like all books, it's been a mixture of inspiration and perspiration, flights of imaginative fancy and what seemed like days and days of careful, plodding writing. As always, there are people to thank, including Sisters in Crime and all the special Sisters (and the Mister) I was lucky enough to spend time with in Charlotte; great writer and friend Shelley Costa, who helped me talk my way through any number of plot problems; email buddies Emilie Richards and Maureen Child, who all too often have to read about what's happening in a book but are always willing to brainstorm; the great folks at Berkley Prime Crime; my agent; and, of course, my family.

❮❮ 1 ❯❯

I wish I could say that the worst thing that happened that fall was Jerry Garcia peeing on Marianne Littlejohn's manuscript.

Jerry Garcia? He's the cat next door, the one whose bathroom habits have always been questionable and whose attention is perpetually trained on the potted flowers on my front porch.

Until that afternoon, that is.

That day, Jerry bypassed the flowers and went straight for the wicker couch on the porch, the one where, until the phone rang inside the B and B, I'd been reading Marianne's manuscript because she wanted one more set of eyes to take a look before she sent it off to a small academic press that specializes in local history. Yeah, that was the couch where I'd left the pages neatly stacked and—this is vital to the telling of the story—completely dry and odor-free.

Jerry, see, had motive, means, and opportunity.

Jerry had mayhem in his kitty cat heart, and at the risk of sounding just the teeniest bit paranoid, I was pretty sure Jerry had it out for me, too.

It was the perfect storm of circumstance and timing, and the results were so predictable, I shouldn't have walked back out onto the porch, taken one look at the puddle quickly soaking through Marianne's tidy manuscript pages, and stood, pikestaffed, with my mouth hanging open.

Jerry, it should be pointed out, could not have cared less. In fact, I think he enjoyed watching my jaw flap in the breeze that blew from Lake Erie across the street. But then, Jerry's that kind of cat. He leapt onto the porch railing, paused to give one paw a lick, and looked over his shoulder at me with what I would call disdain if I weren't convinced it was more devious than that.

A second later, he bounded into the yard and disappeared, leaving me to watch in horror as the liquid disaster spread. From the manuscript to the purple and turquoise floral print cushions. From the cushions to the wicker couch. From the couch to the porch floor.

Oh yes, at the time, it did seem like the worst of all possible disasters.

But then, that was my first October on South Bass Island and I had yet to hear about the legend.

Or the ghost.

And there was no way I could have imagined the murder.

"Visit from Jerry?"

I didn't realize Luella Zak had walked up the steps and onto the porch until I heard her behind me. I shrieked and spun around just in time to see her eye the smelly disaster.

"I was only gone two minutes," I wailed. "I swear. It was only two minutes."

"And Jerry managed to stop by." Luella is captain of a fishing charter service that works out of Put-in-Bay, the one and only town on South Bass Island. She's short, wiry, and as crusty an old thing (don't tell her I said that about the old) as any sailor who plied any of the Great Lakes, but when she stepped nearer to have a look at the mess, she wrinkled her nose.

"I hope those papers were nothing you planned on keeping," Luella said.

The reality of the situation dawned with all the subtlety of a dump truck bumpety-bumping over railroad tracks, and I shook out of my daze and darted to the couch. Before I even thought about what it would do to my green sweatshirt and my jeans, I scooped up the pile of yellow-stained pages and shook them out.

"It's Marianne's manuscript," I groaned. "Marianne asked me to look for typos and—"

Luella didn't say a word. In fact, she ducked into the house, and a minute later, she was back with a garbage bag in hand.

"We can't." Cat pee dripped off my hands and rained onto my sneakers, but still, I refused to relinquish the soggy manuscript. "We can't throw it away. I promised Marianne—"

Careful to keep it from dripping on her Carhartt bib overalls, Luella snatched the bundle away from me and deposited it in the bag. "Marianne can reprint it."

"But if I tell her to do that, I'll have to explain—"

"So what, you're going to take this back to her?" Luella hefted the garbage bag. "And you think she won't notice the stains? Or the smell?"

My shoulders drooped. "I think I need to find a way to tell her I'm really, really sorry."

"I think . . ." Luella thought about clapping a hand to my shoulder and I could tell when she changed her mind because she made a face and backed away. But then, I was standing downwind. "I hate to tell you this, Bea, but I think that you smell really bad."

I didn't doubt it for a minute, but really, there were more important things to consider. "Poor Marianne. All that work and all that paper and now she'll need do it all over again. Printing out an entire book takes a lot of time."

"Marianne wrote a book?" The instant I looked her way, Luella was contrite. "Oh, it's not like I'm doubting how smart she is or anything. She's a good librarian. But Marianne doesn't exactly strike me as the type who'd have enough imagination to write a book."

"It's history. Island history. I didn't get more than a couple pages into it, but I know it's about some old-timer, Charles Harlow."

"Sleepy!" Luella laughed. "Well, that explains it. Word is that Marianne's family is distantly related. I'd bet a dime to a donut she devotes at least one chapter to trying to disprove that. Sleepy has quite a reputation around here, and it's not exactly politically correct for the wife of the town magistrate to be related to an old-time gangster and bootlegger."

"I dunno." My shoulders rose and fell. "I mean about the gangster part. I never got that far. I'd just started reading and then the phone rang and then—"

"Jerry." Luella shook her head. "Chandra really needs to do something about that cat."

"I've been saying that for nearly a year."

"We'll talk to Chandra," Luella promised. "Next Monday at book discussion group. And as far as Marianne, maybe if you just explain what Jerry did—"

I dreaded the thought. "She's so proud of her book. You should have seen her when she brought the manuscript over here. She was just about bursting at the seams." My stomach swooped. "She asked for one little favor and I messed up."

"Not the end of the world. She'll reprint, you'll reread—"

"Inside the house."

"Inside the house. And then—"

And then three black SUVs slowed in front of the house and, one by one, turned into my driveway.

"You've got guests coming in today?" Luella asked.

I did, a full house, and what with the manuscript disaster and fantasizing about the ingenious (and completely untraceable) demise of a certain feline neighbor, I'd forgotten all about them.

"Go!" Luella shooed me into the house. "You go change. And a quick shower wouldn't hurt, either. I'll let your guests in and get them settled and tell them you'll be with them pronto."

OK, so it wasn't exactly pronto, but I did manage what I hoped was a less smelly transformation in record time. When I was done, curly, dark hair damp and in a clean pair of jeans and a yellow long-sleeved top (dang, I didn't even make the Jerry Garcia and yellow connection until it was too late!), I lifted my chin, pasted a smile on my face, and strode into my parlor.

Straight into what looked like the staging for D-day.

Two women, two guys. Another . . . I glanced out the window and counted the men on my front porch. Another four out there. Each one of them carried at least two duffel bags or a suitcase or a camera of some sort, and each one of those was plastered with bumper sticker–variety labels. Black, emblazoned with icy blue letters: *EGG*.

"Welcome!" I tried for my best innkeeper smile and thanked whatever lucky stars had made it possible for Luella to take a few moments and swab down the front porch; through the window, I saw that the floral cushions were missing from the couch, and the water she'd splashed on the porch floor gleamed in the autumn afternoon sunshine. "I'm Bea, your hostess. You must be—"

"EGG." The woman closest to where I stood in the doorway was at least a half dozen years older than my thirty-five, and taller than me by six inches. She was square-jawed, dark-haired, pear-shaped, and more than equipped for whatever situation might present itself. The pockets of her camouflage pants bulged, and the vest she wore over a black EGG T-shirt was one of those that fishermen sometimes sport. It had a dozen little pockets, and I saw batteries, flash drives, and other assorted gear peeking out of each one.

"Noreen Turner. I'm lead investigator for EGG, the Elkhart Ghost Getters." When Noreen pumped my hand, it felt as if my fingers had been gripped by a vise. Her dark gaze stayed steady on mine in a firm—and sort of disquieting—way. "I'm the leader of this jolly little band, and—" She must have had first-class peripheral vision, because though I hadn't even noticed the activity going on over in the direction of the fireplace, Noreen didn't miss a thing.

She whirled toward a young, redheaded woman, and a muscle jumped at the base of her jaw.

"Thermal camera, full spectrum camera, Mel meter, IR light." Noreen's laser gaze flashed from the redhead to the cases of equipment she was busy stacking. "Really, Fiona? Really?"

Fiona's cheeks shot through with color. She chewed her lower lip. "I thought—"

"Exactly your problem." Noreen marched over, unstacked the equipment, and, fists on hips, gave it all a careful look. "Thermal camera on the bottom," she said, setting that case down on the floor first. "Then the Mel meter on top of that." The case with the thermal camera in it was larger than the one that contained the Mel meter, and she set the second case on top of the first, adjusting and readjusting so that the second case was exactly in the center. "Then full spectrum, then IR light." She positioned those cases until they were just right, too, and, finished, she turned her full attention on Fiona, who held her breath and looked as if she was about to burst into tears. "You see what I'm getting at here, don't you?"

Fiona didn't answer fast enough, and Noreen lifted her chin and took a step toward her. "Don't you? Top to bottom, kid. Top to bottom. IR on top, then full spectrum, then Mel, then—"

The oldest of the men in the room (I'd learn later that his name was Rick) was maybe fifty, a reed-thin guy with a receding hairline and a gold stud in his right earlobe. He stood closest to Fiona and he leaned in like he wanted to share a confidence, but since he didn't lower his voice, whatever he had to say wasn't much of a secret. "She wants it alphabetical," he rasped. "She always has to have equipment stacked alphabetically."

"So it's easy to find what we need," Noreen snapped.

"Whatever." The man waved a hand and turned his back on us to look out the window.

"Well, it makes sense. And it's the right way to do things. You can see that, can't you?" She swiveled her gaze to me. "You're a businesswoman. You can see the sense of it."

Fortunately, I didn't have a chance to answer. One of the men who'd been on the front porch came into the house pushing a two-wheeler with a big rectangular box on it. He parked the two-wheeler in the hallway before he joined us in the parlor. The man was about my age, with black, wavy hair and the kind of face generally reserved for statues of Greek gods. Dimpled chin, straight nose, high cheekbones. A picture flashed through my mind: Mediterranean island, whitewashed cottage, aquamarine water. A loaf of bread, a jug of wine, and—

"I didn't ask you to bring that in."

Noreen's growl yanked me back to reality, and I found her glaring at Mr. Greek God. "We're not ready for it," she said, and pointed toward the box, which was maybe three feet high and another couple feet wide. Like the rest of the gear, it was plastered with EGG stickers. "I told you to leave it in the truck, Dimitri. That means . . . well, duh, I dunno. I guess it means you should have left it in the truck."

"You said you wanted it in your room with you," the man sucked in a breath and shot back. "And that means—"

"What it means is that you're not listening. When I'm ready for it, that's when I'll tell you to bring it in."

"In like, what, ten minutes?" Dimitri ran a hand through his mane of glorious hair. "I'll tell you what, Noreen, you want it back in the truck, you take it back to the truck. I'm not moving it another inch. Not now, not ten minutes from now. I'm not stacking anything alphabetically, either, or measuring stuff to make sure it's precisely two inches apart. You want to waste your time with your crazy organizing—"

"It's not a waste of time, it's a system." Noreen held her arms close to her sides, her fingers curled into fists. "And so far, it's worked pretty well, hasn't it? If it wasn't for me—"

Was that a collective groan I heard?

From everyone but Fiona, who was so ashen I had no doubt she wanted to fade into the woodwork.

And Noreen, of course. With a look, Noreen dared them all to say another word.

We'd been introduced like three minutes earlier and already I knew Noreen wasn't the type of person who backed down from anyone. Or anything.

Fine by me. I wasn't, either.

And it was about time I proved it.

"I've got all your rooms set and your room keys ready," I said, deftly sidestepping their bickering. I darted into the hallway and grabbed the keys I'd left on a table at the bottom of the stairs. "Each one's marked," I said, handing them around. "All the rooms are on the second floor."

I'd received room instructions along with the group's reservations and I knew that the only two guys bunking together were Ben and Eddie. Since I had six guest rooms, that meant Noreen and Dimitri each had their own room as well as the other three men, who, according to their reservations forms, were Liam McCarthy, David Ashton, and Rick Hopkins.

"I know. That leaves me with no room." Fiona Blake watched as the others stacked their equipment cases (alphabetically, I presumed) and headed upstairs. She scraped her palms against her jeans. "Noreen"—her gaze darted across the room to where Noreen was doing another once-over of the equipment and checking off a list on a clipboard— "Noreen told me I wouldn't be staying here. That there aren't enough rooms. You don't have to apologize."

"I wasn't going to." I softened the statement with a smile and would have gotten one back if Fiona's gaze didn't shoot Noreen's way again.

"It's not like I didn't know you were coming," I told the

kid. "Ms. Turner told me you'd need a room. I've got everything arranged."

Fiona squinched up her nose in a way that told me that whatever I was going to say, she had heard it all before. "I know, some little no-tell motel on the other side of the island. That's fine, really. I'm used to it. It's not always possible for me to stay with the rest of the crew. I get it." Her gaze landed on Noreen, who was so busy restacking the equipment the others had just stacked, she didn't notice. "I just joined the group and I'm only the intern and I don't rate the same perks the rest of the crew gets."

"Which doesn't mean you shouldn't be comfortable." I waved a hand, directing Fiona to look out the window. "That's why I was able to arrange a room for you next door, at my friend Chandra's house."

"Right next door?" Some of the stiffness went out of Fiona's shoulders.

"And you'll be joining us here every morning," I told Fiona, loud enough to make sure Noreen heard. After all, Noreen had made the original reservations and agreed (begrudgingly, as I remember) to pay an extra small charge for Fiona's breakfasts. "Breakfast is every morning at nine, and we've got coffee and tea available all day, too, and cookies in the afternoon. Anything you want, just stop in."

Fiona would never be described as pretty, but when she smiled, she was cute. She was taller than me (most people are) and in her early twenties, a gangly kid with wide blue eyes that were set a little too close together and a sprinkling of freckles on her nose that made her look as if she'd been dusted with cinnamon sugar. Her hair was a wonderful dark mahogany color that I suspected wasn't natural, and she wore it pulled back in a ponytail. Like the rest of the crew, she was dressed casually in jeans and an EGG

T-shirt, but she'd added a filmy pea green scarf that gave a pop of color to her outfit and perfectly framed the unusual necklace she wore: a white stone about the size of a walnut that was crisscrossed with black veins. The stone was wrapped with a spider web mesh of silver wire, and the whole thing dangled from a black leather loop that hung around Fiona's neck.

"Is that howlite?" I asked her.

Automatically, Fiona's hand went to the stone. "You recognize it? Most people have never heard of howlite." Again, she slid a look to Noreen, who was now counting the equipment and acted like we didn't exist. Fiona's hand fluttered back down to her side. "It's just something I like to wear."

"Well, it's very nice. I've seen similar stones used in Native American jewelry. Is it from the Southwest?"

I don't think I imagined it; Fiona really did look Noreen's way again.

And I couldn't help but think that like my ol' buddy Jerry Garcia, Noreen really couldn't care less.

Fiona's smile withered around the edges. "The necklace is from New Mexico. Can we stop at the truck on our way next door?" she asked, effectively changing the subject. "I'll get my suitcase."

Together, we walked out to the front porch. I was quickly finding out that October on South Bass is a feast for the senses—and I was enjoying every minute of it. The wineries were in full production, and farmers sold cider and pumpkins from roadside stands. Goldenrod danced in the lake breeze, and the lake itself, as smooth as glass that afternoon, reflected the kaleidoscope mood swings of the sky: gray one day, sapphire the next, and when the clouds were low and the winds calm, ghostly white.

In wonderful counterpoint to it all, the trees between my house and Chandra's were a riot of rich color: golden elms, rusty oaks, and fiery red maples, all of their glory like an exclamation mark to Chandra's purple house with its yellow windows, orange doors, and teal garage.

Though I hardly knew her at all, something told me Fiona appreciated all of that as much as I did. Once I ushered her down the steps and she retrieved her suitcase from the truck, we closed in on Chandra's and she caught sight of the windchimes and the sun catchers, the gnomes that filled Chandra's garden, and the gigantic pumpkin near the front door carved with wide, round eyes and a huge grin. Her smile came back full force.

"Cool!" Pink shot through Fiona's cheeks. "Not that I don't like your place. It's a great house, but . . ." she stammered, looking back at my B and B. Believe me, I did not take offense. I know hulking Victorians aren't everyone's cup of tea, but this one was my pride and joy, from the teal color accented with rose, terra cotta, and purple to the distinctive chimney that caressed the outside of the house all the way from the first floor to the slate roof. I'd lived there less than a year and my business had been up and running for just one season, but already the house and the island felt like home. After a hectic life in New York and a past I was anxious to put behind me, a home was exactly what I was looking for.

I laughed. "No worries. There's a lot to like about Chandra's, and I figured being close by was better than you staying all the way downtown at the hotel." I didn't bother to explain that, technically, *all the way downtown* was less than a mile. "Chandra's so excited to have a guest. She's . . ." I wondered how to explain and decided it was best just to lay things on the line. Fiona would know all about Chandra soon enough—Chandra would make sure of that—so she might as well get the truth from me.

"Chandra's our resident island-crystal-and-tarot-card reader," I warned Fiona. "If you have any problem—"

The kid actually skipped across the next few feet of lawn. "This is going to be so much fun! I read tarot, too. And I meditate every evening. I have for years. It sounds like Chandra and I will have a lot in common."

I didn't doubt it, especially when Chandra's front door flew open and a plume of patchouli incense streamed outside. It was quickly followed by Chandra, resplendent (as always) that day in an orange turban that hid her bobbed blond hair and showed her earrings—witch hats studded with purple beads—to best advantage. The earrings looked just right with her diaphanous purple top, which was painted with orange jack-o'-lanterns and cute black cats.

Chandra took one look at Fiona—and that T-shirt she wore with the icy EGG logo—and her welcoming smile vanished in a flash.

"EGG? Bea, you didn't tell me EGG was here again."

I wasn't sure who was suddenly more pale, Chandra or Fiona.

The kid backstepped away from the house. "I . . . I can stay s-somewhere else. I don't want to . . . want to inconvenience you . . . or . . . or anything . . . or . . ."

Feeling a bit as if the sidewalk had been pulled out from under me, I put a hand on the kid's shoulder to keep her from bolting. "EGG's been to South Bass before?" I asked Chandra.

Chandra is nothing if not the friendliest and the most accepting of all the people I'd met on the island. With a start, she realized she'd made Fiona uncomfortable, and she smiled. Or at least she tried.

"I don't remember you from last year." Chandra stuck out a hand and, as if she wasn't sure what was going to happen when she took it, Fiona stepped forward for a quick shake. "Sorry! I was just surprised to see your shirt. That's all. Bea, you didn't tell me EGG was back."

I hoped my laugh didn't sound as phony as it felt. "I didn't know this was a return visit. Besides, EGG might have been here, but Fiona never has. She's new with EGG." Did the look I gave Chandra send the right message? That we had to make sure Fiona felt welcome and at home?

"Sorry." Chandra's weak little laugh was an echo of my own. "I just . . . oh, never mind!" She backed up a step to allow Fiona to walk into the house. "Come on in and we'll make a pot of white tea. How does that sound? It's nice and mild and fruity and—"

"I love white tea!" Fiona turned misty eyes toward me. "Thank you, Bea. I think I'm going to like it here. And sorry . . ." She turned that puppy dog look on Chandra. "I'm sorry I surprised you."

Peace.

I was grateful for it, even if I was a little confused by Chandra's reaction to her guest.

I promised myself I'd have a talk with Chandra, told them both I'd see them later, and headed back home, only to find Noreen rearranging the equipment. Again.

I poked my head into the parlor. "Need anything?"

"No, we're all set. At least for now." Noreen set down her clipboard, picked it up, swiped a hand over the top of the case where she'd just deposited it, and set it down again. "We're anxious to get started, of course."

"You never told me"—I looked around at the equipment cases and cameras—"you've been here before. What exactly are you doing back here on the island?" I asked Noreen.

She barked out a laugh. "Elkhart Ghost Getters?" She looked at me hard. "You've never heard of us? Well, it doesn't matter," she decided even before I could tell her she was right. "We're paranormal investigators."

It all made sense now, the thermal cameras and the Mel meters and such. Though I was not a fan of reality TV shows of any kind, I didn't live under a rock. I knew cable television was fat with shows that followed the adventures of crews who were out to prove—or disprove—the existence of things that go bump in the night.

"You're filming a TV show." It never hurts to state the obvious.

Noreen nodded. "Not just a show. The first episode of our new series."

"And you're doing it here on South Bass?" I realized my mistake immediately and, with a quick smile, apologized for the skepticism in my voice. "It's not that I don't think it's great, but South Bass? I never associated South Bass with—"

"Never saw our pilot episode we filmed here last fall, did you?" Noreen wasn't just happy to show how completely out of it I was; she was downright smug. She crossed the room, flipped open one of the equipment cases, and pulled out an iPad. A few taps of the keys and she flipped the screen around so I could see it.

Except for the glow of what looked like a gigantic camping lantern on the floor in the center of the scene, the video was dark and grainy, a mishmash of gray and black shadows, and I bent nearer, the better to focus.

"You?" I asked, looking up briefly from the shot of the woman standing just outside the eerie beam of light. "You're standing behind what looks like—"

"Wine barrels."

"And this was taken here on South Bass?" It wasn't really a surprise; there are any number of wineries on the island. "What am I supposed to be watching for?"

"You'll know it when you see it," Noreen assured me.

She was right. Fifteen seconds in, there was a movement to Noreen's left that reminded me of the wave of heat that comes off a candle. It rippled and shifted, and the shadows darkened for a moment. That giant lanternlike object in front of Noreen flashed, and a second later—

"You're kidding me, right?"

I stared at the screen for a couple seconds, then stood up straight and fastened the same sort of sucker-punched look on Noreen. "You're kidding me, right?"

"Want to see it again?" Before I could tell her I did, she restarted the video, and this time, just like last time, I saw what I thought it was impossible to see.

In those couple seconds after the light flashed, a figure materialized out of nowhere.

It was a man. I could tell that much from the cut of his clothes. He was tall and completely transparent and he was missing—

I swallowed hard. "Where's his head?"

Noreen clicked out of the video. "No head."

"And he's a—"

"He is the best video evidence of a full-body apparition anybody anywhere has ever recorded."

"And you—"

"Filmed it last fall. Right here on South Bass. This is the video we showed at a paranormal investigation conference last fall, and let me tell you"—Noreen's eyes took on a dreamy look that told me she savored every moment of the memory—"that made the other investigators in our

field stand up and take notice. Got the cable networks
to finally come to their senses, too. I'd been sending them
film of our investigations for years, and it showed some
good evidence, too. But TV producers, they aren't interested in what's good. They only want what's fantastic.
This." She tapped the iPad. "This is fantastic. This is what
got us our show."

"Because it's—"

"Like I said, the best video evidence of a full-body
apparition anybody anywhere has ever recorded."

In an effort to clear it, I shook my head. "A ghost here
on South Bass?"

Noreen tossed her head. "Not into island legends, are
you? It's why we came out to the middle of nowhere last
year in the first place. You know, because of the legend."

"Of the headless ghost."

She slapped my back so hard, I nearly toppled. "You got
that right, girlfriend. And that's exactly why we came back
this year. You know, to get more evidence. We're headed
out to find the ghost of Sleepy Harlow."

❖ 2 ❖

"I'm not sure how many other ways I can say it. No means no. It means absolutely, positively not. No, no, no!"

I'd been going over utility bills, tax statements, and the accounting ledger for Bea & Bees in my private suite, and the sound of the voice in the hallway just outside my door snapped me out of the foggy, groggy daze I'd fallen into. (It was, after all, boring paperwork.)

My head snapped up and I bent an ear to try and hear more, but the only thing I got for my effort was the sound of another voice, lower-pitched than the first, quieter and so undecipherable.

"You're kidding, right?" That was the first voice again. Blame it on the haze of numbers that clogged my brain, but it took me a couple seconds to realize it sounded familiar and another couple seconds after that to place it.

"Kate?" I popped out of my chair and went out into the hallway, where I found one of my fellow members of the League of Literary Ladies, Kate Wilder, at the bottom of the stairs, fists propped on either side of the stylish brown and gold tweed pencil skirt she wore with a matching jacket. Kate's cheeks were the same color as her flaming hair, and her eyes shot green fire across the hallway toward the spot where none other than Noreen Turner looked just as miffed.

Chin out, jaw stiff, eyes narrowed, Noreen barely spared me a glance.

But then, the full force of her fury was trained on Kate.

"You don't mean it," Noreen growled. "You can't possibly mean it. We made you famous."

"You made me angry. Then, and now." In one movement as graceful as a dancer's, Kate turned on her stylish pumps and yanked open the door. "I'll talk to you later, Bea," she called back to me, right before she stepped outside and slammed the door closed.

"She can't . . . She wouldn't . . . You can't let her . . ."

I turned away from Kate's dramatic exit just in time to see Noreen's jaw pump like a piston. The vibration of the banging door still echoed from the high ceiling when she looked my way. "You have to help me," she said.

"Help you . . . ?"

"Talk some sense into that crazy lady, for one thing!" Noreen scraped a hand through her short-cropped hair. "She's a hothead! A prima donna! She's—"

"She's my friend."

A smarter person would have taken the warning for what it was worth and been very careful about what she said next. Oh, it wasn't like Noreen was wrong. Kate was high maintenance, all right. But it was one thing for her friends to point that out (and believe me, we did, frequently—and just as frequently, Kate ignored us). It was another altogether to hear that kind of criticism from a stranger to the island who was also a guest in my home. Noreen, her eyes lit with a fervor that was even more disconcerting than her anger, closed in on me.

"She's a friend of yours? Then it's perfect," she said, and even though she stood three feet away, I couldn't help but notice that she vibrated with excitement. "You can talk to Ms. Wilder. You can convince her. You can talk some sense into her."

It wasn't fair to laugh, but then, it was the most ridiculous thing I'd heard in as long as I could remember. "You don't know Kate well, do you?"

"I do know her. We met last year when EGG was here. Wilder Winery, that's where we shot the video."

"Of the ghost?" I just about kicked myself the moment the words were out of my mouth. Sure, that video Noreen had shown me earlier in the day was startling, but it was also . . .

I searched for the right word and came up with more than just one.

Peculiar.

Suspicious.

Unbelievable.

Improbable.

Unlikely.

I may have seen the transparent shape without a head, but there was no way this girl was ready to believe it was what it looked like it was. Not without a huge helping of proof that amounted to more than a quick glimpse obscured by a swirl of shadows and the flash of that bright pulsing lantern on the floor in front of Noreen.

I shook my head, the better to send the message that I'd misspoken. "The video you showed me earlier," I said, firmly refusing to use the G-word again. "That was taken at Wilder Winery?"

"If you watched our pilot . . . !" Noreen swallowed the rest of what I was sure was going to be a scathing criticism of my TV-watching habits. Good thing. She was already walking on thin ice, what with taking over my parlor with her alphabetically arranged equipment, then with insulting my friend. Maybe she knew it, because she clutched her hands at her waist and bit her lower lip.

Contrite?

Maybe.

Or maybe Noreen was just cagey enough to see an opportunity and didn't want to let it pass.

"If Ms. Wilder's your friend, you could talk to her on my behalf," she said.

"Talk to her about . . . ?"

Noreen's sigh was so deep, all those flash drives in all those pockets of her fishing vest rattled. "We're here to gather more evidence. To see if we can capture another video of the apparition. You know, Sleepy Harlow."

I refused to groan, but let's face it, had I been so inclined, no one could have blamed me. First I find out the island is supposedly haunted by the ghost of a Prohibition-era bootlegger, then I discover it's the same Prohibition-era bootlegger that Marianne Littlejohn's book is about? It was only natural that from there, my thoughts would scamper to the phone call I'd been putting off, the one I had to make to Marianne to deliver the news about the manuscript that was spoiled, soiled, and soggy.

This time, I did groan. "You shot that video at Wilder Winery." I didn't ask Noreen the question because I had no doubt it was true. "And you came back to the island to film there again."

The smile I got from Noreen told me that maybe I wasn't as completely dense as she'd thought. "Exactly. We're here. We're all set to film. And now she says—"

"Why?"

As if I'd slapped her rather than just asked a question, Noreen flinched.

I pressed my advantage. "Why?" I asked again. "I heard what she said. Why did Kate tell you not to come back to the winery?"

Her shrug wasn't exactly convincing. "Like I said, she's crazy. You'd think after we put that tacky little winery on the map—"

"Their really good wine already did that. Long before you showed up here last year."

"Sure. Yeah. Of course." When she flashed me a quick smile, Noreen's teeth showed. "Good wine. I get that. But when a place is a hotbed of paranormal activity, the people who own that place owe it to the public in general and to the scientific community in particular to—"

"You think?" I stepped back and cocked my head, as if I really had to think about it. "You don't suppose that private property is private property and the person who owns that private property has the right to say who comes and goes and what they do there?"

"I would. I do. But we gave the winery plenty of publicity in our pilot, and we've talked it up in the promo spots for the new show, too. We said we'd be filming there. The network's already airing the commercial for our first show. And in it, we talk about returning to the winery."

"But you never actually asked Kate's permission."

"We did." Noreen nodded. "I wrote to her and—"

"She said no."

"I figured there was no way she actually meant it. Not with all the publicity she's going to get. Our show is going to be huge. You'd think she'd understand that. That's what I was going to tell her. That's why I asked her to stop by. You know, so I could explain all that to her and try to get it through that thick skull of hers that there are only a very few spots, really, where the paranormal activity is that powerful. I figured she'd understand."

I glanced at the door Kate had so recently slammed behind her. "She didn't."

"But if you'd just talk to her." Noreen looked out one of the long, narrow windows that flanked the door on either side. "She's just crossing the street. If you hurry, you can still catch her. You can talk to her. If you're her friend, you can convince her, right?"

I was pretty sure I couldn't, but there is something about a woman in camo and a fishing vest that gives a whole new and pitiful meaning to needy and pathetic. I gave in and walked out the door.

"Hey, Kate!" When I called out to her, Kate stopped and turned my way. She'd just crossed the street and was on her way over to her house, which was catty-corner from mine. Kate's backyard is a bluff that overlooks the lake and her front yard is pretty much nonexistent: a streamer of grass that undulates between the road and the single-story cedar-sided house with its deep front porch and low-maintenance and very minimal landscaping.

When I caught up to her, Kate was breathing hard. I knew it had nothing to do with the stroll toward her house and everything to do with the pushy EGG-head who was my guest.

"Sorry," I said, even though she had no idea what I

was about to say. "Noreen Turner asked me to talk to you and—"

The rest of my sentence was lost beneath Kate's aggravated screech. "That woman . . ." She pointed one perfectly manicured finger back toward my house. "The woman is a nutcase. You know that, don't you?"

"I know she's a guest, and I told her I'd try to smooth things over. Except I don't really understand what went wrong. They filmed at the winery last year?"

When Kate nodded, her fiery hair glistened in the late afternoon light. "They showed up here. You know, because of the ghost." Kate studied my blank expression. "You don't know."

"Not about a ghost. Come on, Kate. You don't really believe—"

She waved away my concern. "Of course I don't. But hey, what's a little legend going to hurt? There really was a gangster named Charlie Harlow around here back during Prohibition. And everyone really did call him Sleepy. If you don't believe me, stop at the cemetery and check out his grave. He died on October third, nineteen thirty." She barked out a laugh. "Don't look at me like that. I'm not some sort of Sleepy groupie. Anybody who grew up on the island knows Sleepy's history. He's our local celebrity. You know—Al Capone, South Bass–style."

"But you believe his headless ghost haunts the island?"

"When I was a kid and I'd go to sleepovers at friends' houses, we'd sit up all night and see who could tell the spookiest Sleepy story. Then when we were teenagers . . ." Kate shivered. "Well, you don't have to believe in ghosts to get scared when your friends drag you out to a cemetery in the middle of the night to try and see if they can raise Sleepy from the dead. Looking back on it, it was crazy and fun. But at the time, I'll tell you, it's like the book we're reading for the discussion group, right? *The Legend of Sleepy Hollow*. This story's got Washington Irving beat. Ichabod Crane only had to deal with the headless horseman scaring him as he walked through the woods at night. But our ghost . . . They say a rival gang killed ol' Sleepy and cut off his head." Kate slid a finger across her throat and made a face. "Every year in October, his ghost comes back to the island in search of his head."

"And last October, Noreen says she got a video of the ghost. At your winery."

Kate's lips twisted. "If you believe that sort of hogwash!"

"Last fall, you let them film at the winery."

"I figured it would be good for business. And it's not like I thought they'd find anything. There's no such thing as ghosts. Except . . ."

A cloud scuttled across the sun and, for a moment, we were plunged into cold shadow. A second later, the sun was back, but Kate's mind was still a million miles away.

"Except?" I asked.

She twitched away her misgivings. "It was nothing. Really. It's just that last night I worked late and when I was leaving the winery . . . well, like I said, it was nothing. Maybe a stray cat got in. Or a car went by and threw some crazy light against the wall and that caused the shadows to look weird for a second. I thought I saw . . . something."

Of all the Ladies in the League, Kate is the most practical and the most hardheaded. She is not prone to flights of fancy, and not inclined to believe what she doesn't see, hear, taste, and feel. If asked, I'd have to admit it was one of the reasons Kate was having such a hard time falling as much in love with ferryboat captain Jayce Martin as he was with her. But I hadn't been asked. I stuck to the matter at hand.

"It wasn't a headless ghost, was it?" I asked her.

"It wasn't anything." To put an end to the thought, she turned and headed toward her house, and I walked along at her side. "I just heard a noise and I got spooked, that's all."

"So you've never actually seen this ghost that Noreen says she has video of."

Kate glanced at me out of the corner of her eye. "There are people who say they have. But I'm not one of them."

"So you let EGG come in last year and film. But not this year."

"You got that right, sister. You know, because of what they did." Kate grumbled under her breath. "But of course, you don't know what they did. I keep forgetting you weren't here last fall. It feels like you've lived here forever."

I took it as a compliment. Like in most isolated communities, the folks of South Bass are a close-knit bunch, and though I'd lived there less than a year, I was honored to be considered one of the old-timers.

Unlike my front porch—a riot of wicker furniture, floral cushions, and those flower pots Jerry Garcia found oh-so-irresistible—Kate's porch was as clean and as sparse as an operating room. There was a white Adirondack chair on either side of the front door, and though she motioned me into one, Kate didn't sit down. Her arms crossed over her chest, she paced the length of the porch and back again.

"Last fall when those ghost idiots were here, they filmed at the winery, all right," she said when she got back to where I sat. "And while they were at it, they trampled my entire crop of Lambrusco grapes."

Pretty much the extent of my knowledge about wine is that I enjoy drinking it. Still, even I knew . . .

"Lambrusco grapes are only grown in Italy," I said, looking up at Kate. "In Lombardy. I've been there. I've seen the vineyards. Are you telling me you're growing them here in Ohio?"

"It's just an experiment," she said. Kate hugged her arms around herself and started pacing again, the fingers of her right hand beating out a frantic rhythm against her left arm. "Lombardy is in the north of Italy; our climates are similar. I know other winery owners who thought I was nuts when I mentioned giving it a go, but hey, I figured we'd never know if we didn't try. So I planted a crop."

"And EGG destroyed them."

She froze and stared out at the lake, her rusty brows low over her eyes. "They claim they were so overcome by the excitement of the ghost hunt, they didn't notice the newly planted vines. They cost me a lot of money."

"You've replanted?"

Kate nodded. "And the money I used to buy a new crop of Lambrusco vines was money I'd earmarked for a faster bottling system. So technically, those idiots affected my production capabilities, too. And that means they've messed with my bottom line. They're rude, they're inconsiderate, and that Noreen is the worst of the bunch."

Suddenly, Chandra's reaction to seeing the EGG logo on Fiona's T-shirt made perfect sense. Chandra and Kate might have their differences—how loud Kate plays opera, how Chandra builds bonfires at the full moon—but deep down inside, they were friends, and loyal to a fault.

"Honestly, Bea." Kate's laser look banished my thoughts. "If I knew they were staying at your place, I would have told you to toss them out on their ghostly tushies."

I slapped the arms of my chair and stood. "After what they did, I don't blame you for not wanting them to come back. I'll tell Noreen I talked to you and that you explained what happened, and while I'm at it, I'll tell them that they don't have to keep their reservations for the rest of the week if they want to go back to the mainland."

"The mainland, yeah." Kate's top lip curled. "The rest of them can go back to the mainland. That pushy Noreen, I'd like to see her go somewhere else. Like right to the bottom of Lake Erie."

I couldn't blame her, but rather than encourage Kate's murderous thoughts, I told her I'd see her later in the week at the big party planned for Friday. It was a yearly tradition, I'd learned, a good-natured and boisterous wake—complete with a funeral procession and a coffin painted in garish colors—to mark the passing of summer and the beginning of a few long, quiet months on the island free from all visitors but a few hearty ice fishermen who braved the weather after Christmas. Like everyone else who lived here and the flocks of tourists who'd be arriving for the event, I was looking forward to it.

Honestly, I wasn't surprised when Kate didn't answer. With her gaze still fastened to the lake and her expression thunderous, I was pretty sure she'd forgotten I was even there.

No such luck with Noreen.

She was waiting for me on my front porch when I got back to the house.

"So?" Noreen looked across the street toward Kate's, and I looked that way, too, only to see that Kate had gone into the house. "Did you get her to agree? You did, right? You talked some sense into that uppity little snob. She's going to let us—"

One hand out like a traffic cop, I stopped her before she

could annoy me even more. "Kate's not going to change her mind."

"But you said—"

"I said I'd talk to her. I did. And she told me what happened last fall. She lost an entire crop of grapes because of you."

"Oh, like that was our fault!" Noreen could sneer with the best of them. "Like we were supposed to know that those grapes were there. Those plants were small and it was dark and—"

"And it doesn't matter." I pulled open the front door and stepped into the house. "Once Kate makes up her mind about something, she doesn't change it. And she's made up her mind. There's no way you're going to get near that winery to film."

"Well, that's just great!" Dimitri said, stepping out of the parlor. He had a magazine in his hand, something called *Dead Time,* and one look at Noreen and he flung it back over his shoulder. The magazine skidded across the Oriental rug and landed with a slap against a stack of ghost-hunting equipment. "I've been waiting for you, Noreen. We need to talk."

Noreen clamped her lips shut and marched into the parlor, where she snatched up the magazine, smoothed its pages and set it—precisely—in the center of the coffee table in front of the couch.

"I doubt we have anything much to say to each other."

"Yeah, well . . ." He shot me a look. "Maybe not here. Maybe not now. But we do need to talk. The new issue of *Dead Time*—"

"I have an article in the issue," Noreen cooed, and since Dimitri had apparently already seen it, she added, for my benefit, "It's about the way entities attach themselves to cabinets of curiosities. You know, the collections people used to make of rocks and gems or art or artifacts. They were like mini-museums, and it's a well-known fact, isn't it, Dimitri, that if you find one of those old collections, you'll find evidence of the paranormal?"

I could just about hear Dimitri's teeth grind together. He breathed hard when he growled, "We'll talk about it later."

"Such a sweetie!" I swear, Noreen nearly pinched his cheek. Good thing she stopped herself just in time; I wouldn't have liked to see what would have happened if she took the chance. "I'll handle it," she purred, her voice low. "Just like I handle everything else."

"Yeah, like you handled our chance to get back to the winery?" He backed away from her and grabbed the smart phone that was on top of one of the equipment cases. "While you were wasting your time, Noreen . . ." He coughed. "While you were wasting your time, I was doing some research," he said, and tapped his way through various screens.

"The lighthouse . . ." He flipped the phone around so that both Noreen and I could see the picture on the screen. I'd been to the lighthouse since I'd moved to the island, so I recognized it right away, of course. It was built at a place known as Parker Point on the southwest corner of the island, a two-story brick house with a three-story square light tower attached. The lighthouse hadn't been in service for years and these days, it was used to house the scientists who visited a university aquatic research station that wasn't far away.

Dimitri's dark eyes lit and he gave the phone a little waggle. "There were some weird things that happened when the first lighthouse keeper moved in, and now it's haunted. So is"—he flipped through more pictures—"the hotel over near the park. And this bar." He found that picture and flashed it our way. "There's plenty here for us to investigate," he said, his eyes on Noreen. "We don't need the winery."

Noreen crinkled her nose. "Are you that stupid, Dimitri? Of course we need the winery if we're going to deliver what we promised. And we need the winery"—when she stomped her foot, the Waterford vase on the fireplace mantel protested with a high-pitched ring—"we need the winery because I don't care about the lighthouse or the bar or the hotel. I don't care about anything, not anything except the ghost of Sleepy Harlow."

❖ 3 ❖

I like to think that I am nothing if not true to my word.

That didn't make it any easier for me to talk myself into going to see Marianne Littlejohn the next day.

What I had to tell her, I hoped, would be easier to say in person than it would be on the phone, where the full impact of those infamous words, "peed on by a nasty cat," might not have been conveyed with all the solemnity—or all the contrition—I felt they deserved.

Thus armed with nothing but my good intentions and a box of really expensive chocolates I'd gone all the way over to the mainland to get the evening before, I headed out in the direction of downtown, toward the school that housed our local library. Since it was another warm and glorious fall afternoon, I decided to walk. Talk about symbolism! Yes, I was dragging my feet when it came to seeing Marianne, and I knew it.

I'd gotten exactly as far as Kate's house when I stopped cold. It was that or get flattened by Kate's BMW when she raced out of her driveway.

"Sorry!" She slammed on the brakes and stopped long enough to roll down her window. "I didn't see you."

"Good thing I saw you, or I'd be roadkill!"

She didn't take this personally, which was a good thing, because I didn't, either. Kate was usually a good driver, so in addition to this aberration, what struck me as odd was that it was four in the afternoon.

"Why aren't you working?" I asked her.

"I am working." Kate checked the time on her phone, then tossed the phone down on the front seat next to her. "I'm on my way to the ferry right now. Jayce is holding it for me."

"You don't work on the ferry."

I was going for funny; Kate didn't laugh. She tilted the rearview mirror and checked her lipstick. "I need to get to the mainland. ASAP. I got a call, Bea. From Deidra Mannington, you know, the reporter for *Wine*! It's the hottest new magazine about the business. She's over on the mainland in Vermilion, doing an article about some of the wineries there, and she wants to have dinner at six and talk about Wilder's. She's going to feature us in an upcoming issue. I zipped home to change." She glanced down and I saw that Kate was wearing a black dress with a nipped waist and short sleeves. It was just chichi enough for a special occasion and still businesslike enough that the reporter was bound to take her seriously. "But now I've got to go. I've got to hurry. I don't want to be late."

It really was terrific, and Kate might actually have heard me say so if she didn't burn rubber, race down the street, and disappear in the direction of the ferry dock.

Truth be told, I was glad for this distraction and thrilled that Wilder's—and Kate—was finally getting the recognition it deserved. For too long, Ohio wineries were pooh-poohed by the snooty oenophiles of the world. From what Kate told me, that perception was finally changing, and having Wilder's featured in a prominent magazine was bound to help. Besides, thinking about Kate's good fortune kept me from thinking about what I had to say to Marianne.

Fifteen minutes later, my speech (mostly) prepared and the box of chocolates at the ready, I walked into the library and stopped short.

Marianne wasn't behind the front desk. Her husband, Alvin, was.

I'd met Alvin Littlejohn soon after I first moved to the island at a potluck dinner; and later, I'd appeared before him in magistrate's court more than just a couple times. Believe me when I say I no longer hold this against Kate or Chandra, the ones who'd dragged me into court in the first place with their petty complaints about the construction traffic at the B and B. They were just as guilty as I was of letting our neighborhood squabbles escalate, and they were just as outraged as I was (and I was plenty outraged) when Alvin told us we needed to stop fighting and start talking. He's the one who sentenced us to attend a year's worth of book discussion groups.

Don't tell Alvin, but the way things turned out, we were all grateful.

Even if it did mean reading this month's selection, *The Legend of Sleepy Hollow*, and even if thinking about that Sleepy made me think about the other Sleepy, and—

When I gulped, Alvin didn't look up. He was a tall, skinny guy whose thinning hair was the color of a field mouse, and like a mouse, he was busy rooting through a desk drawer and making a little pile of things nearby: an address book, a lipstick, a desk calendar.

"Hey, Alvin. I was hoping to see your better half."

Startled, he stood and blinked at me for a couple moments while he tugged at his left earlobe. "Oh, Bea. It's you. You haven't heard."

I didn't like the sound of that. "Marianne? Something's happened to–"

"In Cleveland. In the hospital. She's got a detached retina, Bea. She's having surgery first thing tomorrow morning. She asked me to stop in and pick up some things for her before I head over to the mainland this evening."

"I'm so sorry." I handed the box of chocolates across the desk to him. "When you go to see her, give her this."

"Well, it looks like you did know about Marianne!" He took the chocolates out of my hands. "How else would you have known to bring candy?!"

"Actually . . ." I pulled in a deep breath and let it out slowly. "The candy is sort of an apology."

"Because you haven't finished reading that book of hers yet!" Alvin had prominent ears and a long, thin mouth. When he smiled, he reminded me of a ventriloquist's dummy. "It was so nice of you to agree to do that for her, Bea! Marianne, she's just as proud as punch of that little book of hers. Imagine, her being a published author! I swear, knowing you had the book and were giving it a last look, that's the only thing that's made these few days bearable for her, because what with her eye problems, there's no way she could read it herself. She's so excited to see her book in print, she can't wait to get through the surgery and get the manuscript to her publisher."

"Well, that's just it, Alvin, see—"

"That's the only thing that kept me from telling her, of

course." Alvin's expression fell like the soufflé I'd once been foolish enough to try and serve at a dinner party back in New York. "I mean, about the computer."

My stomach swooped. "Computer?"

We were the only ones in the library: one small room with a children's section along the windows to my right and the rest of the books—fiction and nonfiction—in two rows of shelves on my left. Still, Alvin leaned closer and lowered his voice as if, even though she was all the way across the lake and in Cleveland, Marianne might catch wind of our conversation.

"Crashed," he said.

My swooping stomach froze somewhere right between where it was supposed to be and my heart. I pressed a fist to the painful lump. "You're not talking about Marianne's computer?"

He nodded. "Last night. I came back from Cleveland to wrap up some work today and collect these things for her and I promised her I'd be back at the hospital this evening. She said as long as I was coming home . . . she said she knew it was silly of her to be nervous, that it was foolish and superstitious . . . but she asked if I'd please make a backup of her manuscript. And then—"

"No backup?" The words were sand in my mouth.

"I can't worry her. Not before the surgery. I'll tell her once it's all over and she's on the road to recovering. For now, it's our little secret, Bea." He emphasized this with a wink. "But you know . . ." Alvin's smile blossomed. "I guess as it turns out, with everything that's happened, Marianne will be really grateful. She'll see how lucky it was that she gave you a copy of that manuscript of hers! Otherwise, it would be completely lost!" He slipped the box of chocolates in a plastic grocery bag along with the other things he'd collected. "So, what was it you wanted me to tell her?" Alvin asked.

My smile wasn't nearly as bright as his. Or as genuine. In fact, it was so wide and so stiff, the corners of my mouth hurt. "I just had a couple questions. About the manuscript. Tell her not to worry. In fact, don't tell her anything at all. Whatever I have to ask her, it can wait until she's feeling better again."

"Thanks, Bea. You're a lifesaver." Alvin slipped out from behind the desk and headed for the door. "If it wasn't for the fact that you have the only copy of that book of hers . . . Well, I don't even want to think how poor Marianne would be feeling right about now."

By six that evening, I had a roaring fire going in the parlor and I'd taken it upon myself to restack (alphabet be damned!) the ghost getters' equipment out in the hallway to get it out of the way. The painters and plasterers, wood finishers and roofers who'd refurbished the house the year before and returned it to its full Victorian glory had left tarps neatly stacked in the basement, and I'd retrieved them and lined the floor near the table I'd set within arm's reach of the fire. I adjusted the screen on my laptop until it was just right, took a deep breath, and reached down to the floor near my feet and the white kitchen garbage bag where, the day before, Luella had tossed Marianne's manuscript. Thank goodness it wasn't garbage day or I would have already thrown out the bag! I undid the twist tie and held my breath, but of course, that plan was doomed right from the start. The coughing wasn't too bad. Nor was the wheezing. The face I made . . . well, there was nobody around to see it, so I didn't care.

With thumb and forefingers, I plucked the first soggy page of the manuscript off the even soggier pile and held it up to the light to read it, then started typing.

By the time I was done with the page and consigned it to the fire, the computer screen in front of me read:

```
Charles Sleep_ Har___
The Stud_ of an Island Leg____
by
Mari____ _____john
```

This method of decoding was obviously not going to work.

My shoulders drooped, but I refused to be discouraged. It was like a game, wasn't it? Like playing hangman. All I needed to do was fill in the blanks. Lucky for me, it wasn't too tough; not for that first page, anyway. But by the time I'd transcribed what I could and thrown the next three pages of Marianne's soggy tome into the flames, my eyes were spinning and my head was woozy.

Then again, breathing in ammonia will do that to you.

I yanked off my glasses and scrubbed my eyes with my fists, looking back over those first four pages and what I'd been able to decipher.

It was pitifully little.

A word here, a word there.

A full sentence on page two. Hallelujah! Except that it didn't make the least bit of sense with what I could read of the sentences before and after it.

I considered the possibility that Marianne was simply a really bad writer, but honestly, that theory just didn't hold water. As Luella had mentioned the day of the latest unfortunate incident with Jerry, Marianne wasn't exactly the most imaginative person in the world. What she was, though, was thorough. And capable. Like most librarians I'd met, Marianne could rule the world if she chose to. She was that organized, that energetic. She might not be a ball of innovative fire, but she was plenty intelligent and dedicated to both her job and this book about Sleepy. She saw the book as her contribution to island history, her legacy, and I knew she'd never allow herself to be sloppy. She was too proud of what she'd produced.

I owed it to Marianne to give it my best. I needed to try and read the sodden words more carefully and (hopefully) fill in the blanks, and I'd just picked another wet page from the garbage bag when I heard the bang of footsteps on the hallway stairs.

"What the hell?"

Noreen's high-pitched keening preceded her into the parlor.

"You messed with our equipment."

I was in the middle of trying to determine if a word smeared across the middle of page five was *robust* or *rosebush* and I didn't spare her a look. "It's all there," I said, typing out *rosebush* and immediately deciding it should have been *robust*. I glanced over my shoulder at Noreen. "I needed the fireplace. And your equipment was in the way. It's an emergency."

She sniffed the air. "I'll say. No! Not that case, Fiona!" she yelled when she caught sight of something in the hallway and whirled around that way. "Take that other one first. It's bigger."

Apparently, Fiona did, because when Noreen looked back at me, she was smug. "It makes more sense for the bigger equipment cases to go into the trucks first," she said.

"And it would make even more sense," I suggested, "if

you kept all the equipment out in the trucks when you got back. That way, you wouldn't have to load and unload."

I'm pretty sure she would have admitted this was actually a good idea if she'd thought of it herself. The way it was, Noreen's lips puckered like she'd sucked on a lemon. "It's expensive equipment," she said.

"We have a very low crime rate here on South Bass. You don't have a thing to worry about."

"Well . . ." She pretended to consider my plan. "We'll see. For now—"

Dimitri came down the steps so fast, he was huffing and puffing by the time he got to the bottom. "Everything's set," he said, stopping to catch his breath. "Liam, get the cameras into the truck and—"

Noreen cleared her throat. "I've got everything under control," she told Dimitri, then turned to Liam. "Get the cameras into the truck, and Dimitri"—she gave him a rattlesnake smile—"don't worry about it."

Without a word, he elbowed his way past her and into the parlor, checking to see that all the equipment that had been in there had already been moved. Tonight, Dimitri was dressed much like Noreen was, in a heavy jacket emblazoned with the blue EGG lettering. Like Noreen, he wore a fisherman's vest over his jacket and, just like hers, his was crammed with wires and batteries and what I could only imagine were bits and pieces of ghost-finding gear.

"Good luck," I told them when they went to the door, then wondered if that was the proper parlance in the woo-woo world. If these were theater people, I'd say, "Break a leg." If they were sailors, I'd wish them "Bon voyage."

I called after Noreen and Dimitri, "Or should I say I hope you've got a ghost of a chance of finding something!"

When she grimaced, Noreen was not especially attractive. "Yeah," she grumbled, "like we've never heard that one before."

They tumbled out of the house and took their equipment with them, and I got back to work.

"Charles Harlow was born on South Beach in ____," I typed, then figured that should actually say South Bass and made the correction even as I reminded myself that I'd have to double-check county records to make sure this was true.

And so it went. At one point, I had to come up for air, and stepped out on the front porch for a minute or two. At another, I did an Internet search to find the proper spellings of some places Marianne mentioned that I couldn't quite make out.

The next time I looked at the antique mahogany clock on the mantel, it was nearly nine and my eyes felt as if they were about to ooze right out of my head. My temples pounded and the fire that had been fed by the soggy pages was nearly out. I was getting nowhere fast, and in the hopes of tomorrow being another (and better) day, I twist-tied the garbage bag with Marianne's manuscript in it closed and looked over the pitifully few pages I'd transcribed. There were more blank spaces than words on them, and the words that were there hardly made sense. There was no way I could re-create Marianne's manuscript, not like this, and the realization settled inside me like a lead weight.

I massaged the bridge of my nose with the tips of my fingers. "I'm doomed," I groaned, and dropped my head into my hands when I realized the project wasn't going to get any easier. The longer Marianne's manuscript marinated, the soggier it got, and the soggier it got, the more difficult it was for me to read.

Doomed, indeed.

I would have gone right on feeling by turns either sorry for myself or in a complete panic if I didn't hear the sounds of a car out on the road. Not so unusual, except that its brakes squealed against the pavement and the reflection of headlights skimmed the parlor walls when the car turned into my driveway.

"Ghost getters," I grumbled, closing my laptop. "Back from the hunt. I hope they found something they're excited about so they don't spend the rest of the night bickering."

"Bea!" My front door slammed open. "You've got to come. Now!"

I spun around and found Kate standing in the hallway, one hand pressed to her heart. She was pale, and breathing fast.

I popped out of my chair. "What's wrong?"

"Wrong?" Her voice shook, just like her hands did. Her teeth clenched around the word. She took one wobbly step into the parlor and put a hand against the wall to steady herself. "I just got back from the mainland," Kate growled. "It was . . ." Kate is the most practical and levelheaded person I know. I guess that's why it felt like a fist to the gut when I saw that she had tears in her eyes. "It was a wild goose chase," she said. "A big ol' waste of time."

This, of course, made no sense. Unless . . .

I closed in on Kate. "Your wine reporter never showed."

"My wine reporter . . ." She folded her fingers against her palms and tucked her thumbs over them, anger simmering in her every clipped word. "I waited at the restaurant for an hour. Then I decided to give her another half hour. You know, as a professional courtesy. Still no Deidre. That's when I called the magazine office in Chicago, just to make sure I hadn't gotten the time or the place mixed up. And that's when I found out"—the color in Kate's cheeks was the same flaming red as her hair—"that's when I found out Deidre Mannington wouldn't be joining me for dinner. See, she's on assignment. In Hong Kong."

The truth dawned on me much as it must have on Kate when she heard the news. I flinched like I'd been slapped. "Noreen?"

"I'd bet any money on it." Kate spun to the door. "I'm going to the winery, Bea, and you'd better come along, because I'm going to need a witness to testify in court about my mental state when I go on trial for Noreen's murder!"

❖ 4 ❖

I've never seen anybody, anytime, anywhere, turn the color Kate did when we pulled around to the side of Wilder Winery and saw the EGG trucks tucked against the back wall, where I'd bet any money they thought no one would ever see them.

Kate's cheeks were maroon. With purple tinges.

The way she slammed on the brakes, I was pretty sure I'd have a bruise in all the same rainbow hues across my torso courtesy of my seat belt.

"I'm going to kill her, Bea." Kate's words were punctuated by her heavy breaths.

I would have grabbed on to her and urged caution if she had given me the chance. Instead, she pushed open the door and jumped out of the car.

Turns out a woman in fashionable black stilettos can walk pretty fast when she's fueled by pure anger.

This woman in her sneakers had a hard time keeping up when Kate zipped along the side of the building and on toward the front entrance.

Wilder Winery had been built back in the late 1800s. From what I'd heard from folks on the island and from Kate herself, the original building had been a grand and glorious Old World sort of monstrosity, complete with half timber framing, plenty of stucco and even a gigantic cuckoo clock in a tower above the main door. Because of an electrical fire soon after Kate's parents stepped back from running the business and she took over, Kate had been forced to start anew. Kate being Kate, she'd rebuilt with practicality—rather than historical ambiance—in mind.

The current building was a pleasant, farmy-looking place, a lovely slate blue in the daylight that, now that it was dark, looked gray and (dare I say it?) ghostly. The building had a peaked roof above the spacious entryway and a wide foyer that opened to a sleek and modern showroom and tasting bar where there was plenty of room for wine sippers— most of whom turned into buyers—to mix and mingle. Kate had her fingers in every aspect of the business, including the gift shop, which was quickly gaining a reputation on the island for unique and elegant products that included local artists' works.

The front porch of Wilder's was scattered with benches, and picnic tables were strewn around the lawn under the gigantic oak trees that dotted the property.

I was breathing hard when I caught up to Kate right outside the front door, where there was a massive planter jam-packed with mums. I'd been to Wilder's just a week earlier to pick up a case of wine; I knew the mums were yellow and orange. In the pale light of a sliver of a moon, they looked anemic. Like eyes that swayed and bobbed in the breeze off the lake. Eyes that watched our every move.

"Don't do anything stupid." I grabbed Kate's arm just as she was about to open the door. "Don't do anything you'll regret."

"Oh, come on, Bea!" In the glow from a security light somewhere behind me, the smile she flashed was predatory. "If I got to draw and quarter Noreen Turner . . . if I burned her at the stake . . . or used that guillotine to chop off her head, the one that weird rock band brought to the island last summer for the Bastille Day celebration"—she released a long, slow breath—"honest, Bea, I wouldn't regret any of that. Not one little bit."

I didn't doubt it for a moment.

Which is why I wedged myself in front of her and dashed into the winery the instant Kate had the door unlocked.

She flipped on a phalanx of overhead lights and a startled voice cried out, "The lights out there came on all by themselves. Nobody touched them. It has to be paranormal. There's no other explanation!" I followed the sound past the tasting bar and back toward the room where the newly fermented grape juice was stored in rows of gigantic stainless steel tanks.

No explanation?

Au contraire!

EGG should have figured that out when they heard the crack of Kate's footsteps against the hardwood floor, along with the noise she made from deep in her throat—the one that sounded a whole lot like thunder.

Call me crazy, but when I touched a hand to the light switch on the wall in the fermenting room, I thought the ghost hunters would look a little less disappointed to see good ol' corporeal me—and a little more nervous about the whole breaking and entering thing.

Instead, Ben and Eddie simply took the cameras off their shoulders and stepped back to watch.

Liam and David and Rick paused, Mel meters and whatnots at the ready. Dimitri flicked off the digital tape recorder he held in one hand. And Noreen—

"We were in the middle of filming," Noreen said when she saw me, puffing out a breath of annoyance. "You can't just walk in here like that and turn on all the lights. We work in the dark for a reason, you know. The UV rays from light make it harder for spirits to manifest. You ruined the shot and maybe a chance for a spirit to communicate!"

"I'll ruin *you*." Do I need to say that this comment came from Kate? Fire in her eyes, she raced into the room and pushed right past me and that gigantic lantern-looking thing I'd seen in the purported ghost video. Step by infuriated step, she backed Noreen toward one of the stainless steel tanks. "You're trespassing. You're breaking laws. You're—"

"Wait a minute!" Dimitri stepped forward. "Chill out, honey. We've got permission to be here."

If I thought Kate was upset before, I was as wrong as wrong can be. She stopped, and when all the color drained from her face, she looked like an ice queen. Dimitri must have felt the transformation, too; when Kate spun his way, he froze.

"I own this winery, *honey*," she snapped. "That's my name on the front door. And I'm the only one who can give you permission to be here." Kate's voice was so controlled and quiet, it terrified even me. "I never did that."

Dimitri's gaze shot to Noreen, his cheeks flushed and

his breaths coming in long, hard puffs. "You . . . you liar! You told us—"

"That's for sure." I didn't know if it was Ben or Eddie who spoke up, I only knew it was one of the cameramen and that both of them backed up a step, distancing themselves from the confrontation. "She told us it was okay," the cameraman said, glancing from Kate to Noreen. "Don't blame us, lady. Noreen told us that after you two had your little . . . er . . . disagreement back at the B and B yesterday, she talked to you again and that she arranged everything with you. That you told her—"

"Oh, I told her, all right." Kate took another couple steps forward, until Noreen was as flat as a camouflaged pancake against that stainless tank. "I told her no. In fact, I told her no, no, and no again. I told her to stay away. And never to darken my doorstep again." Kate glanced around at the crew. "So if she told the rest of you any different, Dimitri here, he's right. You are a liar, Noreen."

She swiveled a gaze that could have cut through steel in Noreen's direction. "Is that what you did, Noreen? Because if you just forgot what I told you, you have one short memory, lady. But if you flat-out lied to your crew, then you just got yourself and them in some really hot water."

"Now, wait a minute!" Dimitri put a hand out toward Kate, then thought better of the move and tucked his hand in the pocket of his jacket. "You can't blame us for what Noreen . . . for what this lunatic did. We didn't know. She told us—"

"Shut up!" Noreen's voice shot up to the high ceiling and echoed back at us. "She's got it all wrong." She swung her gaze from Dimitri back to Kate. "You've got it all wrong. I remember what you said, and—"

"And I said no."

Was that a smile Noreen attempted? It came and went so fast, I wasn't sure. But hey, after years in New York in a high-powered, high-pressured, high-income profession, I was sure I recognized kissing up when I saw it, and what happened next was so classic, it turned my stomach.

Noreen tucked her meter into her pocket so she could scrape her palms against her camo pants, and I swear, I could just about see the effort it cost her to lower her voice. Like she was standing in front of a firing squad, she pulled back her shoulders. "I know what you said, Ms. Wilder, and believe me, I thought about it plenty and I understand why you feel the way you do. What we did last fall when we were here . . . well, that was wrong. We were wrong. If we hadn't gotten so carried away by catching that video of Sleepy Harlow, it never would have happened. I swear. But that's what it all comes down to, don't you see?" Noreen made a swirly sort of motion with her hand and, for a moment, I thought maybe she was twitching because she was nervous.

I should have known better.

No sooner did Noreen gesture than both Ben and Eddie lifted their cameras to their shoulders and started filming again.

Perfect timing, especially when Noreen looked right at one of the cameras and said, "We caught that video of that apparition last year and now, we owe it to ourselves and to the scientific community as a whole to see if we can find more evidence. It's not just something we want to do; it's something we have to do. It's our mission, our duty. That's why I knew you wouldn't mind. Look around!" Noreen did, but Kate sure didn't. Like a sniper homing in on a target, Kate's gaze was trained on the leader of the ghost getters.

"We haven't touched a thing," Noreen assured her. "We've been very careful and, of course, respectful of you and your business. Between that and all the publicity you're going to get from our TV show—"

The screech rose out of Kate like a banshee's wail and cut Noreen off. She immediately signaled to the cameramen to stop filming. Too bad. Had they kept on, they would have gotten some darned sensational footage of Kate when she darted forward, her hands raised and her fists clenched.

Time for me to insinuate myself into the middle of the tiff.

"You're going to have to leave," I told Noreen, one hand on Kate's shoulder to calm her. "You heard Kate. She doesn't want you here."

"She'll change her mind when she hears what we've already found tonight." Noreen was so sure of herself, she lifted her chin and signaled that the filming could recommence. "I think all the paranormal activity has something to do with the geological makeup of the island. It's mostly limestone, you know. And limestone near running water is known to increase the incidents of paranormal activity. That's because limestone can hold information. You know, like a camera recording historic events. The limestone records it, then releases it, and that information plays back over and over again as what we call a residual haunting."

"They call it the stone tape . . . theory," Dimitri added, breathless at the very thought. He would have been better served realizing that neither Kate nor I cared. The cameramen did. They swiveled around and began recording Dimitri. "It works because . . ." He gathered his thoughts. "Because limestone can trap vibrations and then, if conditions are right, the vibrations play back, like a tape recorder or, you know, a DVR."

"And some theories even say the limestone is like a

battery." This came from David, a tall, good-looking African American who, when it came to vibrations, had apparently missed the whole I'm-going-to-kill-her vibe coming off Kate and thought that an actual discussion about all this horse hockey was appropriate. With the cameras rolling on him now, he said, "The limestone holds energy and that energy keeps the haunting going. But like Noreen said, this only works when it comes to residual hauntings. It's important to remember that. These aren't intelligent hauntings, not entities you can interact with. These are residuals, like watching a movie projected into the air. They don't know we're here. They just keep playing over and over. Like the apparition we caught last year. Which is why, with the help of the plasmometer there"—he looked at the big lanternlike contraption—"we're pretty sure we can catch the apparition on film again."

"Or the whole stone tape theory might actually work because electromagnectic fields are generated by water flowing over the limestone," Liam put in, stepping in front of David and, not incidentally, in front of the camera, too. "You know, like—"

"Like are you all deaf?" I whirled around, taking them all in, and at the sound of my voice ping-ponging against the stainless steel, both Ben and Eddie lowered their cameras. "Limestone, batteries, residual whatevers . . . the only thing that matters is that you get out of here. Now."

"Yeah." Kate followed my example and gave each of them a look until they squirmed. "Before I call the police."

"You can't. You can't do that. Not until we have a chance to film. Just a few hours' worth of footage. What difference is a few hours going to make?" Noreen made the mistake of trying to plead her case by putting a hand on Kate's arm.

I felt the change in Kate's attitude rather than saw it—a shift in the anger that simmered in the air around her, a flare like when wind stokes the flames of a fire. Before I had a chance to respond to it and grab hold of her so she couldn't do Noreen any real physical damage, a voice called out from the tasting area.

"Trouble here?"

We all looked that way just in time to see Hank Florentine, the local police chief, saunter in, one hand laid casually on the butt of the gun in his belt holster. "Kate, I saw all the lights on and pulled around back and saw the cars. Funny time of night for you to be working. Thought I'd better stop and see what was going on. Trouble here?"

"I don't know, Hank. As a matter of fact, I was just going to ask." She pinned her gaze on the leader of EGG. "Is there trouble here, Noreen?"

Noreen gurgled and burbled. Her cheeks shot through with vivid color, then went as pale as the moonlight outside. She bit her lower lip. "Somebody go find Fiona," she grumbled. "She's getting equipment out of the truck. Tell her to get everything put away again. And then let's get out of here. Paranormal activity?" Her snort put an accent on her mood. "No self-respecting ghost would bother with this place."

The smile Kate turned on her wasn't as much about relief as it was about one-upmanship. "No trouble at all, Hank," she told him while she kept her eyes on Noreen. "Noreen and her EGG-heads were just leaving."

Noreen commanded Liam and David to grab the plasmometer and, under the careful gaze of Hank, they all marched out. A few minutes later, we heard the engines on the EGG SUVs start up and saw their headlights skim the wall when they pulled out of the parking lot.

"Want to explain?" Hank asked Kate.

I had to give Kate credit for handling the situation with so much poise, and I could only imagine how much strength it took for her to hold it together. Rather than make her relive it all for Hank, I stepped forward. "Just a mix-up," I said, and paused to give Kate a chance to contradict me. When she didn't, I went on, "The ghost getters were just leaving when you got here."

"Well, all right then." Hank, his gaze still fastened to Kate, stepped back toward the tasting room. "You want me to have a look around before I leave?"

Kate snapped to. "No. It's fine, Hank. They're gone. I'll lock up. Bea's here with me."

"All right then, ladies." Hank wasn't wearing a hat, but he touched his hand to his buzz-cut hair. "I'll see you both at the wake on Friday, right? Last days of summer!" His sigh vibrated through the vast room. "I for one am happy summer's over. We can get rid of the tourists and have the island all to ourselves for a while."

With that, Hank banged out of the front door.

"Come on." Kate led the way. "I want to check things out and make sure those idiots didn't break anything." She screeched her frustration. "The nerve of that woman. She told her people they had permission? She said it was all right for them to be here? I swear, Bea, if you weren't here with me, I would have dumped her in one of these tanks and let her ferment for a month or two. Then maybe she'd get the message."

We crossed that room and headed into a back corridor. Ahead of us, a series of hallways led to the rooms where the wine was bottled, packed, and shipped, and we found and locked the back door that the ghost getters had jimmied open to get in. I wondered what Noreen had told them to explain the inconvenience, then instantly knew: Kate had forgotten to leave a key. I'd bet anything she told them Kate had forgotten to leave a key.

In the other direction was Kate's office, and she went that way.

"They better not have been in here," she said, flicking on the light.

Kate's office was a lot like Kate's house, and a lot like Kate herself. Plain enough to let the world know she was no-nonsense. Stylish enough to be attractive. She zipped right past the sleek Scandinavian-inspired desk that dominated the room in front of a wide window that looked out over the vineyards and went right over to a cabinet that she unlocked. She came back across the room holding an old-fashioned oil lamp, the kind with a fat, round bottom and a tall, conical chimney.

"It might be more efficient if we just turned on all the lights in the winery," I suggested.

Kate set down the lamp on the windowsill. "Huh?"

"An oil lamp." I pointed even though I didn't have to. "We don't need that to search the winery. We could just turn on the lights."

"Oh, the lamp!" She laugh, and truthfully, I was grateful. Though Kate might be hardheaded when it comes to business, I had never known her to be cruel or hard-hearted (okay, with the exception of the times she took me to court because she said my remodeling at the B and B brought too much traffic through our neighborhood). Watching her seethe in anger had not only been uncomfortable; it left me feeling as if I should have/could have done more.

"The lamp has nothing to do with looking around the winery. It's just . . ." Her grin was sheepish. "I guess it's kind of a family tradition," she said. "See, when my great-grandmother, Carrie Wilder, ran the winery, she always put the lamp out when she came to work in the morning. And she always put it away again when she left for the evening. Sometimes she lit it and sometimes she didn't." Kate shrugged as a way of saying she had no idea what her great-grandmother might have been thinking.

"And she always set the lamp on the window ledge. Lucky for us, my office wasn't touched by the fire and this part of the building is original. I put the lamp out every time I walk in. I know it's silly, but hey, force of habit! When my grandparents took over the winery, that was the first and last thing they did every day. And my parents, too. In fact, when Mom and Dad retired to Florida, they told me never to forget to put out the lamp. Nobody knows when Great-Grandma Carrie started the tradition and nobody knows why. But it can't hurt anything."

"It's really kind of nice," I told her. "It keeps you connected with the past and with the family."

"And it reminds me that no matter what that idiot Noreen did, I'm still the boss around here." Fists on hips, Kate did a turn around the office. "It doesn't look like anything was touched," she said. "Noreen can thank her lucky stars for that. If I saw anything messed with in here, I'd get Hank back over here in a heartbeat and have him arrest her camouflaged butt for breaking and entering."

"And I wouldn't blame you in the least. In fact, I was surprised when you didn't."

Kate tried to control a smile. It didn't exactly work. "Don't tell anybody, okay? Most people around the island are convinced I'm as hard as nails. I'd hate to burst their bubbles. Besides, what use is it for them to be thrown in jail? I'd rather have them over at your B and B, with you charging them the fortune you charge and them not being able to get close to the one place they're just itching to investigate. That's real revenge!"

While Kate was busy checking every corner of the office, I went to the window to look over the lamp. I like antiques. I own plenty of them. I knew this one wasn't unusual, and at a flea market, it wouldn't have sold for more than fifty dollars, in spite of its age. But the fact that it belonged to Kate's great-grandmother and that it was involved in such a charming family ritual made the lamp special.

It was a foot and a half tall and made of clear glass, and the kerosene that had once gone into the bulbous bottom part of the lamp had evaporated long ago.

"Ready?" Kate came up from behind me, picked up the lamp, and put it back in the cabinet. "Everything's okay in here. We can check out the rest of the place on our way out."

We did a quick search of the winery, from the bottling room to the gift shop and from the gift shop to the office where a small staff of dedicated workers took care of Internet and wholesale orders. Our last stop was the warehouse, and as soon as we stepped into the cavernous room, I shivered.

"Somebody left a window open."

We checked. They hadn't.

"And not the door into the old back storage rooms, either," Kate said, with a look toward the back of the warehouse. "That's closed, too. It must just be getting colder outside."

And I knew she was right.

Which didn't explain why after she'd already turned out the lights and I took one second to glance over my shoulder into the warehouse, I thought I saw . . .

Something.

I closed my eyes and looked again—and again, I swear I saw a shimmer in the deepest shadows along the far wall. Not a light exactly. And certainly not a full-blown movement. It was more of a flicker. A flutter in the darkness that morphed from black to gray and back to black again so quickly, I couldn't say for sure what it could have been.

Legs.

A torso.

Not a person, surely. Because people have heads.

And I know it sounds crazy, but I swear, the figure that flashed in front of my eyes one second and was gone the next was missing his.

❮ 5 ❯

I t was a trick of the light.
  A trick of the shadows.
  A trick of my imagination.
  And I refused to think about it.
  In fact, the next morning I put breakfast out for my guests and immediately retreated into my private suite. For one thing, after what they had pulled the night before, I didn't want to deal with pushy Noreen and her compadres. They could serve themselves, and considering I provided pumpkin muffins, a couple of carafes of coffee, fresh fruit, and a platter of perfectly cooked bacon, they should have been more than able to.
  More importantly, I wanted to look over what I had done—and the epic amount of work I had yet to do—on Marianne's manuscript.

This was the only Sleepy Harlow who mattered, I reminded myself, glancing over the pitifully few pages I'd managed to re-create.

The real man. The real criminal from back in the days of Prohibition. The person who, according to the little I'd been able to find out about him online and in those few words I'd been able to cobble together from Marianne's manuscript, was responsible for running boatloads of liquor out of Canada and delivering it to any number of mobbed-up gangs in Ohio and Michigan. The man who was viciously murdered by rival bootleggers and whose body—and legacy—had been buried here on the island for more than eighty years.

Not the ghost I thought I saw at the winery the night before.

Which couldn't have been a ghost.

Because there is no such thing.

Right?

My mind made up (even though my irrational self kept replaying that flash of weird, headless shadow I'd seen at the winery), I concentrated on the pages of Marianne's book and realized I had to work fast. They were getting soggier and smellier by the hour.

By ten o'clock, I was talking to myself.

By eleven, the talk had degraded into mumbling, and by noon, that mumbling was punctuated with a whole lot of words I never use in public.

I needed a break and I needed one bad, and since the weather was still glorious and the sun shone golden against the multicolored trees, I opted for a walk.

While I was at it, I decided I could acquaint myself with the (pitifully few) places I'd been able to decipher in

Marianne's manuscript, locations that played a part in Sleepy Harlow's daily life, his life of crime, and his death.

I pulled a black sweater over the red, long-sleeved T-shirt I was wearing with jeans and headed downtown. I'd just been able to make out the address of the place Sleepy had once lived, and though I knew Put-in-Bay had plenty more bars and restaurants per square inch than it had back in the 1920s and '30s, I also knew that many of the old buildings downtown had been preserved and repurposed.

If I could locate and explore Sleepy's old haunts—honest, I didn't mean it, the word just popped into my head—I would hopefully be able to start to get a better sense of the man.

It was a great plan, and it would have worked.

If I hadn't found the address of Sleepy's apartment and seen the sign that hung above the first-floor establishment: *Levi's Bar.*

It was Thursday afternoon and the Wake to Summer would be held the next evening. Already the streets were filled with partiers. Boats bobbed next to the dock at the marina and the park directly across the street was crammed with picnickers. As a last salute to summer, a nearby bar blared Jimmy Buffett and a couple out front improvised a snappy little line dance. They gave me strange looks when I interrupted the fun by barking out one of those words I said I never use in public.

Why?

It's one of those simple questions that's not so simple to answer.

See, Levi Kozlov, owner of the abovementioned establishment, is the bane of my island existence.

And the most delicious man to come into my life in as long as I can remember.

Which, for the record, is pretty darned long.

As for why I wasn't acting on the baser instincts that reared their ugly (and very appealing) heads every time Levi was around . . .

Well, I had my reasons.

Not the least of which was that after he'd kissed me a few months earlier, Levi had told me the whole thing was a mistake.

Since I thought it was a mistake, too, this should have cheered me. It did cheer me. Except for the part about how it didn't. That part of me was only appeased by me reminding myself that I had come to the island to get away from the glare of the public eye and all things associated with it. Like the stalker who'd made my life a living hell back in New York. I wanted peace in my life, and that would come only with anonymity. I couldn't start a relationship—with anyone—without revealing things about myself I'd rather keep hidden.

Anonymity.

It was my motto.

Do not get involved.

That was my mantra.

It all made sense and it all sounded good and I knew it was the right thing to do.

Except that every time Levi was anywhere near, all that good sense went flying out the window.

Just like it did right then and there when just thinking about Levi sent heat racing into my cheeks.

Fortunately, a distraction came along in the form of Dimitri, who I saw up ahead walking away from the ferry dock. He looked more like an A-lister than ever in a stylish pair of aviator sunglasses and with his EGG jacket slung over one shoulder. At his side was a woman every bit as attractive as he was. She was long-legged, dark-haired, and gorgeous enough to turn heads. Curious, I watched them walk slowly over to the park and stop to check out the huge, showy, and very kitschy display of mums and pumpkins and smiling scarecrows that would surround the coffin of summer after it was paraded around the park with great ceremony.

When Dimitri caught sight of me, he stepped away from the woman and waved me over.

"I'm glad I ran into you. What Noreen did last night . . ." He coughed away his discomfort. "I need to apologize on behalf of EGG."

"Not to me."

"I'll talk to Ms. Wilder, too. I was hoping to see her tomorrow at the wake."

"You're lucky she didn't have you all thrown in jail."

"That's exactly what I'm planning to tell her. That, and how much I appreciate her understanding. Not to mention her compassion."

His smile shimmered like the sun reflecting off the Aegean, and it was impossible for me not to smile back.

"That's better," Dimitri said. "I hate to think . . ." He was obviously not a man who was used to apologizing. Not about anything. He pulled in a steadying breath. "After what happened last night, I hated to think that we made you uncomfortable."

"You didn't make me uncomfortable. You made me angry."

"Then that's even worse. Which is why—"

Before he had a chance to finish, the woman stepped up to his side and slipped her hand into his.

"Oh, there's someone here I'd like you to meet," Dimitri said. "This is Jacklyn Bichot. She was one of us back in the day. You know, a member of EGG."

I figured it wasn't politically correct to congratulate her for not associating with the group anymore, so I kept my words to a friendly hello and a welcome to the island.

Jacklyn had hair that was even darker than mine. When she looked over the display and the volunteers who scampered around making sure everything would be just right for the ceremony the next day, her eyes danced. "If there's a wake, can ghosts be very far behind? I can't wait to find out."

"So you're still hunting ghosts?" I asked her.

I did not expect a look that could have shattered glass. "I used to hunt ghosts," Jacklyn said. Her voice went along with the whole tall, lithe, and good-looking package. It was husky, and there was just the tiniest trace of North Carolina backwoods in her elongated vowels. "That is, until Noreen realized I look way better on camera than she ever will."

"Now, Jacklyn!" The warning from Dimitri was friendly enough, but Jacklyn didn't respond with a smile.

"She may as well know the truth," she said, and turned a knowing look in my direction. "I bet you already do. Dimitri tells me that the crew is staying at your place. That means you've met Noreen. You look like a reasonably smart woman. How long did it take you to figure out that Noreen is a self-centered, self-righteous, annoying cow with OCD and an ego as big as all of the great outdoors?"

I was saved from saying *practically no time at all* when Dimitri looped one arm through Jacklyn's and another through mine. "Come on. We're going for coffee. And Bea, it's my treat. It's the least I can do to show you how bad I feel about what happened last night."

Jacklyn's smile was sleek. "Let me guess—that something you feel bad about has something to do with Noreen. Am I right?"

Instead of answering, Dimitri piloted us over to the coffee shop near the park and left us at a table on the patio while he went up to the window to place our orders. He came back and put one cup of coffee in front of me and one in front of Jacklyn before he went back up to the window to get his own.

"So . . ." Dimitri sat down, and without a word, Jacklyn popped the top off his coffee, added two bags of sugar and stirred. "Has Jacklyn chewed your ear off yet? About how much she hates Noreen?"

"We haven't had time to talk about anything at all," I told him, and it wasn't like I wasn't curious, but I did have to admit, I was getting uncomfortable, like I'd stepped into the middle of a family feud I didn't understand and didn't want to get involved in.

Dimitri took a sip of his coffee before he leaned closer to me. "Jacklyn hates Noreen almost as much as I do. With a fiery passion," he said quietly, though not so quietly that Jacklyn couldn't hear it. "Jacklyn would like to boil Noreen in oil."

"I wouldn't waste perfectly good oil." Jacklyn sat up and put an arm across the back of Dimitri's chair, a sort of half smile on her face that made it impossible for me to tell if she was kidding or not. "I'd just as soon whack her over the head with a big old boulder. Then I wouldn't be squandering resources."

"You keep talking like that and Bea's going to think you're some kind of nutcase. Tell her the truth, Jacki. Tell her what you told me a little while ago."

The way Jacklyn's smile wilted, I knew she was sorry the fun was over. "Truth," she said. "The truth is, Noreen is the reason I came to the island. I heard EGG would be here filming, and I came over from the mainland to thank

Noreen." She sat up a little straighter. "Call me shallow. I knew it would be a heck of a lot more fun in person than it would ever be via text message."

My coffee was hot. I popped the top and blew on it. "You came all the way over here to thank her for firing you?"

Jacklyn's dark eyes gleamed. "Absolutely. You see, if it wasn't for Noreen—"

"We'd all be a little less crazy and a whole lot less stressed," Dimitri said, then laughed so hard, he ended up coughing, and he pounded his chest.

"True," Jacklyn acknowledged when he'd finally settled down. "But that's not what I was going to say. I was going to say that if it wasn't for Noreen kicking me off the show, my schedule wouldn't have been nice and open when my agent called a few months ago. I'm just back from California." Her shoulders shot back. "I got a part on *Brains and Beauty*."

"The soap?" I was impressed, and I told Jacklyn so. "That couldn't have been easy."

"It would have been impossible if I was still hanging with these losers." I can't say for sure if the smile she tossed at Dimitri was genuine or not; I only knew that like the sun that shone overhead, it warmed him through and through. I could practically see him turn to mush right before my eyes.

"It's not officially a recurring role," she added. "Not yet, anyway. But my agent says there's a good possibility they're going to write my character into a new story line. Cool, huh? I can't wait to tell Noreen and watch her turn neon green with envy! Turns out when she got jealous and dumped me off the show, she was actually doing me a favor." Jacklyn finished her coffee. "In fact, I'm going to find her and tell her right now. Bea, are you going back to the B and B? If you're not, I'm sure Dimitri will take me over there."

I told her I was heading home and the three of us started out, but either my timing was off or my luck was just plain bad. No sooner had we gotten over to the park again than Levi stepped out from behind the stage he was helping set up.

He caught my eye. Which is a better way of saying it than *he saw me and I was trapped like a dirty rat.*

Trapped like a dirty rat, I told Dimitri and Jacklyn that I'd catch up with them later, and when Levi closed in on me, I forced myself to keep my cool.

"Hey." It was Levi's standard greeting, so I didn't even bother to *hey* back. "I hear you've got some TV stars staying at your place."

"Wannabe stars. They're looking for ghosts."

He laughed. Levi is tall and blond and did I mention gorgeous? While Dimitri had the whole Greek islands/dark and dangerous thing going for him, Levi's good looks seem to rise out of a place where there is a permanent chill in the air. It may have been the icy glint of his incredible blue eyes that made me think that way. Or maybe it was because I never could quite tell what was going on inside his head, and that made me feel left out in the cold.

"Not finding any at your place, are they?"

I snapped out of my thoughts and remembered what we were talking about.

"Ghosts? They haven't asked to investigate the B and B, thank goodness. But speaking of ghosts . . ."

I shook my head to remind myself that's exactly what we *weren't* talking about.

"Sleepy Harlow used to live in your apartment," I told Levi.

"The gangster?" Thinking, he pursed the lips that were the lips I had dreamt about these last couple months. "Cool. But I can't say I've seen his ghost around."

"I didn't think you would have. But I was wondering . . ." I debated about telling him the truth. It was, in fact, the only fair thing to do, especially when I was asking for his help. "You see, Marianne Littlejohn's writing a book about Sleepy, and . . ."

And what?

And I destroyed it thanks to a little help from my furry friend Jerry?

I swallowed the rest of the explanation and went with, "If I could take a look at the place where he used to live, it would help me out."

"Sure." Levi poked his hands into the pockets of the jeans he was wearing with a slate gray sweatshirt. "I can't see how you looking around my place is going to help Marianne, but if you say it is, it is." His eyes sparked. "You could stop by for a drink after the party tomorrow."

"I could, but I think we both know that would be a mistake."

I could have kicked myself the moment the word was out of my mouth. I didn't mean to bring up the subject because, let's face it, Levi didn't need to know that it meant so much to me that I actually remembered it. Or that it still stung. "What I meant is—"

"I know what you meant." His shoulders were suddenly rigid.

"Then you can see why it wouldn't be a good idea."

"You didn't say it wouldn't be a good idea. You said it would be a mistake."

"Because it would be."

"You're probably right."

"So maybe we should just forget the whole thing."

I'd just turned to walk away when Danny Portman, the man who owned one of the local bars and was chairing this year's wake committee, called out for help.

Levi darted over to the stage. "Stop by," he called back over his shoulder to me. "Anytime."

"Right." I wasn't sure why knowing I had a standing invitation to Levi's made me feel a little like the world had tipped on its axis.

Or maybe I was.

And maybe I didn't even want to think about it.

Just when I stepped out to the sidewalk, I heard a voice cry out from somewhere over near the stage where Levi, Danny, and two other men had a brightly painted wooden coffin with the word *Summer* written on it in large yellow letters up on their shoulders.

"It's heavy!" Danny called out. He was shorter than Levi and not nearly as broad, and even as I watched, he lost his grip. Since I'm even shorter than Danny, I wasn't at all sure what I thought I was going to do, but I darted forward to lend a hand.

"The stupid thing's just made of plywood!" one of the other men cried out, trying to adjust his stance when his feet slid. "There's no way it should be this heavy." He stepped forward, shifting his weight, then stepped back again just as I arrived on the scene, my hands out.

"Better not," Levi called and, with a look, urged me to keep my distance. "We're off balance. We're going to—"

The coffin slipped off Danny's shoulder, and after that, it was impossible for the others to hold on.

It hit the ground with more of a thump than plywood should make, and when one side of the coffin broke away and fell to the ground, it was easy to see why.

"Holy Toledo!" Like the rest of us, Danny saw the arm that flopped out of the casket, but unlike the rest of us, he apparently didn't watch the police shows on TV and remember that things like bodies in fake coffins should be left undisturbed. He darted forward and flipped open the lid.

Noreen Turner looked up at us, dressed in her camouflage, eyes wide open, the left side of her skull smashed in.

It didn't take a ghost getter to see that she was very, very dead.

❖ 6 ❖

It took a couple hours for Hank and the other members of the Put-in-Bay police force to take our statements and be done with those of us who witnessed what happened in the park.

And a couple hours after that for me to calm my shattered nerves.

Which didn't explain why when I raised my hand to knock on the door where Levi had hung a shimmery wreath of silver ghosts, it was shaking.

I knocked anyway.

In the exactly two seconds I gave him to answer, there was no sign of Levi, and I'd just whirled away from the door to go back down the outside stairs that led to the deck off the back of his second-floor apartment when I heard the door click open behind me.

"Going somewhere?"

I paused, one hand on the railing, and tried for casual when I turned to face him. "You said I could stop by. Anytime."

"And I meant it." He stepped back and opened the door farther. "Come on in."

It wasn't quite dinnertime, but I pretended I didn't realize that. "If you're in the middle of eating or something, I can come back another time."

He waved a hand, indicating his spick-and-span kitchen with its oak cabinets and deep green marble countertops. "Too early for dinner. I could be talked into making coffee. Would you like some?"

What I would have liked was not feeling so darned nervous simply because I was in Levi's apartment. After all, I was there on business. Sort of. And if I kept that in mind, maybe I could also remember that I wasn't some kid. I was used to the attention of good-looking guys. I'd gotten plenty of it back in New York.

But never from a guy who told me later that it was all a big ol' mistake.

I washed away the thought with a drink of better-than-average-but-not-quite-as-good-as-mine coffee and watched over the rim of my cup while Levi settled back against the countertop, his long legs out in front of him.

"You're not investigating."

It took me a moment to figure out what he was talking about. "Noreen's murder? Hank's taking care of everything."

He pursed his lips and nodded his approval. "I'm glad to hear it."

I set my cup on the countertop, and honest, I didn't mean to plunk it down so hard. Still, the resulting bang punctuated what I had to say. "You're not going to start that again, are you? You're not going to pretend it's any of your business to tell me what's any of my business."

"I wouldn't dream of it." His mischievous smile said differently, but it was a smile, after all, and if nothing else, it told me he wasn't looking to pick a fight. "I just wondered, that's all. After two murders—"

"Three, technically. I've solved three murders since I came to the island."

He gave in with a tip of his head. "Three. But still, you're telling me number four doesn't interest you?"

"I didn't say it didn't interest me. I said Hank was taking care of everything. What it does do"—I wrapped my arms around myself—"is it creeps me out. Noreen was difficult, sure, but if everyone who was difficult died, there wouldn't be many people left in the world. I saw her just last night, and she was alive and well, even if she was nasty and maddening. To think that she's dead . . . it's just horrible."

"And the thought of another murder here on the island . . ." Levi pushed off from where he'd been leaning. "It's not what I expected when I came here."

"Me, either," I admitted. "I thought this was small-town America, and—"

"Small-town America is supposed to be boring and predictable."

"I'd be perfectly happy with boring and predictable, but I was thinking more like how I always thought a small town would be safe. It is safe, right? You can walk around the island any time of the day or night and not feel the least bit threatened or uncomfortable. But still . . ." I picked up my coffee cup to take another drink, but remembering what we'd seen when the lid of the coffin was pushed back soured my stomach. I set down my cup. "It's terrible."

"But you're not investigating? That's not why you're here? Not to ask me if I know who brought that silly coffin to the park? Or who went anywhere near it? Or if I realized something was wrong the minute I hoisted it up on my shoulders?"

Come to think of it, I was dying (poor choice of words) to know the answers to each and every one of those questions. But no, that wasn't why I was there, and I told myself not to forget it.

"Actually, I'm here because of Sleepy," I told Levi.

"The ghost."

"There are no such things as ghosts." I shouldn't have had to remind him. Or myself, in spite of the fact that the memory of that odd, headless half shadow flitted through my mind. "I'm here because of Charlie Harlow, the real person. I told you, I'm doing some research. I thought it might . . ." My shrug should have said it all, but I knew it wasn't enough. I had to explain. "I thought if I kept busy, maybe I could take my mind off what happened today. What we saw over at the park."

"Yeah." The way Levi twitched those broad shoulders of his, I could tell he was as uncomfortable with the memory as I was. "Poor woman. It looked as if her head had been—"

"Bashed in. Yeah." Now for sure I knew I didn't want any more coffee. To prove it, I pushed the cup farther away. "Rather than think about that," I told him, "I thought I'd get to work on this project I'm helping Marianne with." Technically, it wasn't a lie, so I didn't feel guilty about this part of my explanation. "This was Sleepy's apartment." I glanced around at the sleek countertops, the stainless appliances, the gleaming white ceramic tile floor. "Something tells me it didn't look like this when he lived here."

"Believe me, it didn't look like this when I bought the place last year. Too bad you didn't stop by then. I bet every bit of crumbling linoleum and every chip of peeling paint went all the way back to Sleepy's day."

"That would have been helpful."

"Really?" Levi grabbed my cup and took it, along with his own, to the sink. He rinsed them, put them in the dishwasher, then turned to face me, his arms folded over his chest. "Why do you care? What are you and Marianne up to?"

I knew it would come to this, and I was prepared with a story. "She's writing this book about Sleepy, you see. Not about the whole silly ghost thing; about the real person. She's even got an academic press that's going to publish it. And I'm sort of helping. With the research. And proof-reading."

"Do you know anything about writing a book?"

I hoped my quick smile was noncommittal. "If I could just look around," I suggested. "I know I'm being pushy, but—"

"Not pushy at all." I was grateful when he stepped toward a doorway that led into the living room at the front of the apartment, because for a moment there, I thought he was going to press his point. He led me into the living room, which, like the kitchen, had obviously been redone recently, and by someone whose taste was above average and whose budget could support it. The walls were painted an understated, just-barely-there color that reminded me of the stainless appliances in the kitchen. Except for the doorway in the middle of the wall that opened into a hallway that led to a bathroom and bedrooms beyond, the wall on my right was lined with bookshelves. Always curious about peoples' reading habits, I headed that way.

A smattering of history: Civil War and World War II. A

few books about baseball. A book or two on sailing. A variety of cookbooks that promised interesting things would be happening at Levi's sometime soon: street-food tacos, Southern cooking, waffles both savory and sweet. A couple novels.

"FX O'Grady." Levi came up behind me and put a hand against the shelf nearest to where I stood, the circle of his arm only inches from my shoulder. The temperature in the room shot up a degree or two, and I knew if I leaned just a tiny bit to my left . . .

I stopped myself before I could succumb, and concentrated instead on the lurid titles of the novels nearest my nose. They were splashed across the hardcover spines in shades of red, dusty gray, and bilious green, in fonts that looked like blood and smoke and drool: *A Demon's Wrath*, *Minions of Misery*, *Blood Ties*. If ever there was a time for stating the obvious, this was it.

"You like to read horror."

Since I refused to look Levi's way, I didn't know for sure, but I imagined he smiled when he said, "And you don't like reading scary stories. At least that's what I've heard." He shifted his stance just a tad, a move that made his hip brush mine when he plucked the nearest book from the shelf. He opened it to the inside back cover. "Look at that. The best selling of all the best-selling authors and the guy doesn't even get his picture in the book."

I wasn't sure what I was supposed to say about this so I didn't say anything at all.

"Think he's shy?" Levi asked.

"Maybe he's embarrassed that he writes books that scare so many people."

"So, you and the other Ladies in the League won't be reading FX O'Grady in honor of Halloween?"

I tried to make it look perfectly natural when I took a step to my right, the better to put some distance between me and the heat generated by his body. Still, it was impossible to ignore the heady smell of his aftershave. It was as bracing as the fall afternoon, and I wondered if I'd simply missed the scent back at the park, or if he'd splashed it on when he got home to get the smell of death out of his nose.

"We're reading Washington Irving," I said, and prayed my voice didn't sound as breathy to him as it did to me. It might have been the memory of what happened at the park that made my lungs feel as if there were a hand inside my chest, squeezing and twisting.

It might have been something else.

"Sleepy Hollow." Levi chuckled. "A headless horseman and a terrified schoolteacher. At least we don't have to worry about our Sleepy chasing anyone through the woods at night."

"Not as far as we know."

"But I hear your ghost hunters were looking for him, anyway."

Another side step and I was far enough away to turn to him. "They're not my ghost hunters."

"Hank says he thought he was going to have to haul them all into jail last night."

"Kate showed a great deal of restraint."

"Except I heard she and Noreen had a rip-roaring fight before that."

"You're not saying—?" Of course he wasn't. Rather than take the bait, I bit my tongue and stepped around him and to the front of the apartment. There, three tall windows looked toward the Orient Express across the street, the now-closed restaurant where Peter Chan had been killed the spring before. I ignored the memory of Peter's dead eyes staring up at me from behind the front counter where I discovered his body and, instead, forced myself to picture what Sleepy might have seen when he looked out his front windows.

A milk truck, maybe?

A deliveryman bringing blocks of ice?

Swimmers in their knee-length bathing suits made of scratchy wool. Fishermen with their gear. The plume of steam rising out of the funnel of one of the ferries that, back in the day, plied the waters between Detroit and Put-in-Bay, jammed with jaunty day-trippers.

"See anything interesting?" Levi's voice came from right behind me.

"Just thinking about what Sleepy may have seen when he looked out these windows."

"Probably visions of money dancing in his head." Levi chuckled. "From what I heard, the place that used to be the Orient Express—"

"Was a bait and tackle shop before that."

"And probably a dozen other things between then and back when Sleepy lived here. But back in those days, I hear it was a speakeasy."

"Really?" This was news to me, and I wondered if Marianne knew it and talked about it in her book. Don't get me wrong, I know in my head that Prohibition spawned any number of criminal enterprises, and some of them were ruthless and violent. Just ask Sleepy. But like a lot of people, I couldn't help but be caught up in the romance of the speakeasy, an illegal hideaway where you needed the friends—and the right password—to get by security and into a place where you could purchase and drink liquor.

These days, it all seems so impossible, but in the thirteen

years that it was the law of the land, Prohibition—what President Herbert Hoover once called the Noble Experiment—made it impossible to manufacture, sell, or transport beer, wine, and liquor.

Legally, that is.

That didn't stop criminals like Charlie Harlow or the thousands of others who made gin in their bathtubs or smuggled booze over the borders and into the US.

"What do you think?" I asked Levi. "Do you suppose Sleepy brought the booze here, then simply walked it across the street to the speakeasy?"

"That doesn't seem like the smartest plan, even for back in the nineteen twenties before there were any sophisticated surveillance techniques." The furniture in the living room was cushy leather, a couch and chair, both black. There was a TV on the wall opposite the bookshelves and a glass and metal coffee table in front of the couch that was scattered with sports and restaurant management magazines, a remote control, and an iPad. Levi perched on the arm of the couch.

"From what I've heard some of the old-timers at the bar say, there are supposed to be caves around the island where the smugglers stored their booze."

It made sense. After all, as the ghost getters had so recently reminded me, South Bass is made up of limestone, and there are caves all over the island. "So he'd bring in the booze—"

"Probably from Middle Island, north of here," Levi said, then shrugged and glanced at his iPad. "All right, I admit it. After you told me Sleepy used to live here, I was intrigued. I did a little online research about Prohibition in these parts. The island was a hotbed of activity."

"We're less than ten miles from Canadian waters."

"Exactly. Which means Sleepy and other bootleggers

like him could easily pick up alcohol in Canada, where it was perfectly legal, and bring it back here, where it was illegal and all the more lucrative because of it."

"Sounds perfect, but remember, things didn't end happily for our Sleepy."

"Done in by a rival gang," Levi said. "At least that's what my research says. Sleepy was scheduled to hand over a load of Canadian liquor at a spot not far from your B and B. Your house would have been there at the time, of course. It was built well before Sleepy's time. But most of the other places, like Kate's and Chandra's—"

"They're too new. They wouldn't have been there."

"Which meant that was the perfect spot," Levi said. "They would need to make the exchange someplace where they wouldn't get interrupted by the local boys in blue. Sleepy went to the meet thinking it was nothing more than that, but he'd apparently ticked off some of the other bad guys. They killed him."

"And cut off his head." Not a good thought on the best of days. Coming so soon after we found Noreen, bludgeoned and bloody, the thought made my stomach swoop.

"Sorry." Levi popped up, grabbed my elbow, and escorted me into the nearest chair. "You look a little green, and I don't blame you. The other gangsters killing Sleepy, that was one thing. But even for Prohibition-era mobsters, the whole beheading thing, that was pretty out there. They really must have been mad at Sleepy about something."

"I'm fine. Really. I mean, it is part of Sleepy's story. You can't have a headless ghost if he's still got his head."

"You want water?" Levi asked, and before I could tell him I didn't need it, he disappeared into the kitchen and I heard the tap running. When he came back, he held out the glass to me, but even when I took it in my hands, he didn't let go.

"Somehow, I can't think of Marianne having enough imagination to care about what Sleepy saw when he looked out these windows," he said.

I tried for a smile. "That's why I'm helping."

"Because you're the one with imagination."

"Because I'm being thorough." I refused to play tug-of-war. If he wasn't going to relinquish the glass of water, I didn't really much care. I stood, and when I did, Levi had no choice but to back up a step. "Marianne will be grateful that you let me look around."

"And you're not."

"Of course I'm grateful. Taking a look at the apartment gives me a better sense of who Sleepy was."

"He worked at Wilder's, you know."

Though I'm sure Marianne must have mentioned it, I'd yet to find that in the pee-soaked pages. "If it was illegal to make liquor—"

"There were a few exceptions." I guess Levi realized that he sounded like a know-it-all, because he grinned. "Just more of what I was reading about online. A few wineries were allowed to stay in business to produce church wine. And all of them were allowed to keep making grape juice. If customers bought that juice and chose to take it home and ferment it . . ."

"Living that way—it's all so hard to imagine."

"But not hard to imagine how smuggling booze would appeal to someone with a sense of daring."

"Would you have done it?" I asked him. "If you lived back then, would you have taken the chance and pushed the envelope? A lot of people did, but would you? Would you have been a bootlegger?"

The fact that Levi didn't answer right away told me all I needed to know.

"I've bothered you long enough." I stepped away from the chair, and behind my back, I crossed my fingers. "I'll let Marianne know what I found out, and she'll take it from there." The glint of the setting sun flashed against the front window, and I glanced that way. "Will they still have the wake tomorrow?" I wondered.

He shrugged. "Try explaining canceling a major event to a few thousand tourists who are ready to party hearty. If you ask me, the powers that be are going to sweep Noreen's murder under the rug. At least for the next couple days. The party will go on, and Hank will work quietly behind the scenes."

"There's bound to be talk."

"And speculation." When he looked at me hard, as if trying to determine if I would be one of those speculating, and if I'd be acting on whatever it was I might find out, I strolled toward the window. "Do you have any theories?"

"I told you, that's Hank's job. I'd be happy to tell him what I've seen."

"Which is . . ?"

It was my turn to shrug, not because what I had to say was unimportant, but because at this point, I wasn't sure what any of it really meant.

"Dimitri—he's a member of EGG—he didn't get along with Noreen at all. In fact, yesterday afternoon, he was plenty mad at her about something. She told him they'd talk about it later. And there's another woman, but there's no way she could have done it. She arrived on the ferry right before we found Noreen's body. Jacklyn didn't like Noreen, either."

"You mean that gorgeous brunette you were talking to in the park."

I thought back to the way Jacklyn had made it loud and

clear—with a look, with the way she fixed Dimitri's cof-fee, with the casual way she rubbed against him or took his hand or flung an arm across the back of his chair—that she was warning me to keep my distance. "She says she didn't like Noreen because Noreen fired her from the show. I wonder if there was more to it than that. Jacklyn's just about the most jealous woman I've ever met."

"Jealous, huh?" Levi thought this over. "Still, she's mighty good-looking!"

I shouldn't have minded hearing Levi talk about Jack-lyn that way. I wasn't, I told myself. After all, if I allowed a pang of envy to enter into the picture, then it would mean something I didn't want it to mean. About someone I didn't want it to mean something about.

Which, believe it or not, actually made sense to me at that moment.

"And there's Kate, of course," Levi suggested.

Just as he spoke her name, I caught sight of Kate walk-ing down the sidewalk outside Levi's bar. She was dressed in jeans and a navy sweater, and her coppery hair was the exact color of the blazing maple across the street. A few of our fellow island residents walked past, but Kate didn't even bother to nod hello. She sidestepped a group of tour-ists who'd stopped to consult a map, and completely ignored Mike Lawrence, once a murder suspect, who was helping to unload a beer delivery truck parked outside the bar.

"Kate is hardly the murdering type," I said.

"I never said she was. But there was bad blood between Kate and Noreen."

"Because Noreen was an idiot." I shot him a look. "There, now you know I didn't like Noreen, either. Are you going to tell me I'm a suspect, too?"

"Just joining in the speculation."

Apparently, Levi wasn't the only one.

I was just about to turn away from the window when I saw Hank's red, white, and blue police SUV cruise down the street. He spotted Kate, slowed to a stop, and got out of the truck.

"Of course Hank is going to talk to Kate," I mumbled when I saw the police chief approach my friend, more to reassure myself than because I thought I had to provide Levi with some sort of explanation. "Hank was at the winery last night. He saw what went on."

At my shoulder, Levi peered out of the window. "She's getting into his car with him."

Kate did, and the car turned down a street that we both knew led to the police station.

"It doesn't mean a thing," I said, whirling from the window. "Just because Hank is talking to Kate, it doesn't mean—"

"No, but that might."

I turned back around and looked where Levi was pointing. Dominic Bender was a fixture on South Bass, an attorney whose clients included many of the island's most well-to-do families, some of its biggest businesses, and, coincidentally, Kate Wilder. Dominic was a big man and he drove a big car that was instantly recognizable by anyone who'd spent any time at all on the island: a black Lincoln that was always waxed to a finish that made the sun shimmer off its sleek surfaces like light on water.

The Lincoln pulled around the corner from the direction of the park.

"That doesn't mean a thing," I told Levi. "It's not unusual for Dominic to be seen around town."

"Of course not. But you know Dom as well as I do. The

weather is perfect, and he's not out on his boat? I dunno."
When Levi pressed his lips together, his expression was
grim. "It could mean something."

"It doesn't. It can't," I assured him, and I believed it.

Or at least I tried.

I went right on believing it, too.

Right up until I saw Dominic's car follow Hank's to the
police station.

❮❮❖ 7 ❖❯❯

I called the League of Literary Ladies into action.

Well, not the entire League, of course, because one of our members was at the police station, and I had no doubt why—Hank was questioning Kate about Noreen's murder.

"Do you really think we should do this?"

Of all people, I didn't expect Chandra to be the one to protest.

At the front door of Wilder Winery, I paused and looked over my shoulder to find her wide-eyed and dancing from foot to foot.

"The winery is closed," Chandra said. She glanced left, then right, and her pumpkin earrings brushed the black sweater she wore with an orange turtleneck. "Kate always closes the winery the day before the wake. You know, so her employees can get ready for the last official weekend of the summer season and because she knows they'll be slammed tomorrow once all the tourists arrive. That means there's nobody here and the place is all locked up and—"

I didn't wait for her to finish. Instead, I reached behind one of those planters filled with a riot of yellow and orange mums I'd seen looking all ghostly the night before. That evening, with the sun quickly slipping below the horizon and turning the waters of Lake Erie to a fiery orange, the darker flowers took on the color of blood.

So not an image I wanted to think about. Not with the memory of Noreen's body still so fresh in my head.

Rather than dwell, I reached around the flowerpot. Tucked between it and the building was a decorative stone about the size of a softball. Behind that was a smaller, less showy piece of granite, and under that—

I stood up and showed the front door key to Chandra and Luella, who was standing on Chandra's right.

"A couple months ago, Kate told me where to find the extra key. You know, just in case of an emergency," I explained.

"Well, if this isn't an emergency, I don't know what is." Luella stepped forward. "We've got to do something."

"Exactly." I opened the door and stepped inside.

Except for the quickly failing evening light, the winery was dark. Long shadows spilled across the floor from the direction of the windows, and in between the racks of wine bottles, the display of hand-painted stemware, and the cooler where Wilder's offered a variety of cheeses, olives, and other goodies for tourists who wanted snacks with their wine, the shadows were even darker.

I couldn't help myself.

As casually as I could, so that Luella and Chandra wouldn't think I was some sort of nutcase, I checked and double-checked each and every one of those shadows, and, satisfied that none of them looked the least bit like a head-less gangster, I ventured a few more steps into the winery and was enveloped by the silence that filled the place, from the open-beamed ceiling to the hardwood floor. Though Luella and Chandra were only a few feet behind me, I felt suddenly and inexplicably alone.

" 'One of the quietest places in the whole world,' " I murmured.

"What?" From behind me, Chandra's voice bounced against the walls.

When I was done flinching, I managed a smile. "Just a line from *The Legend of Sleepy Hollow*," I said. "You know, right at the beginning, when Washington Irving is describing the little place called Sleepy Hollow. He says it's an enchanted place. That it's quiet and dreamy."

"Too quiet." When she glanced around, Chandra's eyes were big. She wrapped her arms around herself. "Don't forget, Bea, this is where those investigators got the video of Sleepy last year."

"They got a video," I told her, and reminded myself. "That doesn't mean it was a video of Sleepy. Since we both know there's no such thing as ghosts—"

I should have known better. I did know better. But it was impossible to call the words back.

Chandra might still be wide-eyed and on-edge, but her shoulders shot back. "Are you saying that the Egyptians were wrong? That the Romans and the Greeks and the Mesopotamians didn't know what they were talking about? They all believed in ghosts, Bea. People still do. All around the world."

"But not right here. Not right now." I wasn't about to confess that I said this more for my own benefit than for hers. "We've got more important things to worry about."

"Things more important than the shifting veils between the dimensions? Than the vast, unknown universe or the shadows that reside on the Other Side?" Chandra shivered and the witch on the front of her sweater did the hoochie-koochie. "I don't think so, Bea."

"Then I'll tell you what"—I looped an arm through hers, the better to distract her—"we'll worry about Sleepy another time. For now, Kate has to be our first priority."

Chandra might be a little out there (okay, a lot out there) when it came to her beliefs in ghosts and tarot and the power of crystals, but deep down, she had her priorities plenty straight. She knew that friendship came first. Which was why she was so upset at seeing EGG's return in the first place. I was counting on her loyalty, but I guess I underestimated how frightened she was.

"We should go." She stepped toward the door. "I mean all of us. We should go. We shouldn't be poking around where we don't belong. We can come back another time and—"

"You want to explain again why we're here and what you want us to do?" Luella asked, effectively cutting off Chandra.

I hated to admit (again) what I'd already admitted to both Luella and Chandra when I called them thirty minutes earlier. "I don't know. Not for certain. I know we have to figure out a way to help. Hank is talking to Kate and Kate's attorney is in on the conversation."

"Of course he's talking to Kate." The hand Luella put on my arm was supposed to be reassuring, and had we been talking about anyone else but Kate, it might have been. "He knows about the fight Kate had with Noreen last night. You told us Hank walked in here in the middle of it. He's just doing his job, that's all. Just getting his ducks in a row. He'd be crazy not to talk to Kate."

"He is crazy," Chandra added, but neither Luella nor I paid much attention. After all, Chandra had once been married to Hank. Her opinion of his mental status didn't exactly count. "He knows Kate would never kill anyone."

"We know that, too." I was as sure of this as I was of my own name. Funny, that didn't make my voice, echoing back from the ceiling at me, sound any more certain. "I wouldn't think anything of Kate talking to Hank, or of Dominic Bender hanging around, if it wasn't so late in the day. The fact that Hank wants to talk to Kate now and that her attorney is present—"

"Hank just wants to get it out of the way. So he can move on to the real suspects." Luella gave me another reassuring pat.

"Or he's just being a pain in the neck," Chandra insisted.

"Either way, we've got to make sure we've got all the bases covered. I thought we should start here . . ." I twirled around, taking in the winery. "Because this is where Kate and I found Noreen and her crew last night. We know Kate didn't kill Noreen. But whoever did . . . I don't know. Maybe there's some sort of clue here. Something we can tell Hank about. He's too smart to think Kate could actually be guilty, but if word of her being suspected gets around, it could hurt her business, and we can't let that happen."

"Agreed." Luella pulled in a long breath and let it out slowly. "So tell us what to look for."

I only wished I knew.

"We can each take one part of the winery," I suggested, "and just walk. And look. And see if anything is odd or out of place or weird."

"Like the ghost of Sleepy Harlow?" The second Luella and I gave Chandra *that* look, her lower lip protruded. "It's not like I'm the only one who believes in Sleepy. Plenty of people have seen him, and you saw that video, Bea. If it was filmed anywhere else, I wouldn't be so worried. But it happened right here in the winery. If you want us walking around alone, anything could happen. We could see him. Or hear him. Or bump into him." Her gaze darted past me toward the fermenting room and the warehouse beyond, and her shoulders shot back. "All right. If we have to. I'll check back there," she said. "That's where they shot that video last year. Since I'm the only one around here who actually believes in Sleepy—well, maybe he'll take pity on a true believer and he won't jump out of some dark corner and scare me."

I didn't need another ghost getter on my hands. "You and Luella can go together," I said. I made a grab for Chandra's arm so I could send her off with Luella, but she would have none of it. She marched on toward the fermenting room where, the night before, Kate and I had found the ghost getters.

She would have kept right on going if we didn't hear a small sound from the direction of the front door. Chandra froze in her tracks and spun around.

"You heard that, right? Bea, you heard that?"

"I heard a squeak."

"A squeak and a—"

The front door swished open, and Chandra's statement was lost in a burble. I was so busy listening to her, I barely heard the noisy bump of my own heart.

That is, until I saw Kate step into the winery.

"It's you!" I hoped I didn't look or sound as relieved as I felt. I was, after all, trying to put up a brave front. "Hank didn't arrest you."

"Of course he didn't arrest me." Kate flipped on a

phalanx of overhead spots and we squinted at each other through the sudden flood of light. "Don't be ridiculous. Why would Hank arrest me? I haven't done anything wrong."

I believed her. Hook, line, and sinker. But that didn't stop me from noticing the lines of worry at the corners of Kate's mouth or the way she twisted her hands together.

"So you didn't kill Noreen?" Chandra asked.

For once, I thought Kate was perfectly justified in rolling her emerald green eyes.

"Of course she didn't kill Noreen," I reminded Chandra, then, for Kate's benefit, added, "That's why we're here. To look for clues so we can figure out who did."

"Clues, good." Kate paced a nervous little pattern in front of us. She was wearing knee-high boots and her heels clicked like gunshots against the wood floor. "Suspects, better. Because I'll tell you what . . ." She froze in place, and when she looked at the three of us standing there watching her, Kate's eyes filled with tears. "Maybe he didn't arrest me, but Hank thinks I did it. He didn't come right out and say it, but I swear, he actually thinks I killed Noreen. He . . ." Kate's breathing sped up, and she pressed a hand to her chest. "He knows I was mad at her. He made me admit it. About last year and the way Noreen and her friends trampled my grapes, and about how I felt when I found her here last night and saw them and how it all came back to me, all the anger, and how I would have wrung her neck if you weren't here with me, Bea."

"Those are nothing but facts." I kept my voice as calm as possible, which was no easy thing, considering that Chandra had tears rolling down her cheeks, Luella was wringing her hands, and I was close to losing it. "None of that means a thing. Facts are just facts, and facts help Hank build a timeline. You know, so he can figure out where Noreen went when she left here. I just assumed she came back to the B and B."

"You mean that's where she was killed?"

I hadn't even considered it, so Chandra's question gave me an extra-special case of the creeps. I twitched it away with a shake. "I think someone would have noticed," I said. "My cleaning people were in this morning and they didn't say anything about blood. The way Noreen looked . . ." The memory washed over me and left me cold. "Wherever she was killed, there must have been a whole lot of blood."

I was already edgy enough; this was not something I wanted to think about. It was better to stay focused, stay centered, stay objective. I tried. "You have nothing to worry about," I told Kate. "Before Hank can make an arrest, he needs proof. You might have been mad at Noreen. Nobody can blame you. But before Hank can say you did it, he needs to prove you had means, motive, and opportunity."

"Means." Kate nodded, and her complexion turned green. "I heard her head was bashed in. Anybody could have done that, I guess. With anything. A rock. Or a bat. Or a brick. Or a—"

"We get it," Luella told her.

Kate nodded again, and paced some more. Faster. Harder. Her heels banged against the floor. "Motive. Okay, yeah, I admit that part. I did have motive. Last year's destruction, for one thing. And this year, with her coming here without my permission. I guess so-angry-my-head-was-going-to-pop-off is a legitimate motive. But don't forget, there have to be a bunch of other people who have motives, too. There can't be anyone anywhere who actually liked Noreen. She was pushy and rude and—"

"And compulsive and ornery and bossy," I added. "I've already got a short list of the people who didn't like her. We'll check out each and every one of them."

The nods were coming faster, and Kate's left eye twitched. She swallowed hard. "Opportunity. Well, we know I couldn't have done it, Bea. We left here, and I drove you home, and—"

"And when I got home, EGG was back," I said. "At least, all their trucks were. I didn't see any of them; I figured they'd all gone to bed. And I didn't stick around for breakfast this morning. I guess Noreen missed it."

"Well, I can vouch for Fiona," Chandra said, and nodded. "She was in her room listening to a CD of Tibetan monks chanting. You know, while she did her meditation."

Frustrated, I twirled a wayward strand of my unruly hair. "I wish I'd been paying more attention," I mumbled. "I wonder if Noreen came home with everyone else."

"Well, I went home and stayed home." Kate crossed her arms over her navy sweater. "I was so mad, I couldn't see straight. I had a little glass of sherry to calm my nerves and I went right to bed. I didn't work today. I stayed home and enjoyed the day, just like I told all my employees to do."

"That's all you need to tell Hank." In the hope of calming her down, I made eye contact with Kate and refused to look away. "Just the truth. And when he talks to me—and I'm sure he'll get around to it eventually—I'll tell him I was with you as soon as you got back from the mainland. I was with you the whole time you were here at the winery, too, and Noreen and her bunch left here before we did. I'll tell him you dropped me off at home after we left here last night. Then you went home and went to bed. You never had the chance to murder Noreen. Hank will see that. He'll believe it. He'll—"

"He'll slap the cuffs on me and throw me in jail forever and ever!" Kate wailed.

Sure, she was being a little melodramatic, but hey, it's not like I could blame her. It can't be easy being a murder suspect. Especially when you're innocent.

I looked Luella's way and she got the message and moved to Kate's side. "There's an employee lunchroom here at the winery, isn't there?" I asked Kate. I knew there was; I just wanted to ground Kate in reality. Thank goodness, it worked. She pulled herself out of the panic that gripped her and looked past the tasting bar. "Luella, how about if you take Kate in there and get her a cup of tea."

"Or a glass of wine," Luella suggested.

Now that I thought about it, that was the better plan.

"You go do that," I told them. "Chandra and I will—"

"I'll look around for clues. And Sleepy!" Chandra said, and she scurried away.

"Good. Fine," I mumbled to myself once they were gone. "I don't need someone to hold my hand while I look around the winery to keep me from getting the heebie-jeebies. I am, after all, a New Yorker."

I told myself not to forget it, and chin high, shoulders back, and brain absolutely refusing to even consider the fact that there was even the teensiest possibility that I could bump into the ghost of the long-dead bootlegger, I proceeded to look around.

It didn't take long to see that there was nothing out of place in the tasting room or the gift shop. I looked through the fermentation room, too, where a little less than twenty-four hours earlier, we'd discovered the investigators and where Kate and Noreen had had it out.

Nothing.

I breathed a sigh of relief.

It wasn't like I thought I'd really find anything at Wilder's. It wasn't like I wanted to. After all, Noreen and her bunch left the winery before Kate and I had the night before.

That meant that Noreen had been killed somewhere else.

By someone other than Kate.

I left the fermentation room and went into the back hallway, following it past the offices where the accounting people took care of the books, and the packing people handled orders, and the shipping people did their magic to send Wilder's wine to speciality shops in five different states.

I skirted their offices and headed into the warehouse, feeling along the wall for the light switch and breathing a sigh of relief (Okay, I admit it) when I found it and flicked on the overhead lights to banish the inky shadows.

I didn't expect to see Chandra jump out of one of them at the far end of the room.

"You're looking around in the dark?" I asked.

She pressed her back to the door just behind her. "I just thought if I did I might bump into—"

"Sleepy. Yeah, I know." I hurried over to where Chandra stood, glancing around the warehouse as I did.

In the grand scheme of the beverage business, Wilder's is definitely considered a small, boutique winery. But the warehouse—which was part of the original winery complex that hadn't been touched by the fire a few years earlier—was a cavernous space. High ceiling, cement floors, aisle after aisle of metal shelving that rose nearly to the twenty-foot ceiling. Once upon a time, those shelves had been filled with product. These days, with Kate concentrating more on the quality of her wine than the quantity she could produce, most but the shelves nearest to me were empty.

I looked them over anyway, crisscrossing the warehouse from one aisle to the next, and one end to the other. I was all the way over on the far side of the room near where Chandra bounced from foot to foot outside a metal door with a *Do Not Enter* sign on it when I spotted it.

The old metal door was open a fraction of an inch.

"It doesn't make any sense," I mumbled. "Kate told me once that there's nothing beyond this door but some old storage rooms that aren't used anymore."

"That's true." Chandra grabbed my arm and tugged me toward the door we'd come in. "Which means there's nothing here for us to see. Let's get out of here."

"Not so fast!" I untangled myself from her grip. "We owe it to ourselves to check this out. We owe it to Kate."

With that in mind, I pulled open the metal door, and we found ourselves looking into a smaller room where the walls were made of red brick arranged in a basket-weave pattern. I felt around the wall right inside the door and turned on the lights.

Chandra gasped.

I stood perfectly still, staring at the plasmometer—the piece of equipment I'd seen the ghost hunters leave with the night before—where it lay in pieces on the floor. One side of it was bashed in, the metal dark and twisted, and the glass that had once covered a lens of some sort was broken and scattered through the mess of blood and bone and hair nearby.

My stomach lurched, and my hands shook when I reached for my phone.

I hated to do it. I hated to get Kate more involved. But really, I didn't have much of a choice.

I called Hank and told him to get over to Wilder's right away.

❖ 8 ❖

"Well, I think we can say it wasn't a planned murder." When he examined the plasmometer, Hank's expression was grim. "The murderer used something that was on hand to kill Ms. Turner. That means it was a crime of passion, something done at the spur of the moment with no planning involved. The killer didn't bring the weapon with him."

"Except he did," I reminded Hank. "This isn't something that was just hanging around the winery. It's one of EGG's ghost-finding devices. Remember, when the ghost getters left here last night, they took this gizmo with them."

"You're right! I was so worried about Kate hauling off and punching Ms. Turner, I didn't pay a whole lot of attention to anything else." Hank chewed on the end of the pencil he was using to jot notes in a little spiral-bound notebook. "So you're saying—"

"They came back. After Kate and I left. And obviously . . ." I glanced at the battered plasmometer and at the blood caked on it. Hank had already called in a forensics team from the state crime bureau, but until they arrived, I knew better than to touch anything. Still, it didn't take an expert to see the dark, rusty-colored stains on the stone floor around the plasmometer.

Or to know exactly what they were.

I pressed a hand to my stomach. "Noreen came back, and she was killed right here."

"Looks that way."

"Well, that's good for you," I told him, then, since he gave me a quizzical look, I explained, "Now that you have a crime scene, you can collect evidence. But Kate . . ." After I called Hank, I'd escorted poor, shaken Chandra into the lunchroom, and while I was there, I'd left strict orders with Luella: Don't let Kate leave the room. The last thing she needed was to see this terrible scene. "She's going to be very upset," I said. "Once Kate finds out Noreen was murdered here, she's going to feel even worse."

"Unless she already knows."

"You mean because I called you and the place is swarming with cops and—"

Silly me. Reality hit, and I spun away from the beat-up plasmometer and the spilled blood so that I could prop my fists on my hips and give Hank a look that would have intimidated a lesser man. Since Hank was a foot taller than me, at least one hundred pounds heavier, and had the added advantage of years of experience and a lifetime of law enforcement training, he didn't exactly shake in his shoes.

But hey, just because I gave up on being intimidating didn't mean I was any less angry. "You're out of your mind if you think Kate did this. You know Kate, she's not the violent type. She'd never have the heart to—"

"Not even if she was plenty mad?"

I crossed my arms over my chest. "She *was* plenty mad. You know that. And she had a really good reason to be. But she didn't kill Noreen because of it. You saw how she handled things last night. She didn't even want you to arrest Noreen and her bunch, even though they deserved it."

"Maybe because she figured she'd handle things her own way. Maybe she called Ms. Turner and told her she had a change of heart. Maybe she invited Ms. Turner back here, then when Ms. Turner showed up, maybe Kate was waiting for her. You know, to teach her a lesson."

Preposterous!

I didn't bother to say it. Mostly because Hank's fierce glare told me he wasn't in the mood for debate. I went with facts instead.

"Kate and I were here for maybe fifteen minutes after you left last night," I told him. "We went up to the office, made sure nothing there had been touched, did a quick look around the rest of the place. Then we left here together. She dropped me off at home and then she went home herself. She went home, and she stayed there."

Hank rolled back on his heels. "And you know this because you were with her the entire night? Or because you sat up all night long and looked out your front window so you could keep an eye on her house?"

When I glared at him, I narrowed my eyes just for good measure. "I know it because Kate told me that's what happened."

"Uh-huh." It was amazing how much mistrust and disbelief could be packed into two little syllables. "When you've been around people as long as I have—"

"This isn't people, Hank. It's Kate." In an effort to keep the crime scene as uncontaminated as possible, we stepped out of the small, brick-walled room and back into the warehouse, and my voice ricocheted from the high ceilings and the empty metal shelving that surrounded us. "You know Kate wouldn't do this."

"I only know what the facts tell me." He eyed me the way I imagined he checked out the groups of rowdy college students who were known to visit the island on weekends. "So tell me some facts, Bea. What did Kate tell you about Ms. Turner?"

"She told me Noreen was on the island last year. That Noreen and her bunch destroyed a crop of grapes Kate had just planted."

"She say anything about what she was going to do about it?"

I lifted my chin. "That's just how people talk when they're mad," I said. "It's just what people say when they need to let off steam. It doesn't mean—"

"What did Kate say exactly?"

My stomach went cold. "She said she'd like to see Noreen at the bottom of the lake. Or in one of the fermenting tanks. But that doesn't mean anything, Hank. You know that. You know people—"

"You said it yourself: This isn't people. This is Kate. And she's not the type who says things she doesn't mean."

"Well, she's not the only one who talked like that," I added quickly, before any of these crazy ideas could settle in his head. "Jacklyn Bichot—she used to be one of the ghost getters, and she said she wants to boil Noreen in oil. But she wasn't on the island the night of the murder."

Hank made a note of it. "I'll need to talk to her anyway and—"

Before Hank had a chance to finish, every light in the winery went out and we were plunged into darkness.

It wasn't so much scary as it was startling, and I caught my breath, then let it out with a little whoop of surprise when the intercom box on the wall next to me buzzed.

"Don't panic. It's not a problem!" Static punctuated Kate's words. "The lights are computer-controlled. At this time of night, they only stay on for an hour at a time when they're turned on manually. I'll go to my office and—"

"No!" Hank talked before he thought, then grumbled a curse, flicked on his flashlight, and aimed it at the intercom so he could press the proper button to talk. "No, Kate. Don't leave the lunchroom. Bea will go up to your office and take care of the lights." Even before he'd eased his pressure on the button, he'd already grabbed my arm and started dragging me along through the dark.

"Just touch the space bar on my keyboard," Kate told me, her voice growing smaller as we made our way out of the warehouse. "The screen will come on. Click *override* and the lights will come back on and stay on."

In a matter of moments, Hank and I were outside the warehouse and back in the hallway that led past the administrative offices of the winery.

"You know where Kate's office is?" Hank asked.

I nodded, then remembered he couldn't see me. "I'll find it."

"Here." He pressed the flashlight into my hand. "The last thing I need is for you to bump into something. Then we'd have even more drama on our hands."

He turned and stalked off through the darkness in the direction of the lunchroom. I went the other way, following the thin beam of the flashlight to Kate's office. Down the hallway, up the stairs. I'd be there in just a minute.

If, like Hank said, I didn't bump into something.

And if that something wasn't something I couldn't really bump into because it was something that wasn't a real something.

A shiver crawled up my back. Is it any wonder? I'd just tripped over the scene of the murder. I'd just discovered a pool of blood and the weapon used to club Noreen to death. I had a perfectly good excuse for being creeped out.

And it had nothing to do with ghosts.

"No Sleepy," I reminded myself in no uncertain terms. "No ghosts. No—" I opened Kate's office door, turned on the lights, looked around the office, and stopped dead in my tracks.

No telling what you might learn about a friend when you're in that friend's office and she never expected you to be there. Not before her, anyway.

The thought burning through my brain, I overrode the computer command to turn on the lights in the winery, looked around again just to be sure I wasn't mistaken (I wasn't), and hurried back downstairs.

I needed to talk to Kate.

Fast.

Before Hank caught on to what I'd just figured out.

I wasn't sure who looked more miserable, Kate, on Luella's right, whose breaths were coming hard and fast. Or Chandra, on Luella's left, who wept uncontrollably as she took tiny sips of wine from one of the tasting glasses used out at the bar.

I offered Luella my commiseration with a small smile as I zipped past, my attention fixed on the fancy-schmancy latte and espresso machine across the room, the one Kate had installed in the employee lunchroom just a few months before. It was the same sort of machine found in high-end coffeehouses, and from what I'd heard, Kate's employees were thrilled with it. Why wouldn't they be? Kate had unveiled the machine at an employee breakfast and told them it was there for them to enjoy because they worked hard and deserved to be pampered.

That's just the kind of person Kate is.

Good-hearted, though she is disinclined to show it.

Considerate, even though she never makes a big deal out of it.

Kate is aware of how morale affects production and how production affects the bottom line. She's demanding, too, about everything from how the labels are placed on the wine bottles to how each customer is greeted at the front door. This was her family business. It was Kate's name on the label of every bottle of wine that left the building. She had a right to expect hard work and to demand a quality product.

Her attention to detail is just one of the things I admire about Kate. She has a lot of determination. And a great sense of style, for another thing. And though she has been known to push me to my limits when it comes to things like always checking her text messages and always worrying about how she looks and always figuring (though she never comes right out and says it) that she's a Wilder so she's just a little bit better than everyone else on the island, Kate is, deep down, a moral and ethical person, and a hard worker, too. More than once, I'd heard stories about how she'd get right down there in the trenches with her employees when they needed help with everything from packing boxes to unloading trucks.

In other words, Kate Wilder was not exactly the stuff killers are made of.

I forced myself to repeat the thought at the same time I grabbed a coffee mug (Kate's orders—no paper or Styrofoam cups allowed in her lunchroom) and fumbled with the controls on the front of the machine. Truth be told, it wasn't rocket science. That didn't keep me from grumbling a curse.

"Kate!" I spun away from the coffee machine and looked at my friend. "Can you show me how to do this? I need an espresso and I need one bad."

From across the room, Kate stared at me.

"Kate!" I called again.

My appeal sank in, and though she shook herself out of her daze, when she got up and walked over, she still reminded me of a zombie. Glassy-eyed. Stiff. Out of it.

But then, I guess shock does weird things to people.

I waited until we stood side by side at the coffee machine before I said another word.

"We need to talk."

"Sure. Yes." Kate's voice was clogged with tears, and when she pushed the proper buttons on the machine, her hands shook. "But you don't have to tell me. I know what's going on. There's only one reason every member of the Put-in-Bay police force would be here. Noreen . . . she . . ." Kate swallowed hard. "It happened here, didn't it?"

The coffee machine whooshed and glugged. I waited until it was done with its gyrations and my cup was filled. I grabbed it and a couple packs of sweetener and headed over to a table on the other side of the room, one far away from Luella and Chandra and the fresh-faced police officer who stood near the door and eyed us as if he'd just seen our faces on a flyer in the post office.

I waited until Kate sat down at the end of a table. Rather than taking the seat across from hers, I pulled a chair over and sat down next to her.

I made sure to keep my voice down when I said, "You came back here last night."

Her eyes went wide, but she recovered as best she could. There was a paper napkin on the table, and she grabbed it and twisted. "No. I didn't. I told you—"

"You told me that after you dropped me off, you went home and stayed home."

She nodded. "That's right."

"You told me you didn't work today, that the winery was closed so your employees could get ready for the crowds tomorrow."

Kate lifted her chin. "That's right. Ask anybody. It's a tradition. We always close the day before the wake."

"So you didn't work today."

"Not here." Impatient—or maybe she was just royally pissed that someone who was supposed to be a friend had the nerve to question her the way the police had—she tossed the napkin on the table. "I did some paperwork at home. I took a nice, long bubble bath. I went for a walk. And I ended up under a microscope at the police station. You know all that, Bea."

"Yeah, I do. But I also know that you came back here after we left last night."

Kate frowned. "So you're telling me I'm lying?"

"I'm telling you . . ." There was no way anyone else in the lunchroom could hear us, but I wasn't taking any chances. I scooted my chair closer to Kate's and bent my head. "I was just up in your office, Kate. The oil lamp is on the windowsill."

As if she'd been sucker punched, she sank back in her

chair. It took her a moment to catch her breath, and another second before she had the nerve to say, "That doesn't mean anything."

"It means plenty." I drummed my fingers against the table. "You told me yourself, Kate. The first thing you do when you get to your office every day is put the oil lamp on the windowsill. Just like Great-Grandma Carrie used to do. The last thing you do when you leave is put it away, just like you did last night when I was up in the office with you. I can't imagine why you didn't put it away this time. Maybe you were in a hurry. Or maybe you were preoccupied. Or maybe you just plain forgot. That doesn't matter. What does matter is that I know what it means, that oil lamp being out. It means you came back here, Kate. And since you swear it wasn't today, then it has to have been last night. After you and I left here, you came back to the winery."

Kate's gaze shot to the young policeman near the door. "Did you tell them?"

"You're kidding me, right? You don't think I wouldn't give you a chance to explain first?"

She let go a long, unsteady breath. "Yes, of course you would. You're a good friend, Bea. Of course you would."

"So . . . ?" I caught her gaze and held it.

She dared another look at the cop. "They won't understand."

"I don't care about them."

"But they're only going to hear what they want to hear. They're only going to believe what they think they already know. They know I had a fight with Noreen. And they know they found the murder weapon here. When they find out . . ."

Her gaze drifted to the doorway just as another officer

ran by and called out to Hank, "We found a camera! It's down in a pool of some kind of liquid. It's probably ruined. But come on, Chief, take a look."

Kate brushed her hands over her cheeks. "If they find out the truth, it's going to make me look more guilty."

"Not telling the truth is what's going to make you look guilty," I told her.

"You're right." Kate nodded, confirming the thought to herself. "Lies will only make things worse. But the truth . . ." She glanced my way. "Will you believe me?"

"Try me."

She hauled in a breath and let it out slowly. "I dropped you at home. Then I . . . You're right. I came back, Bea. I came back to the winery."

"And you went to your office and you put the oil lamp on the windowsill."

She nodded. "Force of habit. I never even thought about it."

"But why—"

Kate dropped her head in her hands. "It was stupid," she said, her voice muffled. She raised her head. "I see that now. I see that it's going to get me in trouble. Maybe if we don't tell anyone—"

I put a hand on her arm. "You have to tell Hank. You know that. So try out the truth on me first. Why did you come back to the winery?"

She sniffed. "Because I knew that b—" She swallowed the rest of the word. "All right, I know it's not good to speak ill of the dead. I won't say it. But let's face it, we both know what kind of person Noreen was. Sneaky and lying and shifty and nasty and—"

"And we're not going to speak ill of the dead, right?"

She shredded the paper napkin to smithereens. "I knew Noreen was going to come back," she said. "As sure as I'm sitting here, Bea, I knew she would come back to the winery after I tossed her out. All she cared about was getting more video of that ghost of hers." Kate's laugh wasn't as filled with amusement as it was with derision. "You'd think a grown woman would know there's no such things as ghosts!"

"You'd think so." I wonder if my smile convinced her. It sure didn't convince me.

"And I was right, wasn't I?" Kate asked. "From what you said . . . from the look of things around here and all the commotion and all the cops . . . Noreen did come back here. She was murdered here."

"Yes, she was. And you say you were in the building?"

Kate's gaze snapped to mine. "That doesn't mean I killed her."

"It doesn't. It really doesn't. But why were you here, Kate?"

"To catch her, of course." If Kate were feeling more on her game, I had no doubt an eye roll and a tongue click would have gone along with the comment. "I figured she'd sneak back in, and I was going to teach her a lesson. I was waiting for her and I thought when I saw her, then I'd call the cops. This time, I wasn't planning on giving her a break. I was going to file charges and have Noreen and all those other crazy ghost kooks arrested."

"So you were here. In your office. But you didn't see anything? You didn't hear anything?"

"I don't know how I didn't." Kate's shrug spoke to her confusion. "I didn't fall asleep. I mean, I couldn't, could I? Not when I was waiting for Noreen and her buddies to show up. I was in my office, watching the feed from the security cameras. I swear, Bea, I never saw a thing. Did Hank tell you where exactly Noreen was killed?"

"Hank didn't have to tell me. I'm the one who found the scene of the crime." Because I didn't want Kate to get any more upset than she already was, I pretended this was no big deal. "I was just looking around, just checking to see if I could find any evidence that might explain what happened to Noreen, and—"

Kate squeezed my hand. "I'm sorry."

"It's okay. Really." It wasn't, but that's not what mattered. "She was beaten to death with that wacky piece of equipment EGG had with them last night, that plasmometer. It was in the back room. Beyond the warehouse."

"Really?" Kate sat up. "Well, that explains why I never heard anything or saw anything. That's the old storage area that we don't use anymore. There aren't any security cameras in there."

"But how did Noreen get in there?"

Kate's brow furrowed. "She didn't come through the front door, that's for sure. There are cameras there. She didn't come through the back, either. There are stories . . ." She glanced my way, and I had no doubt she was trying to judge if I'd believe her or not. "They say that back during the twenties, the bootleggers used to bring liquor over from Canada and smuggle it through a series of nearby caves. I've heard people say that one of those caves leads into our old storage area—that when Sleepy Harlow worked here, that's where he hid his liquor."

"Sleepy Harlow." I grumbled and folded my hands into fists. "I'm tired of hearing about the man."

"Yeah, but if it's true . . ." Thinking, Kate chewed her lower lip. "Noreen would have had to do research about

Sleepy, right? I mean, if she had any intention of finding his ghost. She might have heard about the caves. That would explain how they got in."

"Why isn't the area secured?"

"Well, it is. Sort of." Kate swept the tiny pieces of paper napkin into a pile. "The warehouse door is one of those that can only be opened from the inside. Nobody can get into the warehouse from the old storage room, and we don't keep anything in there anyway, so there's really no reason to worry about anybody stealing anything."

"But it can't be easy to find that way in."

"You're right. I've never tried it myself. I mean, why would I? But my mom and dad talked about it. And my grandparents. They said it was tricky, but it could be done. They said they used to play hide-and-seek there when they were kids."

"And if Noreen was determined to make her way back inside . . ." I considered the possibility. "It explains how you didn't know she was here."

Kate turned around. There were windows on the far wall, and they looked out over the Wilder vineyards and the lake beyond. "I can't believe I screwed up this bad," she moaned. "If only I'd been paying more attention. Maybe I would have noticed something. If I had called the cops, maybe Noreen wouldn't be . . ." She couldn't make herself say the word.

"Don't beat yourself up." I squeezed her arm. "Everybody knows you would have helped if you could."

"No, they don't." A fresh cascade of tears started down Kate's freckled cheeks. "Everybody thinks I killed her, Bea. And once they find out I was here . . ."

"It doesn't prove a thing." Another thought hit. "It's not at all relevant, but Kate, why didn't you put the oil lamp away?"

She reached for another napkin from the holder at the center of the table and dabbed her cheeks. "I never left here until four this morning," she said. "By that time, I figured I'd just wasted a perfectly good night when I could have been home and snug in my bed. I was so tired I couldn't see straight. I guess . . ." She sniffed. "I guess I just forgot. And if I hadn't, if I put the lamp away, you never would have known, Bea. No one ever would have known that I came back here."

"Somebody would have found out. Somehow. The truth has a way of coming out. Especially when it comes to murder investigations." Hank walked by outside the lunchroom door and I waved him inside. "It needs to come from you," I told Kate.

She looked at Hank and swallowed hard. "You mean I need to tell him—"

I got up to leave. "Kate needs to talk to you," I told Hank, and since I figured my part in the conversation was done, I left the lunchroom.

I wasn't exactly sure where I was going, but I knew I had to get out of there, at least for a few minutes. What with the emotion that was vibrating through the lunchroom (from Kate, and from Chandra, who was still crying her eyes out, and, yes, from Luella, who, even though she was stone-faced and calm, had to be as upset as the rest of us), I needed to give Kate and Hank some privacy—and I needed to clear my head.

I remembered what I'd heard the cop say a little while earlier: They'd found a camera. I wondered if it was Noreen's and what it might show. I wondered where they'd found it, and I retraced my steps back to the warehouse. The heavy metal door between the warehouse and the old storage room was open, but there was no one around. I took the opportunity to step inside.

It was chilly in the old room. The brick in the walls held in the dampness of years of disuse. I shivered and wrapped my arms around myself, then stepped carefully around the plasmometer and the stains on the floor, peering farther into the shadows thrown by the light of the single bulb that hung from the center of the ceiling.

The room was maybe twenty feet wide and half again as long. There were wooden shelves built into the wall on my left, and on the far wall . . .

I peered into the shadows.

There was a deeper shadow in the center of the wall, one that looked like it might be a doorway.

Not that I was about to check it out!

Once Hank talked to Kate, she'd tell him about the caves and he'd get his guys to investigate. Better cops in boots with flashlights and radios poking around in the underbelly of the winery than me in my sneakers and no one around to call for help.

My mind made up, I backed up to head out of the old storage room.

That's when something on the floor along the far wall caught my eye.

Carefully, I made my way over there, and what I found was a magazine.

A *Life* magazine. The cover had a yellow background and showed two stylized and stylish men taking a look at a very little red car.

But it wasn't their old-fashioned clothing that caught my eye and made my breath wedge in my throat.

It wasn't the vintage two-seater car, either.

It was the date up in the left-hand corner of the cover, directly opposite the words that said the magazine cost ten cents.

"October third, nineteen thirty." My voice bumped over the date.

October 3, 1930.

The day Charles Sleepy Harlow was murdered.

❖ 9 ❖

Make no mistake, I saw the gleam in Hank's eyes when he closed in on Kate in the lunchroom. And I saw him later, too, after he'd talked to Kate and she told him how she'd returned to the winery. By then, that gleam was a full-blown conflagration.

Hank thought he had his murderer.

He didn't arrest Kate. Not right then and there. I knew that for certain, because when I got home, I sat by my parlor window and waited, my heart beating double-time and my stomach in my throat, until Kate's car pulled into her driveway. Only then did I breathe easier. But that doesn't mean I thought Kate's troubles were over.

That's why I didn't get much sleep that night, and that's why, by Friday morning, I was groggy and foggy—not to mention more than a tad cranky. The sun was just coming up over the horizon when I finally drifted off. What seemed like only minutes later, I was startled awake by the sounds of a crash from out in the hallway.

I grabbed the plaid flannel robe I'd once bought in Maine, poked my feet into my fuzzy bunny slippers, and raced out of my suite, only to find Dimitri and Jacklyn in the hallway, righting an equipment case that had toppled over.

"Sorry." Dimitri didn't look especially sorry. In fact, his eyes sparked with excitement and he looked pumped and (my editorial opinion here, of course) completely delicious, what with a shadow of dark whiskers outlining the planes and angles of his face, his hair mussed, and his tight-fitting jeans and an equally close-fitting T-shirt that showed off the tattoo of an angel on his left forearm and the Greek-god muscles that were a perfect match to his Mediterranean good looks. It wasn't nearly as early as I had thought it was when I'd jumped out of bed. In fact, the antique tall case clock in the hallway showed that it was just past eight. Still, in spite of the hour, Dimitri didn't look the least bit tired. He zipped over to one side of the equipment case and told Jacklyn to get over on the other side, and they hoisted it.

It didn't take them long to finish, but by the time they did, I had brushed some of the cobwebs out of my brain.

"You're not staying here," I said to Jacklyn.

She had the good sense to look contrite. Or at least to try. There was a little too much twinkle in Jacklyn's dark eyes, a little too much spring in her step, to officially qualify as contrite. "Dimitri, he thought—"

"My decision. I'll take all the blame. Or the credit, if someone's willing to give it to me." Righting that fallen case was a lot of work. He pressed a hand to his chest at the same time he flashed Jacklyn a smile. "I figured no harm, no foul, since Noreen isn't using her room anymore."

Understatement.

I waited for Dimitri to realize it, but he was a little busy. Talking and laughing, David, Liam, and Rick scrambled down the steps, and Dimitri handed out assignments, went over the day's schedule and asked them—in a nice way that still didn't brook any debate—to take various and sundry pieces of equipment out to the front porch so they could be cleaned and tested.

"Not tested! Not here!" I hated myself for saying it, but I knew I'd regret it more if I didn't speak up. (I didn't believe in ghosts, right? So why did I care?) "This is an old house. I don't want to find out that there's something here that I don't want to be here."

"No worries! We promise not to tell." Dimitri gave me a wink that banished any thoughts I'd had about unwanted spooky presences at the same time it made me conscious of the aforementioned plaid robe and bunny slippers. He slipped on his sunglasses, and while he finished moving the equipment case out to the front porch and left Jacklyn in charge of whatever was inside it, I combed my fingers through my hair and automatically reached up to poke my glasses up the bridge of my nose. I would have done it, too, if I hadn't left my glasses on the table next to my bed.

When Dimitri came back inside, he had Fiona with him. The poor kid didn't look any better rested than I felt. There were smudges of sleeplessness under her eyes, and her nose was raw and red. Dimitri instructed her to go up to his room and retrieve a full spectrum camera.

"Like I was saying . . ." Dimitri slipped off his sunglasses, poked his hands in his pockets, and rolled back on the heels of his sneakers. No doubt he knew the move emphasized his six-pack. No doubt he knew I'd see it and appreciate it. No doubt he was right. "With a room open, it only made sense for Jacklyn to stay in it."

I wasn't so sure Fiona agreed with this; that might explain why she froze, one foot on the bottom step, and shot Dimitri a look.

He was not the type of man who noticed such looks. Not from gawky kids like Fiona, anyway.

"It's our room, anyway, right?" Dimitri went on, his words accented by the sounds of Fiona's shoes slapping against the steps and punctuated by the noise of her opening, then slamming shut, the door of his room. "We've got the reservation through the weekend; we might as well use it. And speaking of that"—one corner of his mouth pulled tight—"that cop, the big guy . . ."

"Hank."

"Yeah, Hank. He stopped over here and talked to us yesterday. He said none of us can leave the island. At least not until he gets a handle on what happened to Noreen. If we've got to stay into next week . . . ?"

"I've got two rooms already booked for Thursday and Friday," I told him. "Fishermen. You're good until then. After that if you're still here, and if you don't mind doubling up, we can work something out."

"Terrific." Rick and David shambled back in with news about electromagnetic something-or-others. Fiona came back down the steps as noisily as she'd gone up, punched the front door open, and disappeared.

I waited until the rest of them were all back outside. I would talk to the entire EGG crew in good time, of course. I had to if I had any hopes of clearing Kate's name. Since I had Dimitri all to myself for the moment, it was as good a time as any to start.

"I'll make coffee," I told him. "And get breakfast out on the table in a few minutes. Until then, I wondered if you could tell me—"

His phone rang and he held up one finger to tell me to wait a sec, then answered the call.

I took the opportunity to duck into the kitchen to get breakfast going. Truth be told, I was so sure the members of EGG would be so upset by everything that had happened the day before, I didn't think they'd be up to eating. I hadn't given breakfast much thought except to get some cranberry sour cream muffins out of the freezer.

I checked them and found them nicely thawed, and got some pears and apples out of the fridge to go along with them. That done, I took out a couple dozen eggs to scramble and made the coffee, all the while listening to the burr of Dimitri's voice right outside the kitchen door.

"That's perfect, Al," he told the person on the other end of the phone. "Yeah, my name first, along with that picture we took in Ireland last year. You know, the one of me standing in front of that old castle. That will be a perfect opening shot. Then—"

He paused, listening to whatever it was Al had to say.

"Yeah, that will be fine. But Jacklyn before Rick and the rest of them . . . What?"

Another pause, and Dimitri laughed.

"Yeah, she's back, and now that Noreen won't be around to make sure she doesn't get too much screen time, Jacklyn will be a great addition to the show. Yeah, so me, then Jacklyn, then Rick, Liam, and David. What's that? Oh yeah, then Fiona. I almost forgot about her. But remember to list her as an intern in the credits. I don't want anybody to get the wrong idea that somebody with skills that basic could actually be a full-fledged member of the team. Yeah, yeah. Get right on it, Al. We'll be back in a few days, and we'll have plenty of video to edit. I promise."

I waited until I knew he was off the phone, then raised my voice so he was bound to hear. "Jacklyn's not heading back to Hollywood for that soap opera?"

Dimitri stuck his head into the kitchen.

"Oh. You mean . . ." He gave his phone a look before he put it back in his pocket. "She quit the soap opera. Jacklyn's back on our team. It's good news. She's a good investigator."

There were people who said I was, too, though I spent my time looking for the truth rather than for errant ectoplasm.

"When I talked to her yesterday, she never mentioned joining the team again. Of course, that was before she knew Noreen was dead."

Dimitri grinned. "You got that right! There was no love lost between those two. And you can see why, right?"

I couldn't, and admitted it.

"Well, all you have to do is take one look at Jacklyn." His grin ratcheted up a notch. "She's gorgeous. And Noreen . . ." The grin disappeared completely, and Dimitri's lips puckered like he'd bit into a lemon. "Well, not so much. And don't think I'm just saying that because ol' Noreen isn't here to defend herself. I told her the same thing plenty of times, right to her face."

"And Noreen didn't like it when Jacklyn was around. Because Jacklyn's so pretty."

Dimitri ventured a few more steps into the kitchen. "It got to the point of being ridiculous. Noreen insisted on cutting Jacklyn out of scenes once the tape was edited for our pilot episode. She'd refuse to show evidence when Jacklyn was the one who found it. You know, all sorts of that crazy, jealous thing women are so good at. No offense intended," he added.

Since I'd already taken offense, there seemed little point in arguing. "So now Noreen's gone and Jacklyn's back. Pretty convenient."

"Pretty awesome." Dimitri either didn't see where I was going with this or he had decided I was as easy to ignore as meek and mild Fiona. "We're pumped. I just talked to our producer about the opening credits for the show. You know, to get Jacklyn added."

"And yourself shown first in front of an old Irish castle, the leader of EGG."

This time, his smile wasn't as cocky as it was calculating, and as cold as a January morning. "You're not saying—"

I didn't give him a chance to finish. I poured a cup of coffee and handed it over the breakfast bar to him. "So tell me, what really went on at the winery the other night?"

"You mean with Noreen?" I hadn't offered, but he grabbed one of the cranberry muffins and took a bite. "You were there. You heard what I said then. Noreen, she told us we had permission to be there. None of us knew she was lying. Honest, if we knew she bypassed Ms. Wilder, none of us would have gone near the place. We're not that kind of team. At least we never were before Noreen took over."

I put out a small crystal pitcher of cream on a tray, then added another pitcher of milk, a sugar bowl, a variety of sweeteners and a jar of wonderful, local honey, the kind I hoped to someday produce from the hives I dreamed of installing in my back garden. "So what happened when you left there?" I asked him.

Dimitri was in mid-chew, and he waited to speak until

he swallowed. "After Ms. Wilder kicked us out, we came back here."

"Was Noreen with you?"

He nodded. "We had three vehicles, and we came back here together. Everybody but Fiona, that is."

I grabbed a mixing bowl and the eggs and started cracking and whipping. It was better that than looking too eager to hear whatever he had to say. "What happened to Fiona?"

Dimitri shrugged. "She wasn't inside the winery when you got there, remember. She was getting equipment out of the trucks. We were all in such a hurry to get out of there before that cop changed his mind and hauled us in, we forgot all about her! I don't know where she was or what she was up to, but she wasn't anywhere in sight and we didn't stop to look for her. I hear she hoofed it all the way back here."

"Poor kid."

"She's going to have to learn to suck it up if she plans on being a paranormal investigator." Dimitri's shoulders shot back. "It's not an easy business."

"I don't imagine it is, what with the TV contracts and all."

"Even before we had the TV contract. Old, abandoned buildings. Wet, moldy basements. Deep, dark forests in the middle of the night." Though I was sure he wanted all this to sound sinister, the glimmer in his dark eyes told me this was what Dimitri lived for. "It's not easy, and it's not always safe. Then there are the spirits themselves, of course."

I controlled a laugh. "You don't think spirits can actually—"

"Cause harm to the living? Of course they can. In fact, if you ask me, that might explain what happened to Noreen."

This time, I couldn't help myself, no matter how much I tried. I barked out a laugh. "You think she was killed by a ghost?"

"I believe it's a very real possibility. Think about it. Noreen's been hot on the trail of your local dead celebrity for a couple of years now. She's the one who took that video of Sleepy last year. And being caught on camera . . . Well, we don't understand it all completely yet. But from what I've been able to discover, apparitions don't like to have their ectoplasm disturbed. My own theory is that cameras disrupt the electromagnetic fields around spirits. That they break up their signals. You know, like static on a radio. I wouldn't be surprised if Sleepy wasn't looking for a little revenge."

"Really?" I gave the question all the oomph that could be managed by a woman in a red plaid robe and bunny slippers. "You're telling me that a ghost can—"

"There are plenty of documented cases. Poltergeists, for instance. You've heard of them. They're spirits that cause all sorts of problems. And there's other evidence, too, about ghosts that lure people to their deaths. Your Sleepy just might be one of them."

"He's not *my* Sleepy," I told him, even as I reminded myself that he sort of was. At least until I could re-create his life and times for Marianne's history. With that in mind, I figured Dimitri was fair game. I mean, when it came to finding out more information about Sleepy.

"What about the real Sleepy?" I asked him. "If Noreen and the rest of you were interested in the legend, maybe you know something about the man, too? Could there have been something in his life that someone wanted to keep secret? Something worth killing for?"

"You mean the whole thing about his treasure." Dimitri

said this like it was the most natural thing in the world, then laughed when I froze, mid-egg-whisking.

"You live on this island and don't know about the treasure," he said.

"I'm new to the island, and I don't know about the treasure. Tell me."

"Well . . ." He brushed muffin crumbs from his hands. "They say that Sleepy haunts the island in October because—"

"Because that's when he was murdered."

"Right. That's one of the stories. Another one is that he's looking to get revenge on the rival gangsters who murdered him. Some people say he's actually roaming the island because he's looking for his head. Other people believe that Sleepy's looking for the treasure he buried before he died."

"If he buried it, why does he have to look for it?" I asked. "Why doesn't he know where it is?"

One corner of his mouth pulled into a sneer that should have been enough to tell me this was a stupid question. Still, Dimitri felt obliged to elaborate. "While we've learned a great deal about the Other Side in the last few years, we don't know how it all works. Not yet. Maybe a spirit's memories get all mixed up. Maybe time over there isn't the same as time over here. Maybe Sleepy doesn't know where to find the treasure because on the Other Side, he hasn't even buried it yet!"

Maybe it was time to change the subject, and I guess my expression must have said that, because Dimitri laughed.

"My guess is you don't believe in any of this, right?" He didn't wait for me to answer. "Hey, I'm used to skeptics. In this business, you have to have a thick skin. But the fact of the matter is, what you believe doesn't matter. Our research tells us that people have been seeing Sleepy's ghost on this island for years. Ever since back in nineteen thirty when he was killed."

1930.

I thought about the old magazine I'd found in the storage room and wondered what Hank made of it. I'd told him about it before I left the winery, and no doubt he'd already gathered up the magazine as evidence.

For now, that wasn't my problem. Sleepy's history, on the other hand, was. So was Kate's freedom. "He's been dead a long time, and all that time, you say folks have seen Sleepy. All over the island?"

Dimitri nodded. "Not just at the winery, if that's what you're thinking, though he worked there for a while. Some people think he even used some old caves nearby to store the liquor he smuggled into the country from Canada. I can't say if that's true or not, but Noreen believed it. She claimed if she could find the caves, we'd have a better chance of gathering evidence."

She more than claimed it. She had probably been trying to prove it by finding her way into the old storage room through the series of caves and tunnels that Kate wasn't even sure existed. I did not bother to mention this to Dimitri. The exact place of Noreen's murder was one of the facts Hank wanted to keep from the public as long as he was able.

"What else can you tell me about Sleepy?" I asked Dimitri.

"Not a whole lot." He finished his cup of coffee.

"Then how about Noreen? What else can you tell me about her? You say you came back here together the other night. Did you know she went out again?"

"I had not a clue," he said. "But then, I'm a pretty sound sleeper."

"But when you didn't see her around on Thursday morning, you didn't wonder?"

His shrug tugged that already snug T-shirt across his chest. "Noreen was"—he cocked his head, searching for the right adjective—"difficult. Surly. High-and-mighty. Ornery. Truth be told, I was glad when I didn't see her Friday morning. It meant I didn't have to deal with her craziness . . . Hey, we won't have to arrange the equipment alphabetically anymore!" This was apparently a new thought, because his grin lit the room. "That's perfect, because I've got this way better method for packing and moving the equipment based on what it's for and how much we use it and—" His grin melted into a sheepish expression that would have disarmed a weaker woman. Or one who wasn't as concerned that her friend was going to prison for a murder she didn't commit.

"Sorry. I'm pretty excited to be back in the driver's seat."

"You used to be the head of EGG?"

Dimitri's dark brows dropped low over his eyes. "Seven years ago, I was the one who founded EGG. Let me tell you, it wasn't always easy keeping the group going. We all worked full-time jobs, and we did our investigations at night. Try explaining to your boss why you're falling asleep at your desk when you're falling asleep at your desk because you were up until four in the morning running around some old, abandoned cemetery—and then there are the volunteers!"

He pulled a face. "Sure, lots of people are interested in paranormal investigating, and all those shows on TV make it look so glamorous. But nine times out of ten, our volunteers try it for a week or two, then give up. It's always left to the core group to keep going, and it was always up to me to try and make everybody remember that what we were doing was important. Try being enthusiastic when you're standing in the middle of some ruin of an old orphanage in the middle of the night and you haven't found one shred of evidence and it's raining and everybody you're with knows they've got to be up and out the door and to work in less than three hours."

"Still, you kept the group going."

"You got that right." A muscle jumped at the base of his jaw. "And little by little, every year, we got a little better, a little smoother. We started gathering some really convincing evidence."

"Like that video of Sleepy."

Dimitri grunted. "It was that darned video! It should have been the best thing that ever happened to us, right? And in some ways, it was. I mean, it got us plenty of attention. But once Noreen had that video . . ." He shook his head. "Once that happened, nothing could stop her. Nobody could toot Noreen's horn like Noreen could, and she tooted for all she was worth. There isn't anybody in the field who hasn't seen the video. And not one who doesn't think the Turner Plasmometer is the Holy Grail of paranormal investigation."

"You mean you think that contraption really works?"

" 'That contraption' . . ." Dimitri repeated the phrase but added a certain note of reverence I couldn't have mustered if I tried. "It's the greatest innovation in detection equipment in the last ten years. There's no way we would have gotten that video of Sleepy last year without it. The plasmometer, see, sends out waves of electromagnetic energy that spirits can use to manifest. Other folks have tried similar inventions, and they've had some minimal success. But Noreen—I don't know how she did it, but she got the wavelengths just right. And the radio frequencies. I didn't like the woman. You may have noticed! But I'm the first to give credit where credit is due."

"So that was the plan, just like last year? You take the camera crew and the plasmometer. You lie in wait at the winery and you get more video of Sleepy."

"No." When he shook his head, a curl of inky hair dipped over his forehead. With one hand, he pushed it back in place. "See, last year, we had spread out over the winery to get some base readings and see what we could see. Noreen, she was all alone when she took that video. She caught it with her handheld camera. Since she was back at the winery all by herself when she was murdered, my guess is she thought she could duplicate the conditions. She was after the same thing all over again."

"Sleepy."

"Yeah, Sleepy." Cynicism dripped from every syllable. "And the fame that would come along with getting more footage of him. You see, that's really all Noreen cared about. Not advancing the science. Not illuminating what's been a mystery for millennia. Noreen wanted to be a guest on talk shows. She wanted to be the keynote speaker at paranormal investigation conferences. And she was going to do anything to make that happen, even if it killed her. I guess she got her wish, huh?" Dimitri twitched away the thought. "Hopefully tonight, we'll get some footage of activity here on the island so that we're not wasting our time while we hang around."

"I didn't think you'd want to." When he gave me a blank look, I explained. "I mean, I thought after what happened, you'd take some time off. Or spend your time talking to each other. You know, a little therapy."

"Paranormal investigating is the best therapy known to mankind." He grabbed an apple, tossed it in the air and caught it in one hand, then strolled out the door. "Hey, with any luck, maybe we'll run into Noreen's apparition tonight while we're out. That would be something, huh? Noreen would actually be good for something besides the Turner Plasmometer. And that would be hilarious. You know, because she'd be more useful after she was dead!"

❖ 10 ❖

The next day was Saturday, and I spent all day working on reconstructing Marianne's book about Sleepy.

I know, I know . . . I should have been worried about Kate. I *was* worried about Kate. But worrying would get me nowhere, and I knew that. Neither would trying to get through to Kate. See, Kate being Kate and as single-minded and as stubborn as anyone I'd ever known (except for maybe the possible exception of me), she threw herself into her work to forget her troubles, shutting herself in her office at the winery. Her employees had strict orders that no one—no matter who—could bother her.

At least that's what they told me when I called.

By ten o'clock, I had two dozen more pages for the manuscript. They were mostly blank, with a word here and there that I'd been able to make out. I hoped those words would work like a trail of bread crumbs, leading me to the information that would help me rewrite Marianne's story. I'd talked to Alvin, and learned that Marianne had come through her surgery with flying colors. But the docs on the mainland wanted to keep an eye on her, and they insisted she stay close.

I had a couple days' reprieve.

With that in mind, I waded my way (gagging all the while) through three more chapters. Lucky for me, it was a short book (hurray!) that I assumed would be illustrated with historic photos of the island, the lake, and, of course, Sleepy. After all this time reading about him, thinking about him, and trying to reconstruct his life, I was anxious to see what the man looked like.

With his head.

Thank goodness, the pages I worked on next were slightly more readable. Being farther down in the pile, they weren't as soaked as the earlier ones. It was tough going, but I refused to lose heart. By the time I was done, I'd deciphered enough to know exactly where on the island Charlie Harlow was born, and I'd learned that as a young man, he was a day laborer. Smart guy that he was, he recognized an opportunity to make some real money when Prohibition was enacted. He started out small with a gang of locals who smuggled real liquor (not the nasty bathtub variety) out of a place called Middle Island, Canada, and he soon became their leader. He made contacts (or the word might have been *contracts*, which I guess would have made sense, too) with the larger world and with gangsters on the mainland, both in the US and in Canada. He had the reputation for being quiet (hence the nickname), and once he had a few ill-gotten bucks in his pocket, he was known to

be generous with those who deserved it and less than coop-
erative when it came to explaining to the right side of the
law about where all that money came from.

The rest of those few chapters were fuzzy.

Or I should say, more descriptively, soggy.

I needed a break to clear my head. And my nose. I'd just
made a turkey sandwich and a glass of iced tea and taken it
out to the front porch when Hank pulled in.

He made his way up the front porch steps between the
pots of purple mums and the pumpkins I'd put out in honor
of the season, and when he got over to where I sat, he gave
my lunch the careful sort of once-over that I imagined he
used on perps.

Which made me think about Kate.

Which made me not so hungry anymore.

"Sandwich?" I asked Hank.

He accepted with a nod and scooped up half the turkey
and avocado on wheat. "I already ate lunch," he said
between mouthfuls. "So you have the other half."

I sipped iced tea instead.

"Just thought you should know . . ." Finished with the
half sandwich in three efficient bites, Hank dropped into
the wicker rocker next to the couch where I sat. No matter
how hard the cushions had been scrubbed or how many
times, I swear I could still smell the souvenirs of Jerry
Garcia's disastrous visit to the porch, and I'd tossed the
cushions from all the furniture and ordered new ones
online. Until they arrived, I'd folded up a cushy chenille
throw in a luscious shade of grape that matched the trim
on the house and was ensconced on that. I doubted Hank
was as comfortable in the rocker sans cushions. Then
again, it was a little hard to tell. Hank always had a pained
expression on his pug-ugly face.

"We checked into Kate's phone calls," he said, and maybe he winced because an errant bit of wicker poked him. Or maybe he just didn't like what he had to say. "The other day when she got called to the mainland by that wine critic? That call came from Noreen Turner's cell."

"I'm not surprised." Which didn't mean I wasn't disgusted. "Getting her hopes up like that! What a lousy thing to do to Kate!"

"Yeah, well, Ms. Turner and her bunch wanted to get Kate away from the winery. I guess they figured it was a pretty good way to do it."

"Dimitri claims they didn't know what Noreen was up to."

"That's what he says."

"You don't believe him."

"It doesn't much matter. Kate refused to press charges for the breaking and entering. End of story."

"So why tell me about the phone call?"

He shifted in his seat, and the wicker groaned. "You're a smart woman, Bea."

I swiped a finger along the outside of my glass, getting rid of a drop of condensation. "I'm glad you think so."

"So you know what I'm getting at."

I locked my gaze onto Hank's. "I know you're wrong."

"Are you telling me Kate didn't realize that call was a scam? That she wasn't mad about it?"

"Yes, she realized it. And of course she was mad. You know that. She admits it, and who can blame her? But that doesn't mean—"

"When she figured out where the call really came from and why Noreen made it, she must have just about busted a gasket."

"Maybe, but—"

"And that's when Kate told you she wanted to kill Noreen Turner."

Believe me, if I could take back what I'd told Hank about the conversation I had with Kate after she returned from the mainland, I would have. In a heartbeat. But it was too late for that.

"She didn't mean it," I told him. "Not literally. And even if she did, that certainly doesn't prove she did it."

"You don't think I'm enjoying this, do you?" Hank hauled himself out of the rocker and stalked to the porch railing. It was another glorious fall day, and across the street, the sun glinted off the waves that kissed the shoreline. Tourists were taking advantage of these last wonderful days. The road was busy with buzzing golf carts. Hank might have been watching it all, but I knew it wasn't what he was thinking about. His back to me, he planted his feet and crossed his arms over his broad chest. "So who else do you think could have done it?" he asked.

If he'd been facing me, he would have seen my mouth flap open. There was a time he wouldn't have asked for my opinion. "I don't know," I admitted. "I wish I did."

"Well, we're going to have to find out. It's the only way we've got any hope of helping Kate."

I hadn't even realized there'd been a knot in my chest since I saw Kate get into Hank's SUV. That is, until some of the tension eased. "You don't really think she did it."

He spun to face me. "I don't want to think she really did it. But the facts—"

"Can't be right."

"Until the test results arrive back from the state crime lab and tell me any different, facts are all I have to go on."

I scooted forward in my seat. "I know, but—"

"So unless we find some other facts and those other

facts point us to other people, things aren't looking good for Kate."

"Yes. You're right. Of course you're right." I found myself nodding like a bobblehead and stopped before I made myself dizzy. "What do you want me to do?"

A slow smile relieved some of the surliness of Hank's expression. "I was hoping that's what you'd say. What have you found out so far?"

I didn't bother to ask why he assumed I was digging into things myself. Words like *nosy* and *snooping* tend to rub me the wrong way. Especially since I know they're true.

"I thought they'd all be depressed," I told Hank, with a look at the house that was supposed to indicate the ghost hunters. Since they'd trouped out early in the morning and he didn't know that, I figured I needed to elaborate.

"EGG. They're not the least bit upset," I told him. "Not any of them except maybe for Fiona. In fact, I'd go so far as to say a couple of them are actually thrilled."

"That she's dead?" Even Hank, hardened from years of police work, was surprised.

"Not that she's dead so much as that she's gone," I said. "Dimitri has taken over with a vengeance."

"I suppose someone has to. They have a contract, and they have to produce something for that TV show."

"Yes, I agree. I know a little about the entertainment industry and I know that Noreen's murder is going to give the show a whole lot of publicity. That makes it more important than ever for them to get their filming done and in on time. I get that. Really, I do." I folded my arms around myself. "I just didn't expect that they'd go at it with this much"—I wondered how to describe it to Hank and decided that one word would suffice—"glee."

He narrowed his eyes. "Mostly this Dimitri guy?"

"Mostly. He's back in the driver's seat. He used to be lead investigator for the group. Then when Noreen shot that video of Sleepy that made them famous, he got pushed to the background. He likes being in charge. And he likes the idea of getting first billing on the show and being a star. He'll be good at it."

Hank nodded. "And the rest of them?"

"I haven't had a chance to talk them. I want to, but not until I can get each of them alone. You know, so they can't repeat each other's stories."

Another nod, and I knew he approved.

"But I will say that it's not a coincidence that Jacklyn Bichot is back with the group."

"And maybe not a coincidence that she just happened to show up the day Ms. Turner's body was found?"

This I couldn't say, and I told Hank so. As he'd just reminded me, I could only stick with the facts. "Jacklyn used to be a member of EGG, and she and Noreen didn't get along. Jacklyn went out and found another job. Now that Noreen's gone . . ."

"Made her move and got back in, huh?" Hank's eyes lit. "And the others?" Hank dropped back into the rocker, the better to eyeball me. "They'll be more comfortable talking to you than they would to me. Oh, I've already asked all the usual questions, but I'm thinking you can dig a little deeper. You know, get a little more of the dirt they might not be willing to share with law enforcement."

"I'll try," I promised.

"That's all I can ask." He slapped the arms of the chair and stood. But not before he eyed the other half of the turkey sandwich. "Hey, if you're not gonna eat that . . ."

I gave him permission with a wave, and, sandwich in hand, Hank stomped back down the steps and into his SUV.

I opted for an apple for lunch. Okay, yeah, that sounds healthy enough, but in the interest of full disclosure, I'll admit that after I sliced it, I slathered each piece with peanut butter. Extra crunchy. Thus newly fortified, I made a quick call to Luella to ask for her help with a little Sleepy research, then got back to work on Marianne's manuscript, gagging through another few chapters.

By the time I was done, it was late afternoon, and since I'd left a note by each of the ghost hunters' doors that morning inviting them to tea that afternoon, I wasn't surprised when they were back at four on the dot.

And plenty hungry, as it turned out.

I set out a china pot of nice, strong black English tea, and another of green tea; a variety of tiny sandwiches that Meg, Luella's daughter and my go-to person for all things culinary, had come in to make for me; a platter of sugar cookies; and a selection of really nice chocolates.

Then I stepped back to wait.

I have to admit, I wasn't surprised when the guys and Jacklyn dug right in or that poor Fiona hung back, eyeing the table and quietly waiting her turn. In fact, it was just what I was hoping for.

I caught her eye and waved her into the kitchen.

"By the time they're through, there's not going to be anything left," I said, and I was sure to add a smile, just to gain the kid's confidence. I led the way to the counter, where I'd kept extras of everything. "Go ahead," I said. "Help yourself. I'll get us some tea."

"That's so nice of you!" Fiona plunked down on one of the tall stools at the breakfast bar. Like every time I'd seen her, she was wearing that spectacular howlite necklace, and the light above the counter caught the stone and made it shine like newly fallen snow.

When I handed it to her, she wrapped both her hands around her teacup. "I'm starving! We worked so hard today. We were out at the lighthouse."

"Did you find anything?"

"You mean evidence of paranormal activity?" Fiona gulped down one of the tiny egg salad sandwiches and reached for a second. "Maybe a couple EVPs. You know, Electronic Voice Phenomena. That's when you make a recording and you don't hear anything with your own ears, but when you replay the recording, you pick up the voices of spirits."

"Well, for your sake, I hope you caught plenty of them. Noreen would have liked that."

"Noreen. Yeah." Fiona changed her mind just as she was reaching for another sandwich. She sat back and glanced over her shoulder. From here, we could hear the lively conversation going on in the dining room. "They don't care," she said.

"Maybe they know they don't have the luxury. You've got a TV show to finish producing."

"I guess." Her shoulders rose and fell. "But it seems kind of harsh, doesn't it? I wish the cops could figure out what really happened to Noreen."

"They talked to you?" I knew Hank had, but Fiona didn't know that I knew. "And you told them that when EGG left the winery the other night, they forgot to take you with them?"

She tried for a smile. Oh, how she tried. I actually might have been convinced the expression was genuine if Fiona's eyes didn't get misty. "They were in such a hurry to get out of there, they never even bothered to think about me."

"But you made it back on your own. At least that's what Dimitri told me."

Apparently, now that we weren't talking about Noreen directly, Fiona's appetite returned. She wolfed down a ham salad sandwich. "I walked all the way from the winery to Chandra's."

"But before you got back, did you see anything else at the winery? Anyone else?"

Fiona might have been young, but she was nobody's fool. Her eyes went wide. "You mean, did I see the killer?"

"Something tells me we can't be that lucky. What I mean is think back, Fiona. When you snuck out of the winery, were there any other cars around?"

"You mean other than the EGG trucks and Ms. Wilder's?" She shook her head. "I didn't see any. Maybe if I had . . ." Tears filled her eyes, and I knew I was going to lose her if I didn't get her thinking, and fast.

"How about on the way back to Chandra's?" I asked. "Did you pass anyone on the road?"

She squeezed her eyes shut for a moment, then they flew open. "A golf cart. I know I passed a golf cart. I was wondering what anyone was doing out. You know, because it was late and it was dark."

Golf carts are the island's preferred mode of transportation, for both residents and visitors. Still, we were making progress. "Good," I told Fiona. "And this golf cart, was it headed for the winery?"

Thinking, she wrinkled her nose. "I dunno. I don't think so. I think it turned." She waved an arm in some indeterminate direction. "Sort of that way. Not toward the winery."

Her shoulders dropped. "Sorry. I wish I could be more help. I guess I just wasn't paying a whole lot of attention."

"You're doing great," I assured her. "How about when you got back to Chandra's? Did you notice if the other members of EGG were already back here?"

She nodded. "I saw three trucks in your driveway."

"And did you see one of the trucks leave again that night?"

When she shook her head, her hair glowed like a new penny in the light. "I was kind of upset," she admitted. "I mean, first I thought for sure we were all going to end up in jail. I was just coming back into the winery from the truck, see, with a piece of equipment Noreen had asked me to get, when you and Ms. Wilder showed up. I heard what Noreen and Ms. Wilder said to each other. It was impossible not to, right? There was so much shouting. Then when the cop got there . . ." Color shot through Fiona's cheeks. "Well, I stayed as far back in a dark corner as I could. I figured everybody was going to get hauled into jail and I didn't want the police to find me. Then that Ms. Wilder, she said nobody should get arrested and I was so relieved. And I guess everybody else was, too, because they cleared out so fast, they left me behind. By the time I got back to Chandra's, I was more upset about that than anything else." Fiona shot a look toward the dining room.

"I went to my room, lit some incense, and did my meditation. When I get that upset, it's the only thing that calms me down. After that, I went right to sleep. And I slept really well, too, only . . ." Thinking, Fiona tipped her head.

I scooted closer. "Only what?"

"Now that I think about it, I woke up around midnight. It was so quiet, I could hear the waves swishing against the shore. And I thought about how peaceful it was, and about how lucky I was to be here on the island, doing what I love doing. And then . . . yeah, that's right." Her eyes lit. "I heard a car start up. And I thought that was really weird, because it was so late and it was so quiet, and so I got up, and I looked out the window. Bea . . ." Fiona swallowed hard. "I'm sorry, I forgot. I forgot all about it. I did see something. It was one of the EGG trucks. It was pulling out of your driveway."

Since I knew Noreen had ended up back at the winery, this wasn't a big surprise. Still, I felt obliged to ask, "You didn't see who was driving it, did you?"

She gave me a puppy dog look. "I'm sorry I can't be more helpful."

"Not a problem!" I assured her, because, actually, she had been helpful. She had confirmed what Chandra had already told me: that after the incident at the winery, Fiona had come back to Chandra's and was in her room meditating and playing a CD of chanting monks.

As for Noreen going back to Wilder's, we already knew that. But now we also knew that she drove. And since that's where she died, I think it was a safe bet to say she wasn't the one who returned the truck to my driveway.

Noreen hadn't gone out alone. Or, if she had, she'd been followed by someone who'd returned the truck to exactly where it belonged.

I wasn't sure precisely what any of this meant, but I knew the answers might be in my dining room.

I pushed a plate of cookies closer to Fiona and excused myself with the explanation that I wanted to see if anyone needed anything else.

As it turned out, I didn't have to go far—I met Liam in the doorway. He had the empty sandwich plate in his hands.

"More?" he asked.

"Plenty," I told him as I stepped back to let Fiona scurry out of the kitchen. Like I had with Fiona, I gestured to Liam to follow me and took my time loading the serving dish with a brand-new array of sandwiches.

"Any luck with the ghosts?" I asked him, carefully arranging cucumber sandwiches on the Depression glass platter.

Liam Nash, EGG's technical and equipment specialist, was a guy of thirty or so with short-cropped dark hair and a couple dozen tattoos on his arms, the tops of his hands, and his legs. And those were only the ones I could see thanks to the T-shirt he wore with cutoff denim shorts. "But then, maybe you don't know yet," I added. "Fiona tells me you're never quite sure what you've captured until you have a chance to review the evidence."

"When she's around, we're lucky we capture anything," he grumbled. "She's a cute kid. Okay, I get that, I get that we need someone young on the team to attract a younger demographic of viewer for the show. But Fiona, she's like a bull in a china shop, traipsing through the areas we're investigating, making all kinds of noise. The digital recording I listened to from last night, all I could hear was Fiona in the background, complaining about how cold she was. I'm going to have to talk to Dimitri about it. I hate to cause trouble for the kid, but I really don't have any choice. I can't have Fiona mucking up our investigations."

"Maybe she's just a little too eager?"

He grabbed two egg salad sandwiches, stacked them one on top of the other, and chomped them both down. "That's what I keep telling myself," he said, his mouth full. "But I dunno. I think maybe she's just not cut out for this sort of work, you know?"

"I know Dimitri tells me it looks easy, but it's really hard to be a paranormal investigator."

"Harder not to be." He flashed me an eggy smile. "I mean, some people are in the field for the fame and the glory."

"Some people like Noreen?"

He gave a snort but didn't comment further, so I had no choice but to push.

"And Dimitri?"

"He's a pretty boy," Liam said. "But I'll admit, he knows his stuff."

"Noreen didn't?"

"There are some of us who do this job because we can't help ourselves," he said. "We've got to find out if there's really something out there, something that's left behind when our bodies poof away to dust. Me? I'm pretty sure I'm the luckiest guy in the world because I get to do what I love doing. I just wish we could find more evidence." He stressed the importance of this statement by swallowing down another sandwich. "Noreen was a true believer, but she was smart when it came to marketing. She knew the value of publicity."

"Like that video of Sleepy."

"Man!" Liam's smile was beatific.

"It must have been something to be there and see the ghost, then realize you got the proof on film."

His smile faded and Liam shook his head. "Wish that was true. Fact is, Noreen was all alone when she got that footage. With a handheld camera, of all things." Exactly what Dimitri had told me. I made a mental note of it.

"All that expensive equipment," Liam said, "and Noreen, she gets the Holy Grail on handheld! What I wouldn't give for another piece of footage like that! Say . . ." He glanced my way. "You're one of the locals. I don't suppose you could talk to that cop, the big guy with the attitude. Rumor is that the cops have our plasmometer. I don't suppose you could talk him into giving it back. We were hoping to use it on this investigation. You know, Noreen, she could be a royal pain in the neck. But that plasmometer of hers, it was brilliant."

"So everyone says."

Liam grabbed the plate of sandwiches and headed back toward the dining room. "I'll tell you what, when she showed up with the plans for the plasmometer, I was all set to blow her off. But I'm glad I took a second look, and I'm glad I worked on building it. That plasmometer, it's amazing."

"And now, what if it's gone?"

There was a swinging door between the kitchen and the hallway, and Liam pushed it open with his butt. "That would be a shame, but if that's the case, it will take us a while to get the money together to buy the parts for another one, but have no fear, EGG is on the job! I'll build another plasmometer one of these days." Hanging on to the sandwiches, Liam headed back into the dining room.

I stood in the kitchen for a bit, nibbling on a cookie as I thought about all I'd learned.

The stuff from Hank?

More than interesting, considering one of the things I'd learned was that he wanted to believe that Kate didn't kill Noreen and he was willing to work to prove it.

The information from Fiona?

Pretty much just confirmed what I knew about EGG all along: they were so absorbed in their ghosts and their TV show and their stardom, they never even bothered to worry about the intern who did so much of the grunt work.

And everything Liam had said?

Now that . . .

I brushed cookie crumbs off the front of my sweatshirt and got to work cleaning up the kitchen.

Of everything I'd heard that day, what I heard from Liam was the most interesting.

See, I didn't want to offend, so I didn't say anything, but let's face it, from what I knew of Noreen, she was picky and annoying and a walking poster child for OCD.

Oh yeah, Noreen was a lot of things, but from what I'd seen, she certainly wasn't brilliant.

« 11 »

The witch at my front door looked mighty familiar. And mighty impressive, I must say, in a conical hat decorated with a wild array of orange, gold, and purple silk flowers; a flowing black robe studded with sparkling sequins; scarecrow earrings; and green paint on face and hands that would make the Wicked Witch of the West proud.

I opened the front door wider to allow Chandra to step into the house. "You're a week early for Halloween."

Chandra had a pumpkin tucked under one arm, and she pointed to it. "Pumpkins. You invited us over to carve pumpkins tonight."

I groaned. Right after I was done cringing. "I honestly forgot! With all that's been going on this week, I—"

There is nothing quite so sad as a green witch in full disappointment mode.

"Of course we're carving pumpkins tonight!" I closed the front door and motioned a now-smiling Chandra toward the kitchen. "I've got some sloppy joes in the freezer. We can warm those up, and there are plenty of cookies left from this afternoon's tea, and—"

The doorbell rang.

I opened the door to find Luella waiting on the porch. No costume, but she had a pumpkin, too.

"Come on in." As long as the door was opened, I darted out to the porch and grabbed one of the pumpkins from the front steps. "We're just getting started."

Luella eyed Chandra's getup. "You're going to get pumpkin guts all over your costume."

"Just trying it out." Chandra put her pumpkin on the stairs so she could whisk off her hat and tug her robe over her head. The green makeup on her face and hands looked especially ghastly with her orange sweatshirt, which had the words *Happy Halloween* spelled out across the front of it in frolicking black cats. She shook out her hair and combed her fingers through it, and I didn't have the heart to tell her that even after she was done, there was still one clump suffering from serious witch hat hair. It stood up straight at the very top of her head.

"I have to make sure my costume is perfect for the party on Friday night," Chandra said.

"I'd go with the other earrings." Luella pointed to the cute ceramic scarecrows that dangled from Chandra's ears. "You know, the witch hats you had on the other day. Keeps the spooky theme going."

"Witch hats. Sure." Chandra scurried into the kitchen, and we followed her.

Luella waited until I spread newspaper over the counter, then she set down her pumpkin.

"No Kate?" she asked.

"She's never late," Chandra said, though since she was studying her pumpkin and had a Sharpie in her mouth, it came out sounding more like, "Shsh n lt."

No matter which way she said it, Chandra was right.

"I don't like it," I said. I'd just finished giving my pumpkin a quick rubdown with a damp paper towel, and I scrubbed my hands against the legs of my jeans. "She's shutting everyone out."

"Or she forgot. Just like you did." Chandra took out her phone and gave Kate a call.

"Pumpkins," she said, the moment Kate answered. Chandra listened for a bit. "You can't be serious. It's going to be a whole lot of fun. Bea has margaritas."

I didn't. Not made. But the little get-a-move-on gesture Chandra made told me to get crackin'.

She listened some more. "But it won't be any fun without you. Sure. Yeah. Of course." She set her phone on the counter and when she frowned, green makeup settled into heavy creases around her mouth. "Kate's staying home. She says she's not in the mood to carve pumpkins."

It was exactly what I was afraid of. "Maybe we should go see her," I suggested.

"We could take the pumpkins to her house!" Chandra suggested. "Once she sees me in my witch costume, she's bound to change her mind and want to join in the fun."

"I don't think so." Luella put a hand on Chandra's arm. "Something tells me this is a problem that can't be solved with pumpkins."

I settled on one of the high chairs at the breakfast bar where we were working. "I wish there was something we could do."

Luella shook her head. "Only so much we can do. I know you're looking into the murder, Bea. Kate knows it, too. She knows you'll get to the bottom of things. Just like you always do."

"Hank's working hard, too," I reminded them. "I know he's talked to all my guests." They were gone for the evening, and from what I'd heard when they piled out of the house, they weren't out investigating. Dimitri said something about a night off, and they whooped and scattered. I had no doubts that bar patrons up and down Put-in-Bay would be hearing about ghost hunting tonight.

"They must be done checking out the winery, right?" Chandra drew huge, round eyes on her pumpkin and I hoped for the sake of pumpkin aesthetics that she'd be carving outside the lines, not inside. Her circles wobbled. "I mean, the cops must have found all the evidence they're going to find. By now, I mean. Right?"

"I guess." I gave my pumpkin a careful look. I'd bought a variety of pumpkins, big and small, from a local stand just a week earlier. The one I'd grabbed from the porch was one of the big ones and it was nice and fat and round. I considered what kind of personality I wanted to give it.

Chandra set down her Sharpie with a slap. "Maybe we should go back there."

"The winery?" Luella asked.

At the exact same time I said, "You're not going to find Sleepy. No matter how hard you look for him."

Chandra pouted. Not an especially good look for a woman covered in green. "I just thought we could help."

"We are helping." Luella plunged a knife into the top of her pumpkin and carved around the stem, and when she was done, she lifted it and scooped out seeds and stringy pumpkin innards.

"But we haven't found anything. Not like a real clue," Chandra said.

"Really?" Since Luella was done with the knife, I grabbed it and started in on my pumpkin. "We found the murder weapon," I reminded Chandra. I shouldn't have had to. Chandra has even more imagination than I do; I couldn't believe she'd forgotten the ruined plasmometer. Or the blood.

I knew I'd never forget the blood.

"And I found that old *Life* magazine," I reminded them.

"In that back storeroom." Chandra *tap, tap, tap*ped her fingers against her pumpkin. "If there was anything else back there . . . you know, anything that pointed to someone other than Kate . . . they would have found that, too, right?"

I hoped my shrug said it all, but when Chandra still stood there looking quizzical, I said, "Like I said, I guess they would have."

"And they would have done something about it, right? Like they would have arrested that somebody else."

"I wish," I admitted. "Then Kate would be off the hook."

Luella agreed.

Chandra? She just stood there looking a little green.

Luella and Chandra were gone within a couple of hours and a pumpkin with triangle eyes and a zigzag frown looked out at the world from my front porch. Halloween wasn't until the following Friday, but I lit a candle in the pumpkin when I put it out there, anyway. Like Chandra with her witch costume, I wanted to try out my jack-o'-lantern, and besides, it wasn't too early to contribute to the holiday mood of the neighborhood. Already there were flickering candles in Chandra's front windows, dry ice that billowed out of a cauldron outside her door, and music coming out of the speakers she'd set up outside her garage that was spooky enough to give me the shivers and loud enough to be heard over half the island.

The fact that Kate had yet to complain about the noise said a lot about how worried and depressed she was feeling.

Chandra and Luella had insisted that I keep all the pumpkin seeds, and at Chandra's urging (which was actually more like badgering, and I discovered I had no defenses against her greenness), I had agreed to roast them. They were washed and picked through, and I'd just put them in salted water to soak overnight when Liam and David showed up at the back door.

"I didn't think I'd see you this early," I told them.

"It's never too early when you've had too many beers." David laughed and, with a slap on the back, sent Liam into the hallway and up the stairs. The way he reeled, I hoped he'd make it, and when I heard his room door shut, I breathed a sigh of relief.

"Will he be all right?" I asked David.

He'd grabbed a bottle of water out of the fridge and settled back against the counter to drink it. "He'll be fine once he sleeps it off. When it comes to beer, Liam's a lightweight."

"You're not?"

David grinned. He had a nice smile, great cheekbones, and a strong, square chin. I can't say if it was planned, but I didn't have a shred of doubt that he'd attract plenty of female fans to EGG's TV show.

"I'm smart," David said, and the wink he gave me told

me he was only half kidding. "I know when to stop. Two beers are plenty for me."

"Liam had more than that?"

"Thought they'd have to send to the mainland for more."

He finished his bottle of water, and I pointed him to the recycle container just outside the back door.

"So . . ." Since I couldn't risk looking too eager, I went to the sink and wet down a cloth, then swiped it over the countertop. Yes, I'd just cleaned it. David didn't know that. "No work tonight, huh? That must be a welcome change."

"Everybody scattered the second Dimitri said we deserved a night off. Most of us went to the bars, but I hear he and Jacklyn took off to some fancy restaurant down by the water."

I remembered how I'd heard Dimitri coughing earlier in the day. "I hope he was going to order chicken soup."

David peeled out of his EGG jacket. "His immune system must be shot—guy's always got a cold."

"So he deserves a night off." I hoped I was subtle about getting the conversation back on track. At least back on the track I wanted it to take. "You all deserve a little R & R, what with everything that's happened this week."

"You mean Jacklyn coming back."

"Actually, I meant Noreen's murder."

"Oh yeah. Sure." David was far too self-confident to look embarrassed. "Don't get the wrong impression. It's not like I forgot she was dead or anything. It's just that we're trying to move ahead. You know? Dimitri, he got everyone together this afternoon and he told us we've got to focus. On our investigations. On the show. On our careers. He's right. This is a huge opportunity for all of us, and we can't blow it. What's done is done and what's over is over."

"What about mourning?"

"Noreen?" He scrubbed a hand over his chin. "She was a tough lady."

"And not easy to get along with."

"I don't know anyone who liked her."

"And now she's dead."

"And you'd like to know who did it."

I hoped I wasn't that transparent.

I lifted a shoulder. "It's a small island, and there's nothing like a little gossip to heat things up." I rinsed the cloth and set it in the sink. "Do you have any theories?"

David laughed. "You sound like that cop! He asked me what I thought, too, and I could only tell him the truth. It could have been anyone."

"Anyone but you?"

Another laugh, and he swept a finger, crosswise, over his heart. "I didn't like Noreen any more than anyone else did, but I didn't kill her. She could really get under my skin. And she could make me so mad, it felt like my head would explode. But she wasn't worth going to prison over. That's for sure."

"And you think the person who did this will end up in prison?"

"You don't have to like Noreen to hope for some justice, do you?"

He was right.

"So what can you tell me?" I asked him.

"About the murder?" Thinking, he pursed his lips. "Not a thing. You saw the knock-down-drag-out Noreen had with the woman at the winery."

"Kate."

"Yeah, with Kate. You heard what they said. You saw how mad that Kate was. I guess the cops think she had a good reason to kill Noreen. At least that's what we heard in town tonight. People are talking. You know, about how the cops are looking at Kate and thinking they've got their murderer."

"I think they're wrong." I crossed my arms over my chest. "Kate's not that kind of person."

"That's why you wonder who really did it."

I didn't argue. In fact, now that we had that much out in the open, I didn't feel the least bit self-conscious when I asked, "After that knock-down-drag-out, you all came back here?"

"Absolutely. Except for Fiona. When we were leaving, I tried to tell them she was nowhere around, that we were leaving her behind, but Noreen was so steaming mad at that point, she didn't listen. She didn't care. She screamed at me, told me to get in the truck and start driving."

"Did that make you mad?"

Oh, that smile of his was going to light up TV screens from coast to coast!

"Not mad enough to kill her," David said.

At this point, I wasn't sure if I believed this or not, but there was no use arguing. "When you left the winery, you came right back here?"

He nodded.

"And after you got back here, Noreen came inside with you?"

"She did." There were still some cookies on a platter on the counter and, with a look, David asked if he could take one. When I said yes, he chose peanut butter. The man had good taste; peanut butter were my favorites, too.

"But Noreen left again."

His shrug was barely perceptible and spoke to how much David really didn't care. "She must have."

"Did anyone else?"

Another look, and this time, I gave David permission to go to the fridge and get a glass of milk. While he drank it down, he finished off two more cookies.

"You know I can't say anything with certainty . . ." David began, and I guess the way I stood up like I'd touched an electrical line made him think he better add a caveat. "Just because I couldn't find him, it doesn't mean anything."

"Because you couldn't find . . ." I leaned forward, hoping to egg him on.

"You might have noticed Dimitri was a little out of sorts on Wednesday. Turns out that was the day he got the newest issue of *Dead Time*."

"I know. I heard him say something to Noreen about it. She said she had an article in the new issue, but whatever Dimitri had to say about it, she didn't seem to think it was all that important."

"Well, that's just like her, isn't it?" There was no amusement in David's laugh. "Noreen wrote an article about curiosity cabinets. You know, collections that people used to keep. It was a big deal back in the day. They'd collect rocks or art or gems or bones. And they'd show off their collections to their friends."

"Yes, Noreen mentioned that."

"Well, a year or so ago, Dimitri started talking about how those sorts of collections must hang on to residual energy. You know, so that they attract entities. He did a whole lot of research on the subject on his own, and he was planning on publishing his own article about it."

"And Noreen beat him to it. I get it, I really do. I see why Dimitri was so angry. That must have been a big disappointment."

"What it really was, was a case of Noreen hacking into Dimitri's computer."

I swear, nothing should have surprised me. Not when it came to finding out what Noreen had been up to. Still, the news made my stomach turn cold. "She stole Dimitri's research."

"All the facts. All the figures. All the photographs. Never gave him a shred of credit. Claimed it all as her own and published it before he had a chance. He wasn't just mad. He was mad enough to kill."

That chill in my stomach turned into a block of ice. "You think he did it?"

"That's just it, isn't it?" David scraped his hands through his hair. "I don't think Dimitri's that kind of guy. Don't get me wrong, he can be a jerk sometimes. But that doesn't mean he's a murderer. Except . . ." The pained expression on David's face told me there was more to come.

He let out a long, slow breath. "I wanted to see the article for myself, so after we got back here from the winery, I went to Dimitri's room. You know, to talk to him about it and to borrow the magazine so I could read it."

"And?"

"And"—a muscle bunched at the base of his jaw—"he wasn't there."

"Not in his room?"

"Hey, I'm not accusing the man of anything. Maybe he was down here getting a midnight snack. Maybe he went out to one of the bars. All I can tell you is when I went looking for him, he wasn't in his room." David took his glass to the dishwasher. "I'm not a betting man, but my bet is that it doesn't mean anything at all."

With that, he disappeared upstairs.

My mind buzzing a mile a minute, I thought about

everything I'd just heard. I had to agree with David: the fact that Dimitri wasn't in his room probably didn't mean anything at all.

That didn't keep something that felt very much like hope from blossoming in my chest.

As much as I hated the thought of having a murderer staying at the B and B (it wouldn't be a first, and believe me, I wouldn't like it any more than I had back when I first arrived at the island and the Ladies and I solved a murder at the Orient Express restaurant), I could barely stand still thinking that maybe—just maybe—I'd found what I'd been looking for: a suspect with a strong motive, and along with him, the breakthrough that would finally prove Kate's innocence.

❖ 12 ❖

It was bound to happen.

The next day, a Sunday, dawned chilly and gloomy. The sky was packed with low-hanging clouds as fat as German sausages, and the wind picked up. Across the street from the B and B, the lake churned, peaking into whitecaps that dotted the gray surface with foam. With more fish being brought to the surface by the waves, the flocks of local lake gulls were thrilled. They raced and dove and rose from the water with breakfast in their beaks, all the while calling out a high-pitched creaky chorus.

For the record, I was not nearly as excited.

See, I'd arranged with Luella to go out on the lake that day, and because of her charter schedule and a forecast that promised even worse weather the next day, I knew this was my one and only chance. I am not an especially queasy sailor, but neither am I thrilled with riding a watery roller coaster. *Too bad, so sad,* I told myself. I'd already made arrangements with Meg to come in and take care of breakfast for me. And I'd already taken advantage of Luella's friendship and her skill as a boat captain, and I wouldn't ask her to flip around her schedule to accommodate my whims.

It was now or never.

I pulled on warm clothes, packed an extra sweatshirt and a slicker just in case, and threw together the lunch I'd promised Luella, who'd refused any money for the use of her boat and had been about to refuse my offer of a meal, too, until I crooned the magic word: *caprese.*

Luella is a sucker for fresh mozzarella and tomatoes.

I assembled the ingredients I'd need for our salads, and in light of the weather and the distance we had to travel, added a couple thermoses of hot vegetable soup, too, and the makings for both turkey and ham sandwiches. Since I am a firm believer that, except in dire emergencies, sandwiches cannot be eaten without pickles and potato chips, I packed those, too. Before anyone else in the house was up and moving, I loaded everything into my SUV and headed downtown.

The *Miss Luella,* the thirty-foot fishing boat her late husband had christened in Luella's honor, bobbed next to the dock. It was a gentle sort of seesawing motion. Up and down. Side to side.

I was hypnotized, and my stomach mimicked the rocking.

I told it to stop.

It might actually have listened and behaved if, when I got to the *Miss Luella,* Levi hadn't hopped off the boat.

"Where's Luella?" My gaze darted toward the boat. Up near the front, it had a roof over the spot where the controls were, and windows on three sides. Because of the day's weather, a removable canvas curtain had been fitted and zipped at the back edge of the roof. I couldn't see beyond it to where I assumed Luella was making last-minute preparations. "She's getting everything ready, right?"

Levi grabbed the heavy carry bag I'd brought lunch in and swung it over the side of the boat to set it on deck. "Luella asked me to help her out."

"She didn't say anything about that to me last night when we carved pumpkins." He grabbed for the sweatshirt and slicker in my arms and I had no choice but to hand them over. I followed my belongings onto the boat. It seemed awfully quiet beyond that zipped, canvas curtain. "Where is she?"

He unzipped the barrier and stowed my clothing inside, as well as lunch. No Luella. "Like I said, she asked me to help."

"And she'll be here in a couple minutes, right?"

"Maybe." Levi started the engine and the boat motor roared to life. "But it won't really matter, because in a couple minutes, we'll be gone."

"What do you mean?" I darted forward, a simple enough movement on solid land that turned out to be a little trickier when the deck beneath my sneakers rolled and bucked. I steadied myself, my arms held out from my sides, and took a few careful steps toward the controls. "Luella's taking me to Canada today," I told Levi.

He guided the boat out of its slip and ever-so-cautiously piloted it around the sign that warned, *Slow! No wake!*

I watched the dock grow ever smaller. That's when the reality of the situation hit and I turned to Levi.

"You're taking me to Canada."

For a few minutes, he didn't answer. He was too busy

getting us safely out of the harbor, and for those few minutes, I watched him handle the wheel as if he'd been born on the deck of the *Pequod*. Finally he glanced my way. "Luella—"

"Asked you to help. Yeah, I got that part. But that doesn't explain where she is or why she asked for your help."

He was dressed in jeans and a navy sweatshirt, and he wore a North Face jacket that was the mouse gray color of the lake. In answer to my question, he lifted a shoulder.

We were in more open water by then, and he nudged the boat to go a little faster.

"Do you even know how to operate a boat?" I asked him.

He flashed me a smile, and in that one instant, it wasn't so chilly anymore. "I know how to do a whole lot of interesting things."

My feet far enough apart to brace myself, I crossed my arms over my chest. "Not what I asked."

He stepped away from the controls. "You want to drive?"

"No." To prove it, I backed away. The boat bucked, and I threw out a hand and hung on to the side to keep from toppling over. By the time I got my sea legs, we were out of the harbor and on the open water.

He threw me a sidelong glance. "Canada, huh?"

"Luella didn't tell you where we were going?"

"She did." He checked a navigation chart and made the proper corrections. "She told me to head for Middle Island, the southernmost place in Canada. It's a nature preserve, you know."

"I know."

"The place is completely deserted and boaters are discouraged from docking there. Plus, you need special permission from the Canadian parks people to stop and disembark."

"I got it."

"On a Saturday."

"Today's Sunday," I reminded him.

"Yeah, but you didn't decide to go to Middle Island this morning. You called Luella yesterday, which means—"

"I talked to the proper authorities yesterday. Sure. Okay. I admit it. It's no big deal."

"Bet they wouldn't have talked to me on a weekend if I called them."

I prayed my smile was as charming as I hoped. "Maybe you're just not as persuasive as I am."

"Oh, I'm sure of that!" Levi grinned. He set *Miss Luella's* autopilot and, arms braced behind him, he leaned back and studied me. "That still doesn't tell me why we're going to Middle Island."

I let go of my hold on the boat and faced forward. It was better than meeting that very level, very intense, very blue gaze of his straight on.

Left, right, and dead ahead, all I could see was an endless expanse of gray, roiling water. Now and then, the sun poked through the clouds and gilded the waves.

Though I had been sure I wouldn't need them when I left the house, I was glad I had brought along my sunglasses. I got them out of my pocket and slipped them on.

"This has something to do with Sleepy Harlow, right?" Levi asked.

"Exactly. See, back in the nineteen twenties, Middle Island was owned by a big-time mobster. He built a clubhouse there, and that's where he and his gang lived. Pretty clever, huh? Just inside Canada, where there was no law against producing or selling liquor. And just close enough to the US to be a great distribution point. This mobster, he even had a casino in the basement of his clubhouse, carved out of the limestone bedrock. Middle Island is where Sleepy picked up his Canadian liquor."

"So you're looking for atmosphere again, like you were when you checked out my apartment. You want to get into Sleepy's head and get to know him better."

"That's right."

"Because you're helping out Marianne."

I hadn't had the nerve to tell him the truth before, but there was something about being alone out on the water that invited confidences. I made a face. "More like because I *was* helping Marianne by reading her manuscript. Until Chandra's cat visited and peed on it. It's completely destroyed and Marianne's computer crashed and she didn't have a backup, and she's expecting to get the manuscript back when she returns from the mainland and she needs to get it to her publisher so I'm redoing it, rewriting it. Or at least I'm trying. I'm checking out any of the facts that I can find, and I'm trying to fill in the blanks and—"

I'll give him points for trying to control a smile.

No points for bursting into laughter anyway.

"That's why you're doing this? You're trying to re-create Marianne's book?"

I was the one working with the stinky manuscript, so of course I knew there was nothing to laugh about. "Before she gets back from the mainland."

"Because Marianne's mad about what happened and insists you help."

I bit my lower lip. "Marianne doesn't know about it. She's not going to know about it," I added as a way of warning him that he *would* keep his mouth shut. "I'm going to put the whole thing back together just the way she gave it to me. She'll never know."

"Uh-huh." At least he wasn't laughing anymore. He

was, however, smiling when he said, "I wonder if that's how real authors write books. You know, go to the places where their subjects lived so they can soak in the atmosphere and see what that person saw. Unless they're writing fiction, of course. Then I guess anything goes. Take that FX O'Grady guy. You know, I was reading over one of his old books last night and thinking that he must have one heck of a warped imagination. The book was all about vampires and werewolves. So how do you suppose he gets into their heads?"

Even with the canvas curtain zipped, it was cold out on the water. I reached for my sweatshirt and tugged it on. "I have no idea, but I guess he'd just sort of, you know, play a sort of game of *what if*. What if vampires showed up in modern-day Scotland? What if they won a war with humans and became the governing force of the country? What if someone opposed them?"

"Sounds like you read *Imperfect Creatures*."

I shook off the thought. "I think I saw the movie once. I didn't like it very much."

"Too scary for you?"

"The world's a scary enough place without vampires and werewolves to worry about. Especially when Jerry Garcia's running around ruining manuscripts."

My strategy was to deflect the subject in another direction, and it worked. Levi's smile settled into a grin that reminded me of the glowing embers left after a roaring fire. "At least if you're writing a book, you don't have time to go messing with Noreen's murder investigation."

A chill snaked up my back. It had nothing to do with the weather. To prove it, I pulled back my shoulders. "As a matter of fact, Hank asked for my help."

I had hoped for some sort of reaction that was a little more dramatic than the no-reaction I got.

Which kind of surprised me. That is, until the truth hit. "You knew that." I pointed an accusatory finger in his direction. "You knew Hank asked for my help. That's why you talked Luella into taking her place today. You didn't know the trip to Middle Island had anything to do with Marianne's book. You thought I was going over there as part of the investigation, and you wanted to keep an eye on me."

"Wouldn't dream of it."

Yeah, like that was going to convince me.

"What makes you think you have the right to follow me around like you're some kind of watchdog?" I demanded, right before I thought about telling him to turn right around and head back to Put-in-Bay. I would have, too, except that I knew we'd nearly arrived at our destination. Middle Island is only about seven miles from South Bass, and already I could see the jagged branches of trees etched against the horizon.

"I don't need this," I grumbled. "I don't need you to—"

"You don't." I wasn't sure he believed it, but at least he gave the words a try. "But when Hank told me you were poking around, I thought—whoa!"

Whatever he had been going to say, Levi's words dissolved in the exclamation, and I could see why. Up ahead on Middle Island, thousands of birds rose into the sky like a plume of black smoke.

"Cormorants," I said, as awed as Levi. "They nest on the island."

He gave me a sidelong look. "Are they friendly?"

"What, you're afraid of birds?"

"Not afraid." The way he twitched his shoulders told me otherwise. We watched the mass of birds swing out over the water, their weird, throaty grunts in stark contrast to the high-pitched screaks of the gulls that had followed us from home. Some of the cormorants dove into the water to fish. The rest of them swept back the way they came. They settled in the trees that blanketed the shoreline.

"There are an awful lot of them," Levi said.

"Thousands." I'd done my homework before I made arrangements to travel to the island. "They eat fish, not people. You've got nothing to worry about."

Levi edged the boat to shore and turned off the motor. He hopped off the boat first and helped me down, his hands on my waist.

"They say Sleepy picked up his liquor here." The second I was back on solid ground, I backed out of Levi's reach and looked around the deserted island, because, let's face it, ten feet of beach that was then swallowed by heavy vegetation wasn't a more appealing sight than Levi's gleaming blue eyes, but it was a heck of a lot safer to concentrate on trees and brush than it was to risk getting bewitched.

Apparently, Levi thought so, too. No sooner had I stepped away than he hooked his hands together behind his back.

"He bought the liquor from the gangsters here and brought it over to South Bass," I continued. "From there, Sleepy distributed it to other gangsters on the Ohio mainland. Except"—I reached for my phone and checked the time—"Marianne's manuscript talks about a trip Sleepy made over here and how he left Middle Island with a boat full of liquor at three in the morning. She says he never got back to South Bass until five. It sure didn't take us two hours to get here."

"More like twenty-five minutes," Levi said. "And that's in choppy water. What do you suppose it means?"

"Probably that I read the soggy words wrong," I admitted.

Using the information I'd been given by the Canadian parks official I'd talked to, I'd sketched out a rough map of Middle Island. I pulled it out of my pocket, and together, we stepped off the sandy beach and into the undergrowth.

"Welcome to Canada," Levi said.

Or at least that's what I thought he said. No sooner had we moved toward the trees than the cormorants went up again. Their grunts were deafening.

"Maybe they'll settle down once they get used to us," I yelled.

"Maybe." Levi ducked when one of the birds swooped a little too close, and we scurried farther into the under-growth and away from the trees and the birds nesting in them. "So what do you want to see?"

Armed with my makeshift map, I led the way. Mobsters had romped around Middle Island in the '20s, and after that, there was a hotel somewhere on the island that, up until the 1950s, hosted hunters and fishermen every year. Since then, the island had been allowed to revert back to nature. Stepping over fallen trees and through overgrown foliage, we followed what there was of a path to all that remained of the old lighthouse: a square of stones still blackened by the fire that had destroyed it.

I got out my phone and took some pictures, then walked the perimeter of the building, glancing from the structure to the lake.

"Let me guess." Levi stood back to watch. "You're imagining how Sleepy would have seen the lighthouse."

"Like I said, Marianne talks about the time he left here at three in the morning. When you're smuggling booze, I don't imagine you work nine to five. It's pretty darned dark in the middle of the lake in the middle of the night. Just think about him heading back to South Bass, watching the light of this tower get smaller and smaller as he got farther and farther away."

"So what does that tell you?"

I'd been lost in the thought, and I shook it away. "That it takes nerves of steel to be a bootlegger, for one thing. That Sleepy must have been a decent sailor. That he was a man who was willing to take chances, and that he thought money was worth the risk. It tells me he had guts, even if his energy was misplaced, and it tells me he was tough. He must have been to deal with the kinds of mobsters who ran the liquor trade. It also tells me he was brave. I wouldn't want to be out in the lake alone at night."

"Only you don't know if he was alone."

"True," I admitted. "But for the sake of Marianne's book, we're going to pretend he was. I don't have the time or the patience to find out any information about anyone else."

Done with the lighthouse, we found our way to the site of an old mansion that was said to have once operated as a brothel. Like the lighthouse, there wasn't much left except stones piled here and there. From there, we set out to find what we could of the clubhouse built by the mobster who made a fortune supplying men like Sleepy with liquor.

We were nearly there when we were treated to another chorus of cormorant grunts and screeches. The sky above us grew dark with birds. They eddied, swooped, and turned toward the lake.

"Darn birds." I pretended not to notice how relieved Levi looked once they were gone. "We're not even over there by those trees where they're nesting. Why do they care that we're walking around way over here?"

"Just like they started flapping and squawking before we ever even got to the island."

We stopped and looked at each other, and honestly, I'm not sure which of us spoke the words, I only know that as soon as they were voiced, ice formed in the pit of my stomach.

"We're not alone. There's someone else on the island."

✦ 13 ✦

"Come on!" Levi grabbed my hand and pulled me farther down what there was of a path. I didn't resist. Except for the raucous cormorants, the island was supposed to be deserted. In fact, the park supervisor I'd talked to the day before assured me no one had even called to ask about Middle Island for as long as she could remember.

There was something about knowing we weren't alone there on that tiny spot of land in the middle of nowhere that made a funny sort of rhythm start up inside my rib cage. It wasn't a steady beat so much as it was a clattering. Like a drummed message, a warning.

Or maybe I was just breathing so hard because Levi had long legs and ran so fast.

He stopped as suddenly as he'd started, and I stood beside him, fighting to pull in breath after chilly breath while I watched him scan our surroundings. From my vantage point, there wasn't a whole lot to see other than the foliage that surrounded us, its dry and brittle leaves scraping together in the stiff breeze like skeleton fingers. But then, Levi's a whole lot taller than me. He looked around, his head bent, listening, then pointed to his left. "Over there!"

A heartbeat later, hundreds of birds rose into the sky.

"That's got to be where he is. He's frightening the birds. Quick!" He took off running again, tugging me behind him. By the time we got to the trees, though, whoever we were trailing was long gone. Which didn't make the cormorants any happier about seeing us. They circled over our heads like billows of black smoke. I have to admit, when I'd read about the call of the cormorant, I didn't think a bird could possibly sound like a pig, but they did, honest. Their grunts and gulps provided a sinister backdrop to our rough breathing, like the uh-oh-don't-look-now music of a spooky movie.

I put my hands on my knees and fought to catch my breath. "I'm not afraid of birds. I mean, not like you are." Since I only did this to get his goat, I didn't give Levi a chance to defend himself before I added, "But these birds, they're like something out of a horror movie."

"Yeah." He managed a smile between deep breaths. "Like something your friend FX O'Grady might write about."

"He's not my friend," I reminded him, and then, because I saw another black cloud of cormorants rise from their nests a few hundred yards to our left, I took off running and left Levi to follow in my wake.

But again, by the time we got there, whoever we were following was gone.

The breeze had picked up and brought an icy chill with

it, but sweat tickled my collarbone, and I pulled off my sweatshirt and tied the arms of it around my waist. "Maybe it's just a bird-watcher," I suggested. "Or a fisherman who stopped for a rest. Or—"

From what sounded like a very long way off, we heard the roar of a boat motor.

Levi grumbled a curse. "Well, whoever it is, he's gone." He kicked a nearby clump of fallen leaves. "And if he was just here watching birds, you'd think he'd move a little slower and not cause so much commotion. This guy, he was moving awfully fast."

"Like he knew we were following him."

"Like he knew all along that we were here."

Once again Levi grabbed on to me and we made our way in the direction of the sound of the boat, but by the time we got to the ribbon of beach, that boat was nothing but a speck out on the water.

His eyes shielded with one hand, Levi watched the speck get smaller. "Looks like a twenty-footer. If we're fast—"

He didn't have to tell me twice. I took off like a shot for our own boat, but even on an island that's less than a mile wide, it took too long to get there. That didn't stop us from trying.

Levi jumped on the *Miss Luella* and offered me a hand up.

"We'll never catch him," I said, standing at the back of the boat, my eyes riveted to that speck, watching it getting smaller and smaller by the second.

He raced for the controls. "That doesn't mean we can't try."

Except he didn't try.

One minute, and I waited to hear the sound of our own boat spring to life.

Another minute, and when nothing happened, I marched over to where Levi stood, his fists on his hips.

"What?" I asked. "Why aren't we moving?"

A muscle bunched at the base of his jaw. "The battery's gone."

I heard what he said; I just found it impossible to believe. "Of course it isn't gone. How could it be gone? It can't be gone. Who could have—" I snapped my head around. The boat we'd seen leave the island was long gone.

And Levi and I were stranded.

By the time I had the vegetable soup in mugs I had found down in Luella's galley, Levi had a small fire going on the beach.

"The Canadian Coast Guard says it will be a couple hours." He tucked his phone back into the pocket of his jacket. "They've got a commercial fishing boat somewhere west of here that's having serious problems. They've got to take care of that before they can worry about us."

"Great." I flopped down on one of the blankets Levi had folded near the fire and handed him his soup. "At least we've got food."

"And warmth." He poked the fire with a stick and it flared and shot sparkling embers into the air and toward the clouds that were getting thicker by the minute over our heads. "If it rains, we can hide out on the boat."

While I was getting the soup, Levi had laid out the sandwich fixings. He heaped ham on bread, added swiss cheese and mustard, and took a bite, thinking. He washed it all down with a swallow of soup. "So you're the one investigating," he said. "Having our battery swiped, what does that tell you?"

"Not much," I admitted. "I can't imagine it has anything to do with my investigation, or with Noreen's murder."

He took a few more bites, leaving me to think about what I'd just said.

If I didn't have a mug of soup in one hand and a half a turkey sandwich in the other, I would have slapped my forehead.

"The whole thing must have something to do with Sleepy! Someone was here checking out his old hangouts. If it were the ghost getters, they might have been here because they thought they could find some evidence that Sleepy's still around."

"So why work so hard to stay out of our way? Why strand us?"

This took more careful thought. While I was at it, I sipped my soup, grateful that I'd thought ahead when I was packing for a day on the lake. It was getting chillier by the moment, and the hot soup felt good going down. I scooted closer to the fire. "Maybe . . ." Maybe what? Since we couldn't know for sure, I figured it wouldn't hurt to play that *what-if* game I'd mentioned to Levi when we were on our way to Middle Island.

"What if the person who took our battery didn't want us to find out he was here on the island?"

"The way he was moving, I'd say that was a given."

"So what if he figured that when we heard his boat, we'd naturally follow the sound?"

"So we'd get to the beach—like we did—and watch him head south—like we did. What would make him think we'd care enough to jump in our boat and follow?"

I had no answer for this question, and I made a face and thought about it. It wasn't until I finished my half sandwich, the pickle that went with it, and the handful of potato chips that I figured was my reward for running helter-skelter all over the island that the truth dawned. "We jumped onto the *Miss Luella* and tried to follow because we were curious about who he was and what he was doing here. He couldn't take the chance that might happen. He didn't want us to follow him. More importantly, he didn't want us to see him. That explains both why he was running away from us and why he stranded us. He didn't want us to see him because he knew we'd recognize him. It was someone we know."

"And if it was one of your houseguests, I can't imagine they'd care if we saw them or not," Levi added. "If we caught up to them and questioned why they were here, they'd say they were on the island looking for Sleepy's wandering ectoplasm. There couldn't be any harm in us knowing that."

"Which means whoever was here wasn't here for a reason he could easily explain away."

A blast of wind blew my words away, and I shivered.

Levi patted the blanket beside him. "It's warmer when you add some body heat," he said.

That was exactly what I was afraid of.

I hugged my arms around myself.

Levi gave up with a nod. "So what if . . ." He reached for another couple slices of bread and built another sandwich. Bread, cheese, ham. A whole pile of ham. He finished with mustard. "I don't suppose you brought horseradish?" he asked.

"Next time we get marooned on a deserted island, I promise I will."

Above the sandwich he was about to chomp into, his eyes sparked. "There's going to be a next time?"

"I suppose if we keep getting mixed up in murder, there might be."

"Promise?"

For one quick heartbeat, I actually wanted to.

That is, until I came to my senses.

"Look"—I brushed my hands together and set my mug of soup in the sand, the better to link my fingers and give Levi my full attention—"there's something we really need to talk about."

I'd hoped he'd pick up on the opening and do the talking for me, but instead, he fixed that intense blue gaze on me, chewed his sandwich, and waited for me to make the first verbal move.

"Last summer . . ." I felt my cheeks flush and told myself it was windburn. I mean, it must have been, right? "When you said it was a mistake . . ."

Levi swallowed. "You mean when I kissed you."

My shoulders shot back. I didn't mean to come across as so defensive, so I covered by inching closer to the fire. "That's right. The thing is, we've been dancing around the subject since then."

"And now you don't want to dance."

Another handful of chips gave me something to crunch into to release the tension that had built inside me. "I'm not much of a dancer," I admitted.

"And I happen to be an excellent dancer." He gave me a wink. "Fast on my feet."

"You keep proving that."

"A man's got to play to his strong suit."

"You keep proving that, too."

"I'm glad you've noticed."

How could I not?

Oh, he could dance, all right. He was dancing for all he was worth, right then and there. Not that someone who didn't know Levi well would have noticed. And not that I knew him all that well. But hey, I'm pretty good when it comes to picking up impressions. Call it women's intuition. Call it the product of a mind that far too often is lost in daydreams. Say that I'm always looking for motives behind peoples' actions. Go ahead, say it.

It's absolutely true.

I couldn't help but notice the way his gaze couldn't manage to focus on me. It darted out to the lake—and believe me, the gray and churning waves weren't all that interesting. Neither were the cormorants who kept their distance at the same time as they kept an eye on us, circling overhead like vultures.

Levi was as nervous about the conversation as I was, and realizing it, my courage came back and brought my backbone with it.

"I'm sorry we've been so uneasy around each other since the summer," I said. "I should have told you sooner. You were right."

"Of course I was." His smile faded and he eyed me carefully. "About what?"

"About how you kissing me was a big mistake. It was. A huge mistake. A colossal mistake. A ginormous—"

"Okay. All right. I get the message. So you're telling me you didn't enjoy—"

"Not what I'm talking about." I held out a hand to stop his words in their tracks. It might have been a far more effective gesture if my hand weren't coated with salt. I rubbed it against the leg of my jeans. "There may have been a certain . . . appeal to the situation," I admitted. "But on reflection, it was a mistake. Yes, definitely a mistake. So"—I got up and grabbed both my mug and Levi's to take them back to the boat—"I think the best thing to do is just forget about the whole thing, don't you?"

It was nearly the end of October, and the clocks wouldn't fall back to Eastern Standard Time until the beginning of November. Still, the sun set right around six, and with the clouds being so heavy, evening closed around us in what seemed like no time flat. When the last of our little fire splurted out in a blast of cold Canadian wind, we smothered it with sand and surrendered, gathering our blankets and the remnants of our lunch and climbing back aboard the *Miss Luella*.

Waves pounded the boat and it creaked and rocked. It was too chilly even in the closed-in area near the controls, so Levi and I ducked below deck. There, Luella had a tiny galley, a bunk bed, and benches that fit snugly along either side (I never know which is port and which is starboard) of the boat under the bow. It was warmer, sure, but below the waterline, the power of the waves was more apparent than ever.

I flopped down on the bench. "I suppose we could have dinner while we're waiting. If you feel like eating. If the waves aren't making you too queasy."

"I'm always up for dinner. And don't worry, I'll get it."

A couple minutes later, Levi was back with caprese in one hand. His other hand was tucked behind his back. "Gourmet dining in the middle of nowhere. You think of everything."

"Not everything, or we wouldn't still be here."

"And not wine." Like a magician pulling a rabbit out of a hat, Levi revealed the bottle of pinot noir he'd had hidden behind his back. Good pinot noir.

My tastebuds applauded . . . right before my radar told me a rocking boat, a handsome man, and a few glasses of wine were probably a recipe for trouble.

"You had no idea we were going to get stuck here, and you still thought to bring wine?"

"I told you I know how to do a lot of interesting things. Being prepared for all events is one of them. When you're with a beautiful woman, it never hurts to have a bottle of wine around."

He handed me a glass of the ruby liquid, and I told my radar to shut up. I was a big girl, and nobody's fool. The wine looked heavenly and smelled divine, and besides, I liked being called beautiful.

Levi and I clinked our glasses together and I tasted the wine and nodded my approval. In silence, we ate our dinners.

"You know . . ." He'd already gotten a second helping of caprese and finished with it. Levi sat back, satisfied. "You never gave me a chance to tell my side of the story."

"Which story is that?"

"About why I was sorry I kissed you."

"I thought we were supposed to forget it."

"We are. We will. But only you got to say how you feel about it. You know, the whole ginormous, horrendous, dreadful, appalling, horrific thing."

"I never said any of that. Well, except for the *ginormous* part."

His smile told me he'd just been kidding. It settled into a sizzle. "So my side of the story goes something like this. I said it was a mistake for a couple of different reasons. I'm living in a new place. I've got a start-up business I'm try-ing to keep afloat. I'm busy and I have responsibilities, and I'm not looking for a relationship, and Bea, I knew it the minute it happened—that was the kind of kiss that was definitely going to lead to a relationship."

What was that I said about radar?

Right about then, mine went completely out of whack.

That would be the only thing that could possibly explain why I leaned closer to Levi. It wasn't like I had a lot of choice in the matter. Magnet and steel. Moth and flame. "That's the most romantic thing anyone's ever said to me," I told him.

"Yeah." He had the good sense to at least look a little nervous. That didn't stop him from leaning closer to me. His words brushed my lips along with the heady aroma of the wine. "That's something else I've been accused of. Sometimes I can't help myself. I mean, when I'm with the right woman." He plucked my wineglass out of my hand and set it on the floor along with his, then slipped an arm around my shoulders. "I don't know if it's a mistake or not. And right about now, I don't care. You're the right woman."

When his lips brushed mine, I closed my eyes.

They flew right open again when a voice boomed out on a loudspeaker somewhere very close by, "Canadian Coast Guard. Anyone on board?"

Both Levi and I jumped and scrambled to get up on deck.

A Coast Guard cutter was waiting, its powerful spotlight trained on the *Miss Luella*.

I wonder if they saw the mix of disappointment and relief in my eyes.

Relief, of course, was the wise emotion to stick with, along with the realization that hey, it wasn't the cavalry riding to the rescue. Not exactly, anyway.

But it would do.

❈ 14 ❖

The image on the screen slid and swooped. One second, Marianne was there; then she was gone; then she was back.

"I've never done anything like this before," she said, her voice a little too loud and her words a little too clipped when she fidgeted in her seat and played with the screen in front of her. "Can you all hear me okay?"

We could, I assured her. "And if you'd stop moving around," I added, "we'd be able to see you better, too."

"Sorry." Marianne made a face. "I've never done this before."

"Isn't it the best?" Chandra was sitting on the couch next to me and she slid my iPad over so that Marianne could see her. "Imagine, there you are in Cleveland and here we are at home, and we can all see each other for book discussion group."

"It is wonderful, isn't it?" Marianne looked comfortable in a pink robe, but there was a gauze bandage over her left eye that made her look especially worried when she said, "Except that I hear things haven't been going so well at home. Kate?" Marianne leaned left, then right, as if she could look around and see Kate somewhere in the room. "Kate, I know you're there. Just so you know, Alvin and I, we don't think you did it."

We were in my parlor, and Kate was settled in a chair that sat at a right angle from the couch where I sat. Anyone who knew Kate as well as I did couldn't fail to notice that there wasn't as much of a gleam in her green eyes as usual, and nowhere near the enthusiasm in her voice. She looked stiff, brittle, like the real Kate had been put aside somewhere and a cardboard replica had been sent to book discussion group in her place. In fact, she didn't turn the tablet around so Marianne could see her when she said, "Thanks, Marianne. I wish Hank felt the way you do."

"Hank!" There was a platter of chocolate brownies on the coffee table in front of the couch and Chandra grabbed one and took a chomp. "The man couldn't find a barn with a searchlight. He should look for the real killer and leave Kate alone."

"Well, of course he's just trying to do his job," Marianne said, but as much as she tried to be the voice of reason, she couldn't erase the edge of worry from her words. "Bea, what are you doing about this? You are trying to find the real killer, aren't you?"

"Oh, Bea's been too busy for that!" Even talk of murder couldn't keep Chandra from squealing with delight. "I bet she's been too busy to read our book for the discussion group, too. You should know that, Marianne. Go ahead, ask her. Ask her what she's been up to."

Chandra must have seen me roll my eyes, because instead of giving me a chance to defend myself, she went right on. "Ask her how she could possibly have time for reading or investigating when she spent last night with Levi."

Marianne let out a giggle that would have done a teen-age girl proud. At least I think she did. Since I was grumbling, it was a little hard to tell.

I grabbed the iPad and yanked it back in my direction. "We didn't spend the night together," I insisted, and don't ask me why, but I felt compelled to add, "And I did too read *The Legend of Sleepy Hollow*."

Chandra yanked the tablet away from me and set it on the coffee table in front of her. "Okay, they didn't spend the night together, but it was all day. Alone. On an island," she told Marianne. "And they didn't get home until really late last night."

I snatched the iPad back. "We were stranded," I said in no uncertain terms, not only for Marianne's sake, but just in case Luella and Chandra and Kate (who didn't join in the gentle teasing) had forgotten what I'd already made perfectly clear to them when they showed up at my place for book discussion group and peppered me with questions about why I'd gotten home so late and what Levi and I had been up to out on Middle Island.

Yes, there are plenty of advantages to living in a pictur-esque town on a small and lovely island.

Everyone knowing everyone else's business is not one of them.

"We went to Middle Island yesterday and we got stranded."

"All alone! On a deserted island!" As if she'd been skewered by one of Cupid's arrows, Chandra clapped one hand to the nose of the jack-o'-lantern that adorned her purple sweatshirt and flopped back. She grinned, and the magnanimous part of me knew it was because this was more of her teasing. The less kind and gentler Bea Cartwright suspected it was a ploy; Chandra was determined to get the details of our trip to Middle Island out of me. She thought there were plenty of them and she was convinced they were wonderfully, gloriously, and deliciously steamy.

Wouldn't she be surprised to know how very wrong she was!

Chandra swooped up the tablet, and I imagined all Marianne could see was a close-up of Chandra's face.

"Anything could have happened out there in the middle of nowhere," Chandra purred, fishing for more information, hoping I'd rise to the bait.

"Anything did happen." Luella was in the tobacco-colored chair across from Kate's, and when I glanced her way I saw that she looked thoughtful. "But not the kind of anything Chandra's talking about. Getting stranded like that . . ." Though Luella is as tough as any Great Lakes captain, a shiver skidded across her shoulders. "It's not a joke. The lake can be a dangerous place, and whoever did that—"

"Really? It was on purpose?" Marianne's question reverberated with a frisson of excitement. "You mean the murderer—"

"We don't know that," I assured her, and looked around the group to make sure everyone else got the message, too. I didn't even try and make a grab for the iPad. Even if Marianne couldn't see me from her hotel room in Cleveland, she could hear me plenty clear. "We can't jump to conclusions. We don't know who it was."

"Of course we do." Chandra set the iPad on the coffee

table and sat up straight, her hands on her knees and her shoulders back. "It's about time we stopped kidding ourselves, ladies. We know exactly who stranded you. It was Sleepy Harlow."

In my defense, I wasn't the only one who groaned.

"You can make fun of me all you want." Chandra's voice was as tight as her jaw. "And you can make up all the theories you want, too, but you have to admit, it's the only thing that makes sense."

"Except that it doesn't," I told her. "Somebody else was on the island. That's for sure. But that doesn't mean that somebody else was a ghost. The person could have been there because—"

"Why?" Chandra demanded.

I threw my hands in the air. "Something fishy, obviously," I admitted. "Otherwise he wouldn't have swiped our boat battery so we couldn't follow. But that doesn't mean he was the murderer."

"Of course not," Chandra agreed. "Because it was Sleepy." Her eyes flew open. "Unless Sleepy is the murderer!"

Luella is as good as anyone when it comes to ignoring Chandra's flights of fantastic fantasy, and that's exactly what she did. Instead of giving in and trying to reason with Chandra, Luella cocked her head, thinking. "So someone was on Middle Island. Someone other than you and Levi. That's a given. So what could that someone have been there to see?"

I shrugged. "We explored the whole island."

"When you weren't doing other things," Chandra butted in, her voice a singsong of unspoken anticipation.

I pretended I didn't hear her. "There's not much to see. A few crumbling ruins. A whole lot of cormorants. Nothing of any significance."

"Which proves that it was Sleepy."

It didn't, but I didn't bother to point this out. Instead, I reminded Chandra, "Only if ghosts need boats to go back and forth between islands."

This she found perplexing, and, considering it, she chewed her lower lip and the purple lipstick she'd told us when she arrived was her fashion tribute to the season.

That gave Luella a chance to discuss the problem dispassionately. "So the person might have been looking for something," she suggested. "And if the old structures on the island aren't all that interesting, what else is there?"

"Sleepy's treasure?" I guess Kate was listening, since she roused herself long enough to make the suggestion.

"Except . . ." I thought about the slim pile of manuscript pages in my office. In all of Marianne's book, I had yet to discover one mention of the word treasure. "What do you think, Marianne?" I asked her. "When it comes to Charlie Harlow, you're the expert. Was there really a treasure?"

I turned the tablet so I could see Marianne when she answered. "There's no proof. Which is why I don't devote any time to it in the book. You've probably noticed that, Bea," she added because she assumed I was a conscientious friend who did not let other friends' cats pee on manuscripts. "Oh, I've heard the stories. Just like everyone else on South Bass has. But there's no historical data to back them up."

"But that doesn't mean someone else hasn't heard the story," Luella said. "And that someone else might not care about historical data. Whether the story is true or not, that person might believe there really is a treasure."

"It's possible," Marianne conceded.

"So let's pretend it's more than possible," I suggested, getting back to that *what-if* game I'd played with Levi. No, no, not *that* what-if game! The one about coming up with theories and motives that might help explain why Noreen was murdered and who had done it. "Let's say someone does believe there's a treasure, and that someone wants to find it. What is it, Marianne?"

"You mean, what's the treasure?" She shifted in her easy chair. "Well, it depends who you talk to, doesn't it, Luella? The old guys down at the docks who still talk about Sleepy swear it's money. A whole lot of money."

"Other people say it's a map that shows where Sleepy stored the liquor he brought over from Canada," Luella added. "I'm not much of a connoisseur when it comes to liquor. If it's true and there is old liquor tucked away somewhere, would any of it still be any good after all these years? I suppose even if what was in the bottles wasn't very good, the bottles themselves might be collectors' items. Somebody might want to buy them just because they're associated with bootlegging and the whole mobster culture of the twenties."

"Money, liquor . . ." I thought this over. "Could any of it have anything to do with Noreen?"

"Noreen. You mean the woman Kate *didn't* kill." Marianne made sure she emphasized the *didn't* just to show her support.

"Could Noreen have found something? Could she have known something?" Yes, this particular version of the *what-if* game was pretty pointless, but I couldn't help myself. "Could there be a connection? And what if the person hunting for Sleepy's treasure actually found it? I guess we'll never know. But if he didn't find it, he might . . ."

What?

Honestly, I didn't know. Except that if he hadn't found the treasure out there on Middle Island . . . if there was no treasure to ever find . . . it meant our mysterious treasure hunter would keep looking.

But where? And how would we know?

And even more importantly, what did it have to do with Noreen?

I twitched away the thought. Rain pounded outside the parlor window, and this Monday was even grayer and gloomier than it had been the day before, when Levi and I ventured out onto the lake. I'd made lattes for everyone, and I wrapped my hands around my coffee mug, enjoying the warmth when it spread from my fingers to my hands.

"We're not going to find the answers; not right here, not right now," Luella said, as if she were reading my mind. "And something tells me Marianne needs her rest. So let's do what we're supposed to be here doing. Let's talk about the book." Luella reached for the slim volume she'd dropped at the side of her chair. I wasn't surprised that she was the one who'd so deftly changed the subject. Luella loved to read, and she always had a book with her when she took a fishing charter out on the lake.

"Anybody have anything to say about the Sleepy we're supposed to be talking about?" Luella asked.

"Well, that's the whole point, isn't it?" Chandra said. "In the book, it's the headless ghost that's trying to scare that Isaac guy—"

Kate's voice was flat, sure, but Kate was not one to let a mistake go uncorrected. "Ichabod. Ichabod Crane."

"Yeah, Ichabod, like I said," Chandra breezed on. "The ghost is trying to scare Ichabod away. Just like our head-less ghost was trying to scare you and Levi yesterday. Unless, of course, you and Levi were too busy doing something else to even notice the ghost."

I did not acknowledge this comment because I didn't

want to think about the fact that if the Coast Guard hadn't arrived when it did, Chandra might actually be right.

"But the ghost in the story isn't really a ghost," I reminded Chandra. Heck, *The Legend of Sleepy Hollow* is only something like thirty pages long. The way I figured it, even Chandra should have read the assignment. "What Ichabod thinks is a ghost is really Brom Bones, the local alpha male who's in love with Katrina Van Tassel, the daughter of a rich farmer, just like Ichabod is. Brom wants Ichabod to leave Sleepy Hollow, so he—"

The thought hit and I sat up like a shot. "Brom Bones pretends to be the headless horseman," I said.

To which my fellow book discussion group members— well, except for Chandra, who believed that the Headless Horseman really was a ghost—gave me blank stares that pretty much said, *No duh*.

I scooted forward in my seat. "But don't you see? Brom was trying to scare Ichabod, so Brom pretended to be the ghost. What if someone's pretending to be Sleepy?"

"You mean like a real, living someone?" Chandra asked.

"Exactly."

"But why would anyone do that?" Kate asked at the same time that Luella offered her own comment.

"Well, if that's true," Luella said, "it's somebody who's been pretending to be Sleepy Harlow for a very long time. Even when I was a girl, folks talked about seeing Sleepy's ghost on the island."

I admit, it wasn't the most seamless theory I'd ever had. Still, the idea of someone impersonating Sleepy burned through me like fire. Even after Marianne asked me to call her back once Luella, Kate, and Chandra were gone, I couldn't let go of the thought.

That is, until I realized what Marianne wanted. I hoped I didn't gulp too noticeably when she picked up the phone.

"How is it?" Marianne asked, her excitement vibrating through the air all the way from Cleveland. "What do you think of the book?"

"It's fascinating! Who knew there was a gangster of Charlie's status here on the island."

"Exactly!" I didn't have to see Marianne on the screen in front of me like we had during the discussion group. I knew she was sitting tall, a smile on her face. "That's why I decided on doing the book in the first place. Sleepy's story is an interesting one. It deserves to be told."

"Absolutely." Could I sound any phonier? I told myself to get a grip.

"I'll be home for the Halloween party," Marianne added. "That's on Friday. Then on Monday, I'll send off the manuscript. Will it be ready by then?"

For one instant, panic overwhelmed me, and I thought that somehow, she knew the true story of what had happened to her book. That is, until Marianne added, "Are there a lot of typos and things I have to fix? Because then maybe it will take a couple extra days to send it off."

"No typos." I could pretty much guarantee her that. I am nothing if not a crackerjack typist and proofreader. "You've included so much interesting information, Marianne. But tell me . . . this is something I've always wondered about writers . . . do you remember . . . do you remember everything in your book? Like, every word?"

Her laughter sent chills down my spine. "Every word."

Every word.

Thinking back on the conversation an hour later, I felt

as cold and wet as if I were outside in the storm. I spent the time looking through what I had of a manuscript and deciding what I still needed. But have no fear—just because I was thinking about Sleepy didn't mean I wasn't ready when at ten o'clock the ghost getters got back from what must have been a long, cold, and very wet hunt.

I waited until they'd peeled off their wet slickers and hung them near the back kitchen door, then offered them coffee and the rest of the brownies and bided my time until, one by one, they began to straggle their way up to bed. David and Liam had just said good night and Jacklyn was refilling her coffee cup when I stepped between the kitchen door and her, effectively culling her from the pack.

"So, how did the hunt go tonight?" I asked her.

Jacklyn's hair was soaked, and a shower of raindrops spotted the shoulders of her black EGG sweatshirt. She brushed away a drop that dribbled down her forehead. "Dimitri figures as long as we're stuck here, we might as well do all the investigating we can. He decided on the hotel tonight."

"Any ghosts?"

She stretched a kink from her neck. "Management wasn't exactly thrilled with the possibility. They told us we could investigate all we wanted, as long as we stayed outside."

The way the rain was pounding on the kitchen windows, believe me, I felt her pain.

"I guess Dimitri was telling the truth when he said ghost hunting is a tough business. Sorry you came back to EGG?"

"You're kidding, right?" The sound Jacklyn made wasn't quite a snort of derision. She was way too aware of her status as the group's sex symbol for that. "I'm thrilled to be back with EGG. I just wish that Noreen—" She swallowed the rest of what she was going to say.

Except for Fiona, the other ghost hunters seemed to be decidedly unconcerned that their one-time leader had been bludgeoned to death. The raw emotion on Jacklyn's face was something of a relief.

"You think I care," she said when she noticed me watching her. "The way you looked, all touched when you thought I was about to talk about Noreen. You were all set to tell me how sorry you were that Noreen is dead."

I had been.

"But see, here's what you don't get." I'd turned off most of the lights in the kitchen, but still, Jacklyn's smile was radiant. "You've got it all wrong. I'm thrilled that she's gone. In fact, the only thing I'm sorry about is that I never got a chance to thank Noreen."

"For allowing you back in the group."

"Don't be naive. If Noreen was still here, I wouldn't be part of EGG again. When I came to the island, I didn't think I would be back with the group. I only showed up here so I could tell Noreen in person. You know, about how I got the role on the soap opera. Leave it to Noreen to get killed before I ever had the chance to rub it in her face." Jacklyn twitched away the thought. "But hey, I might not have gotten the chance to thank her for dying, but at least I ended up with second billing on a reality show. That's better than a soap opera walk-on. And I wouldn't have that," she added matter-of-factly, "if I wasn't sleeping with Dimitri."

The first thing I thought was that I wasn't surprised.

The second thing was that if Jacklyn wasn't using her room, she should have offered it to Fiona.

Truth be told, neither was surprising, so it wasn't hard

to say, "Noreen was jealous because you're so much prettier than her."

"Prettier. Better dressed. Way smarter. And a much better actress. Combine that with what I know about the paranormal and with investigating and you've got the perfect fit."

"So were you going to put all that to good use on the soap opera? Were you going to play an investigator?" I'd seen weirder story lines on the daytime dramas. "I didn't know they had that sort of thing on soap operas."

"They have actors on soap operas," Jacklyn said, and looked at me hard. "Oh, come on. How stupid do you think I am? You don't think I believe any of this, do you?"

"I . . . I . . ." I guess this wasn't a surprise, either. I mean, not completely. Yet Jacklyn's frank confession left me feeling a bit as if the proverbial rug had been pulled out from under me. "The ghost-getting thing, it's all made up?"

Jacklyn leaned back, her elbows propped on the counter behind her. "I said, how stupid do you think *I* am. The rest of them, they're plenty stupid. They believe all this hooey. Me, I script it all in my head. You know, before we arrive at a place we're going to investigate. That way, I can decide when I'm going to spin around and gasp, 'What was that?' like I actually heard something. Or when I'm going to jump like some invisible hand touched me. All the usual ghost-hunting garbage!"

First I'd had to suspend my disbelief to wrap my head around the fact that there were people who actually looked for ghosts. Now, Jacklyn was challenging me to turn my opinion another one hundred and eighty degrees. There were people who looked for ghosts who really didn't believe in ghosts.

Well, at least one person.

"What about Noreen?" I asked. "Was she a true believer?"

This time, she did allow an unladylike snort. "Noreen! Noreen would believe in anything that would get her noticed. I saw her fake evidence. You know, she'd get her camera rolling, then stand off to the side and stomp her feet, then pretend she'd heard disembodied footsteps. What a crock!"

"Then that video of Sleepy she got last year . . ." Oh yes, I waded into this tentatively, hoping it would sound as if this were a new thought to me and not that it was what I'd wanted to discuss with Jacklyn all along. "Was someone just pretending to be Sleepy?"

"Well, that's just the thing, isn't it?" Jacklyn's dark (and perfectly shaped, by the way) brows dropped over her eyes. "When Noreen first showed us that stupid video, it's exactly what everyone thought. But Noreen . . . she swore it was the real deal, and none of the experts who've examined the tape have been able to prove otherwise. Pretty ironic, don't you think? There I was making up every minute of every investigation. And there were the guys wanting so much to believe that it hurt and trying so darn hard to find something—anything—that would prove the existence of an afterlife. And in spite of it all, who gets the real evidence? Stupid Noreen."

« 15 »

Don't think I hadn't been paying attention.
Though I was inclined to believe Jacklyn when she said she was faking the whole paranormal investigation experience, I hadn't failed to catch the undercurrent of her each and every word.

She hated Noreen with a fiery passion.

And not for the same reasons the guys hated her.

The guys took exception to Noreen's bossy ways. The guys didn't like dealing with the whole OCD thing, or Noreen usurping leadership of EGG. The guys were jealous that Noreen had caught that video of Sleepy all on her own.

But Jacklyn . . .

I reminded myself that I'd seen Jacklyn at the ferry dock right before we discovered Noreen's body. There was no way she could have killed Noreen. Tell that to my investigatin' instincts! Try as I might to eliminate Jacklyn from a pitifully small pool of suspects, I couldn't forget the way she hovered around Dimitri, brushing her hip against his, lightly touching a hand to his arm.

She might as well have a neon sign flashing over her head: *My Man—Stay Away!*

Since I had no intention, then or now, of making a move on Dimitri, that was fine with me. But believe me, I knew what it meant: Jacklyn was one very jealous woman.

Could her jealousy have extended to Noreen?

Noreen and Dimitri?

As unlikely (not to mention icky) as it seemed, I intended to find out.

I kept that in mind when my ghost-tracking guests arrived at the breakfast table the next morning. They were a sullen and solemn bunch; that is, when they weren't complaining about the evidence—or, more accurately, the lack of it—they'd ended up with after nearly a week on the island.

"Production needs to be finished in three weeks," Dimitri grumbled, pushing scrambled eggs from one side of his plate to the other. "And so far, we don't have much to show."

"We need the plasmometer," Liam said. "At least then we'd have a fighting chance. You've got to talk to the cops, Dimitri. You've got to explain that we can't do our jobs without the plasmometer. There's got to be some kind of law about how they can't keep it. We need to repair it or rebuild it, and that will take time. Tell them that. Tell them we need it to make our living."

"We might have EVPs." Fiona was much too chipper. At least that's what the looks they threw her said. She either didn't realize it or she didn't care. I was going with the she-didn't-realize-it theory. Fiona heaped her plate with scrambled eggs, grabbed a blueberry muffin, and sat down opposite Dimitri. "I spent a few hours listening to the evidence we collected last night. There might be a few EVPs."

Dimitri did not look convinced.

Or maybe he was just distracted when Jacklyn strutted into the room swaddled in a pink kimono, her hair piled up on her head, her skin dewy and trailing the scent of musky bath gel. When she leaned over to get the coffee carafe from the middle of the table, she caressed the back of Dimitri's neck with one hand.

"Fiona thinks we got EVPs," Rick told her.

"Isn't that sweet." Jacklyn's gaze drifted to Fiona for the briefest of moments before it traveled to where I stood in the doorway just waiting for someone to take the last of the bacon off the serving platter so I could refill it. She didn't need to say a word; I knew exactly what the look meant: *See how foolish the poor child is! If she wasn't, she wouldn't be so darned optimistic.*

"We'll need to review all the footage," Dimitri said, daring to be optimistic, too. "And listen to the tapes. After breakfast. My room. Bring everything you have."

I left them to it and went to the kitchen to leave last-minute instructions with Meg, who agreed to take care of the breakfast cleanup duties while I went out for the day.

Time was a'wastin'. Marianne and Alvin would be returning to the island soon. I had more to do, more to find out, before they got back home. I had to finish re-creating the manuscript, then get it typed, edited, and proofread to perfection. And I had to do it all fast.

Thank goodness that though temperatures had cooled, the sun was shining again. Still, I wasn't going to take any chances. Along with my jeans, a long-sleeved T-shirt, and a heavy sweater, I pulled on a jacket thick enough to keep out the wind that blew from the direction of Middle Island, and a pair of knee-high rubber rain boots. Where I needed to go, it was likely to be muddy.

I left the house, and less than fifteen minutes later, I pulled my SUV through the two stone pillars that marked the entrance to Crown Hill Cemetery. According to what I'd been able to decipher from Marianne's manuscript, Charlie Harlow's grave was at the end of the drive. I wouldn't have slammed on my brakes when I arrived there if I didn't see Levi's black Jeep already parked there, or Levi himself waiting for me, a bunch of red carnations in one hand, their long stems swaddled in green tissue.

"What are you doing here?" Yes, it was a little too proprietary. After all, anybody could visit the cemetery. I just didn't like it that Levi was visiting it exactly when I was visiting it. My gaze flickered to the flowers and heat shot into my cheeks. "You're paying your respects to someone buried here."

"Peace offering." He handed the flowers to me.

I was too surprised not to accept them and too unsure how I felt about the whole thing not to be awkward. I tucked the bouquet into the crook of my arm like a Miss America pageant winner. "What do you want?" I asked Levi.

He laughed. "What, you think I have an ulterior motive? You've got trust issues."

"Only if that means I don't trust you to make a peace offering I didn't know I had coming."

"You're right. Technically, you didn't have it coming," he said, and then, because my shoulders automatically shot back just as my chin just naturally shot forward, he laughed again. That is, right before the gleam of amusement in his eyes settled into a warm blue glow.

"Truce?" he suggested.

The word hung in the air between us long enough for me to be tempted to ask him to elaborate. But then, I'm smarter than that, right? I didn't need an explanation. I knew exactly what he was talking about.

It was all about that mistake we both made the summer before.

All about how we'd nearly made it again out at Middle Island.

It was based on the fact that we both believed that this was the wrong time and the wrong place for either one of us to start into a relationship, and about how if we really meant that, it was time to simply admit it and get on with our lives.

I stuck out a hand to shake his. "Truce."

There. Done.

Finally.

Hoping I didn't look too eager to break off the contact, I pulled my hand back to my side and adjusted my hold on the carnations. Their spicy scent tickled my nose.

Maybe Levi was as relieved as I was that we'd finally come to some sort of agreement. He turned and strolled across the grass. It was still wet from the recent rain, and it was slick. I was grateful for my boots.

"Meg's the one who told me, by the way. I called your place a little while ago and she said you were headed over here."

I hadn't asked, but I appreciated the explanation. "Did she tell you why?"

"She didn't have to." He stopped and looked down at the gray granite marker nearest his feet. "This is where Charlie Harlow is buried."

It was, and Sleepy's grave was exactly what I wanted to see.

"I couldn't read the information clearly," I said, bending down so I could brush away fallen leaves and get a better look at the stone. "I know he died on October third, nineteen thirty, but I couldn't read Marianne's pages clearly." I pulled a notebook out of my pocket and jotted down what I needed. "Eighteen ninety-eight. He was born in eighteen ninety-eight. I figured it was pretty important to get that right." I would confirm the information through local county records, but for now, I was satisfied.

"Not a bad spot to spend eternity." Levi tipped back his head and pulled in a deep breath of autumn-crisp air. The small cemetery backed into a grove of trees that were dappled with the same sunlight that danced and glistened against the grass in patterns that changed with the wind. "It's quiet. It's restful. It seems out of character that a man who lived as a gangster could rest so peacefully."

"Unless he's not. If," I added, because I was afraid the look Levi gave me said he was worried about my sanity, "if you believe what some people say."

"I'm pretty sure he's right here." There was a heavy fringe of overgrown grass that hemmed in the headstone from all sides, and Levi tapped the toe of his sneaker on it. "He's always been right here, and this is exactly where he's going to stay."

I was sure of it, too. Pretty sure. What I wasn't so sure about . . .

I looked to where Levi's shoe rested against the thick grass that threatened to smother the stone. The gray granite of Sleepy's marker had survived the years better than many of the marble gravestones nearby. Island weather had worn away many of their inscriptions so that the words were soft and nearly indecipherable, like writing on a foggy mirror.

The information on Sleepy's stone had fared better. Except . . .

Before I jumped to any conclusions, I dropped down on my knees, and, ignoring the way my jeans immediately acted like a wick and started soaking up water, I grabbed at the closest tuft of grass. Thanks to the wet ground, it pulled out with little effort, so when I was done with that patch, I worked on another and another and another. In no time at all, my fingers were slick with mud, and all the grass that had encroached on the marker was torn away and piled nearby.

"Take a look," I told Levi, pointing. "His name, Charles Harlow, is nice and clear and easy to read. So are the dates of his birth and his death. But look at this." I ran a finger over the bottom eight inches of granite. With the sun shining on it, the granite glimmered, throwing Sleepy's name and vitals into relief and making it possible for me to see my own hazy reflection in the stone. But there at the bottom, the granite was rough and pitted. I ran my finger over the grooves that slashed the stone horizontally.

Levi crouched down next to me. "It looks like it was vandalized."

"But if that's the case, why not destroy the whole stone?" I set aside the red carnations, scraped my muddy hands against my jeans, and brushed my fingers against the smooth surface, tracing the name. "Why just part of the stone and not all of it?"

"The cops showed up? The person got interrupted? Or maybe there was some kind of storm damage." There was a gigantic oak tree twenty feet away, and its branches overhung the area. "A branch could have come down and smashed the stone."

"But this isn't smashed." I slid my finger from smooth surface to rough. "These lines were put here deliberately. Like someone . . ." I doubted it would help, but I crouched down even farther, one ear on the tombstone, eager to see it from a different angle and hoping for a better sense of what had happened. "It's like someone was trying to blot something out. Look." I sat up again and traced what I could see of a faint pattern with one finger. Just above the gouges, there was a rounded shape carved into the stone. And just below the rough grooves, a clean, straight line.

"This carving is delicate," I said, following what was left of what had been etched into the stone, first with one finger, then two. "These lines weren't made with force; not like the ones cut into the granite over them."

Levi tilted his head for a better look. "So you think there was something else on the stone? Something someone tried to blot out?"

"I don't suppose it would do any good to contact the monument company that made the headstone," I said, thinking out loud. "Nineteen thirty was a really long time ago. Even if they still had the records, I bet they're stashed away in some moldy warehouse and impossible to access."

"And you think it matters because . . . ?"

"I don't know," I admitted, and sat back on my heels. "But it's weird, and that makes it interesting." I pulled my phone from my pocket. "I wonder if a picture will help." I took a couple. "Or a rubbing."

Levi slid me a look. "You know how to do gravestone rubbings?"

Rather than admit I'd never even tried I said, "How hard can it be? All we need is a sheet of paper big enough to cover the part of the stone that's all chewed up and something to make the impression." Even though I knew there was nothing in my jacket pockets that would help, I patted them down. "Like a pencil lead."

"A pencil won't work. The lead wouldn't be fat enough." Levi jumped to his feet and headed to his car. He was back in a flash, a few sheets of paper in one hand and a box of crayons in the other. He popped open the lid on the crayon box, took out a black crayon and peeled back the paper.

"Halloween," he said, as if it were enough of an explanation. Then, because he knew it wasn't, he grinned. "I figure there will be a lot of families coming to the island for the big costume party on Friday. So I ordered a few dozen boxes of crayons. You know, so I can put them out on the tables in the restaurant along with paper to keep the kids busy while families are waiting for their orders. The morning ferry brought the stuff and I was just over at the dock picking it all up." He finished with the black crayon, stuffed the tiny shreds of its former paper wrapping in his pocket and held up the gleaming, naked crayon for me to see. "What do you think? Will it work?"

I laid the piece of blank paper over the vandalized portion of the headstone and held out my hand for the crayon. "Let's find out."

Holding the crayon on either end, I swiped it lengthwise over the paper. The paper moved. I cursed. Levi leaned over so he could hold either side of the paper and keep it in place.

Good idea.

At least it would have been if it didn't mean we were suddenly in very close proximity. I reached around him to try and rub the crayon across the paper again, and when that didn't work, I laid aside my pride and ducked under his arm. He was kneeling behind me now, one arm on either side of me. Rather than consider how if I moved just a fraction of an inch, our truce would turn out to be the shortest one in history, I got to work on the rubbing.

Done, I sat back.

Or at least I would have if Levi—solid and oh-so-tempting—weren't there.

He jumped to his feet.

I followed.

I don't think I imagined it; he was as breathless as I was. He covered better than I would have been able to, looking over my shoulder at the rubbing, a smear of black against the white paper. "I can still see the gashes in the stone." He pointed to those lines. "And the other parts you pointed out . . ." His finger traced the pattern. "It's just like you said. It looks like there was something else carved into the stone. Something somebody didn't want anyone else to see."

I stared at the fat, black pattern, at the delicate tracery at the bottom and that smooth, round curve at the top that reminded me of—

"It's an oil lamp."

"All right." The way he dragged out the words added to the skepticism that rang through his voice. "I can see the bottom of it and I guess it could be an—"

"An oil lamp." I clutched the rubbing in suddenly trembling fingers. "Just like at the winery."

This, of course, he didn't know, and with my words vibrating with an excitement I didn't quite understand, I gave Levi the *Reader's Digest* condensed version of the story.

When I was finished, he took the paper out of my hands and examined the picture again. "So every day when Kate goes to the winery, she sets an oil lamp on the windowsill."

"Just like her parents did, and their parents did, and their parents did," I explained.

"And you think—"

"I don't know what to think. Except that it's a mighty strange coincidence. Sleepy's ghost has been seen at the winery and—"

"And I thought we don't believe in ghosts."

"We don't. Only if we did, Sleepy's ghost has been seen at the winery. And the oil lamp is always put out at the winery. Do the math, Levi." I did, very quickly, and I came to the conclusion I knew he'd arrive at once he thought about it. "It was Kate's great-grandma Carrie who started the tradition with the oil lamp. The timing is right. I'd bet anything that she was working at Wilder's in the twenties and thirties. It's exactly Sleepy's time period."

"And it means?"

"I have no idea what it means! Maybe there was some sort of tradition in town about oil lamps back then. I'll check with the historical society. Or maybe . . ."

A thought floated through my head, and as foolish as it felt to put it into words, I figured I owed it to Levi. If he was game enough to go through these theories with me, I might as well speak my mind.

"Sleepy worked at Wilder's. He and Carrie Wilder must have known each other." Again, I studied the rubbing. "What if they more than knew each other? What if she put out that oil lamp to signal to Sleepy?"

Levi chuckled. "Maybe what you really should be writing is romance novels," he suggested.

My head shot up and I stared at him. If there weren't a lump that blocked my throat, I might have asked why he was suddenly so pale.

I swallowed the sand in my mouth. "Romance novels instead of—"

"Instead of the book you're doing about Sleepy on Marianne's behalf, of course." Levi's smile came and went. Or maybe I just thought it did because of the way the tree branches above our heads swayed with the next breeze that blew through, spilling sunlight over us, then disappeared, leaving behind a shower of leaves. "Sleepy was a gangster. You know, one of the bad guys. And Kate's great-grandmother . . . well, I'm new to the island, just like you. But even I know the Wilders would never pass the time of day with the likes of Sleepy."

He was right, and I admitted it.

But it didn't explain the carving. Or the fact that someone had tried to eradicate it.

I'd just given up on trying to figure it out and had turned to head back to my car when something in the grove of trees at the far end of the cemetery caught my eye.

I stopped and squinted for a better look. "Did you see that?" I asked Levi.

He looked where my finger was pointing. Looked again. Leaned forward.

"Something's moving over there," he agreed, and since we both knew it was probably something no more threatening than a squirrel, he really didn't need to take my arm and tug me to the side so he could step in front of me. "There!" It was his turn to point.

Since Levi's so much taller than me, I had to step around him to get a better look at the shadow that glided behind the trees.

Not a squirrel. It was too tall to be an animal. Too quiet to be a person. It stepped from sunlight to shadow and again into sunlight, too far into the brush to be clearly seen. It walked like a person, and if I watched it carefully . . .

I'd already moved forward for a better look when a gust of wind whipped through the cemetery. It snaked across my shoulders and whizzed over my head, and when it got to the place just beyond the perimeter of the cemetery where the grass was taller and the brush was thicker, it shivered over a sumac bush, bending its branches with their red leaves toward the ground.

That's when I got a better glimpse of the shadow.

It was man-high and for what couldn't have been more than a second or two I saw clearly that it had two arms, two legs.

And no head.

"Levi!" My fingers were already pressed into his arm before I even realized I'd reached for him. I dared to look away long enough to see that Levi was looking exactly where I was looking.

"I see it," he said, his voice breathless, as if he'd been punched in the stomach. "Come on!" He took off like a shot, taking me along with him.

We zigzagged around headstones and kicked through tall grass, and in less than a minute, we were standing at the spot where we'd seen the shadow.

There was nothing there.

"And no place for anyone to go," Levi said, glancing to his right, where there was a road that led to the state park. If there was someone out there, surely we would have seen him. To our left, another road led to the other side of the island, but there, too, there was no sign of life.

I'm afraid that when I asked, "What the hell just happened?" my voice shook just a little bit.

But then, when he answered, "I don't have the slightest idea," Levi's did, too.

"You don't think—"

He didn't let me finish. Keeping a firm hold on my hand, Levi tugged me back into the cemetery and over to the spot where we'd first seen the shadow: Sleepy Harlow's grave.

He tried to make it look as casual as can be, but I couldn't help noticing the way he looked back into the shady grove when he said, "I've got to get over to the restaurant and work on tonight's dinner menu. Don't forget your flowers."

I picked up the bouquet of carnations, then thought better of it. Don't ask me what gave me the idea, because honestly, I don't know. I only know that when we left Crown Hill Cemetery, the flowers were right where I thought they belonged.

On Charlie Harlow's grave.

❖ 16 ❖

Hank called that afternoon. "Can you get over here to the station, Bea? There's something I want you to see."

He didn't need to ask me twice.

Hank, see, is one cool, calm, collected dude. I mean, he has to be, in his line of work, right? Yet when he called, there was a tiny burr of excitement in his voice. Oh, he tried to hide it under that hard-as-rocks exterior that served him so well when he was keeping the peace on the island. But I was intrigued.

Not to mention grateful.

See, if there was something Hank needed to see me about, it probably had something to do with Noreen's murder.

And if I was thinking about Noreen's murder, I wouldn't have time to think about anything else.

Like what Levi and I saw out at Crown Hill Cemetery that morning.

I kept my mind on the case, and headed for the police station.

"Come on back to my office." The Put-in-Bay Police Department is housed in the basement of the town hall building, and Hank intercepted me as soon as I was down the steps and inside the door. He put a hand on my elbow to guide me, and once we were in his small, tidy office, he closed the door behind us.

"What's up?" I asked him.

He pointed me to a chair opposite his gray metal desk.

"I figured I owed you," he said. "I asked you to poke around to see what you could find out."

"Unfortunately, that hasn't been much."

Hank plunked his little spiral notebook on the desk, but he didn't open it. Apparently, the details of the case were firm in his mind. Just as apparently, he didn't like them. That would explain his frown. "I thought you should know that we checked into that coffin. You know, the one Noreen's body was in. As far as that goes, nobody remembers anything. Nobody saw anything. The coffin had been in the park for a couple days along with everything else they needed for the wake. No one remembers seeing anyone near it."

"Well, the body would have had to have been moved at night. But there was a lot of blood. If you checked—"

"Your ghost hunters' vehicles?" Hank grimaced. "We'd need a warrant, and we don't have enough evidence to get one. I did, however . . ." He sat back, and to tell the truth, Hank didn't do prevarication very well. There was a tinge of pink in his cheeks when he said, "I may have glanced in their trucks when I saw them parked around town."

"And . . . ?"

"And nothing. Nothing I could see, anyway. Whoever moved that body was smart enough to wrap it in plastic first. I guarantee that, just like I guarantee that plastic is long gone. Even had the guys check the landfill. In fact, the only even semi-interesting thing we've found . . ." There was a TV nearby on a stand and, without a word, Hank took a DVD off his desk and slipped it into the player at the front of the TV.

"Remember back at the winery the day you found the body? One of my officers came across a camera."

"One of the ghost getters' cameras?" I sat up like a shot.

"Don't get too excited." Hank sank down in the chair behind his desk. "It's one of theirs, all right, but if you're looking for a smoking gun—"

"I'm not." I wasn't any better a liar than Hank. Of course I was looking for a smoking gun. A smoking gun (or in this case, a battered plasmometer) in someone else's hand would exonerate Kate.

"The camera slid under some old boxes in that back room where you found the body and landed in a stagnant puddle of water. It looked like it would be pretty useless, but we sent it off to the state crime lab and they were able to get something off of it. I want you to take a look at it," Hank said, grabbing the remote. "See if it makes any sense to you."

I couldn't help myself. In spite of Hank's suggestion that I shouldn't get excited, a funny cha-cha rhythm started up inside my chest. With sweaty palms, I clutched the arms of the chair. Better that than letting Hank see that my hands were trembling.

It took only a few more seconds, but by the time he got the video going, I was about to burst.

There was nothing to see on the TV screen in front of me except blackness. I heard a crackle, and a zigzag of gray shot across the screen.

"What the hell do you mean you're not going to do it?"

The voice belonged to Noreen.

The picture bounced, and a second later, Noreen's face filled the screen, then was gone again.

"You can't—" Static crackled and blocked out Noreen's words. "—told me you would. How dare you—"

The screen went black and my spine accordioned and I plopped back in my chair. "Well, I can see why you said I shouldn't get too excited."

"Shhh!" Hank pointed to the TV.

A blob of gray lightened the screen, and a second later, it once again filled with a picture of Noreen's face. No doubt she'd set down her camera and was standing in front of it. The picture went out of, then back into, focus. As she had been the last time I'd seen her—both alive and dead— Noreen was dressed in her ghost-hunting gear: camouflage pants, heavy sweatshirt, fishing vest. The light was terrible and the colors of her clothing were washed out on the video, like an old-fashioned tintype that had been hand-colored. Against the rest of the anemic colors, her cheeks looked too pink.

"Are you finally ready?" Noreen asked.

Like Noreen, I waited for the answer. With my breath caught behind a ball of tension in my throat, I leaned forward in my chair, waiting to see who she was with and what would happen next at the same time I searched the picture for anything that might provide a clue.

"She's in that back room," I said, more to myself than to Hank. "The room where I found her body. You can see the basket-weave pattern of the brickwork behind her."

Hank, no doubt, had already noticed that. He caressed his chin with one hand.

Though Noreen was still the only person in the picture, it was clear someone had joined her. Her head snapped around. Like me, she'd heard the faint shuffle of feet.

"I'm going to switch the plasmometer on," Noreen said. "You better be ready to go as soon as I do. Walk in from back there." She looked over her shoulder into the deeper shadows at the far end of the storeroom. "I'll be scanning the room and I'm going to say that it feels suddenly colder. That's your cue. That's your cue to walk in and leave that old magazine. You know, to prove who you are."

"Cue?" I remembered everything Jacklyn had told me about how she merely acted her way through each investigation. Still, the enormity of what I saw playing out in front of me on the screen felt like a fist to the solar plexus. I sucked in a breath. "Is Noreen saying what I think she's saying?"

"Shh," was Hank's answer.

I gulped back my excitement and propped my elbows on Hank's desk, the better not to miss the flicker of even one shadow on the screen.

"All right. All set." Whoever Noreen was waiting for, now was the time. "I'm switching on the plasmometer, so you'd better step lively. We both know this piece of junk isn't going to stay on for long."

When she leaned over to flip the switch on the plasmometer, Noreen disappeared from the picture. A second later, the screen filled with a flash of chartreuse light and Noreen was back. This close to the plasmometer, her face looked like a caricature of itself, her eye sockets too deep and black, her mouth too much of a slash, her doughy cheeks the texture and color of moldy white bread.

"I'm ready," she said, glancing over her shoulder toward that dark corner where she'd told her coconspirator to make an appearance. "Are you listening? I said, I'm ready." She cleared her throat. "I'm here in one of the old storage rooms at the winery," she said, "and I've been trying to catch EVPs for the last ten minutes. I've played back what I recorded and so far, no luck. But it's suddenly gotten a lot colder in here."

Noreen waited.

Nothing happened.

"It's suddenly gotten a lot colder in here," she said, louder this time.

And still, nothing happened.

Noreen grumbled a word that would definitely have been bleeped if the show ever made it to the air. "Where the hell are you? Come on, do what you're supposed to do and let's get this over with before the cops come back. Do what you're being paid to do and quit acting like a prima donna. I told you I'd make it up to you. I told you I'd—"

A shuffling noise brought Noreen spinning around just as the screen filled with the blinding green light of the plasmometer. The light swirled and arced. Right before the plasmometer knocked into the camera and sent it careening under the shelves and into the puddle of water where Hank said they'd found it, I caught a last glimpse of Noreen's face.

Her eyes were open wide. Her mouth was a gaping hole of terror.

She knew as well as Hank and I did that the plasmometer was about to come down on her head and that in just another second, she'd be dead.

I didn't ask for anything to drink, but Hank was enough of a professional to recognize the first telltale signs of shock when he saw them. I guess my shallow breaths and clammy skin qualified. The next thing I knew, there was an open can of Pepsi on the desk in front of me, and it wasn't the diet version I drank when I drank soda (which was hardly ever because I didn't especially like the way it tasted or the way the bubbles made me feel as if my stomach had been pumped with a tire inflator). This was the high-test stuff, and I knew the sugar and caffeine would pack the punch I needed. I lifted the can with both hands and drank deep.

The bubbles tickled my throat and, yes, my stomach felt as if it had been pumped with a tire inflator. On the upside, the sugar raced through my system like a shot of adrenaline. I may not have been completely coherent by the time I set the empty can back on the desk, but I was getting there.

"Did we just see what I think we just saw?" I asked Hank. Three cheers for me, my voice didn't tremble. Well, at least not too much.

"A murder? I'm afraid we did."

"The murderer couldn't have known Noreen was already filming. If he did, there's no way he would have left the camera there."

"Or he did know it was there and he couldn't find the camera once it was knocked off whatever Ms. Turner had it propped on. I told you, we found it in a puddle of slimy water beneath some very old shelves."

"Or maybe that's when Kate got back to the winery. The killer might have heard her come in and then he panicked. He left without the camera because he couldn't take the chance of sticking around, not once he knew there was someone else on the premises. Either one of those scenarios makes sense. What doesn't . . ."

Like it or not, my gaze drifted back to the TV screen.

Hank had paused the DVD and I found myself staring into Noreen's terrified face. I swallowed hard.

"In that very first bit we saw, it sounded like she was trying to talk someone into something," I said.

"I agree with you there."

"And it sounded like that someone didn't want to be talked into it."

"Agreed. Again."

"But in that second bit . . ." Just thinking about what we'd just seen unfold in front of our very eyes made my insides shimmy. "It's—"

"Yeah." Hank sat back in his chair. I was grateful he'd cut me off. I could think of plenty of words to describe Noreen's murder—brutal, savage, and incredibly disturbing came right to mind—but none of those words was sufficient to describe what we'd just seen, or the emotions that overloaded my senses. Disgust. Outrage. Clinical interest. I'm not sure which disturbed me the most. Maybe it didn't matter.

A flash of memory swam up through the riot of emotions. "Noreen said the plasmometer was junk."

"Yeah, I caught that." Hank had brought over a can of soda for himself, and he popped the top and poured the soda into a paper cup. "You need more?" he asked, and when I shook my head, he finished pouring and sipped. "So you tell me, do your guests think that plasmo-whatever is junk? The way they've been pestering me to get that hunk of metal back, you'd think it was God's gift to mankind."

"Not God's. Noreen's." When Hank gave me a blank look, I explained. "It's called the Turner Plasmometer because Noreen designed it. Every single one of the ghost getters I've talked to has told me that it's the greatest thing since sliced bread, that it puts them one step ahead of every other ghost-hunting team out there, and that they can't live without it. Well . . ." I thought about what I'd said. "Maybe not Jacklyn."

"What did Jacklyn tell you?"

"That she doesn't believe any of this ghost hooey. Except for the video of Sleepy. That, she says, is as real as real can get." In my head, I went over the scene we'd just watched. All told, it couldn't have lasted more than a minute, so it wasn't hard to recall it frame by frame.

"Whoever was there with Noreen, there's no sign of him on the video," I said. Of course, Hank already knew this, so there was no use waiting for him to respond. "I'd bet anything that whoever it was, he was dressed like Sleepy. Noreen was going to get more footage of Sleepy! Isn't that what it sounded like to you? She said she was going to say something about feeling cold, then the person was supposed to walk in. That's the only thing it could mean. Makes me wonder about that video she shot last year. It must have been phony, too."

"Could that be something our murderer didn't want anyone to find out about? That the ghost they claim they caught was nothing but a fake?"

I couldn't help myself—for a second, I pictured Chandra roaming the island, ready to defend Sleepy's ghostly reputation in any way she could. I didn't dare mention the fantasy to Hank; he already had one of my friends under suspicion, and I didn't want his brain latching on to any of the others.

"The ghost isn't the only thing that's a fake," I told Hank. "If just about everybody in EGG thought that plasmometer was the be-all and end-all of ghost hunting, that means that Noreen was a fake, too. She lied to them about everything. The power of the plasmometer, and that video they shot last year, the one that made EGG famous. If one of them found out she faked it all . . . Well, I'll tell you what, Hank, except for Jacklyn, these paranormal investigators take their jobs very seriously. If they found out Noreen wasn't a believer and that she'd lied to them all, it just might be a motive for murder."

Hank let go a long, low whistle at the same time that I mumbled, "Hell hath no fury like a ghost getter scorned."

The EGG-head I really wanted to talk to was Liam, the group's equipment tech, who should have been able to tell me more about the Turner Plasmometer. But when I got home from the police station, he was nowhere around. In fact, the house was empty except for Ben.

Or was it Eddie?

The cameraman—whichever cameraman it was—was sitting out on the front porch steps.

"Not filming today?" I asked.

He'd just finished a cigarette, and one look from me and he knew better than to flick the butt into my flower beds. He stubbed it out and set it on the toe of his sneaker. "Dimitri said we needed another break. Everybody pretty much scattered. I heard a few of them were going to head downtown to party."

"You're not a partier?"

"Thought I'd catch up on my reading."

With his long, stringy, dark hair and a beard that looked as if it could use a good mowing, he didn't exactly strike me as the reading type. But then, I am often surprised by readers and the books they enjoy.

"Anything interesting?" I asked him.

His hand shot to the thick book on the steps next to him.

"Technical stuff. Once this show is up and going and I have a few bucks in my pocket, I'm hoping to finish my MFA in film at UCLA."

Like I said, people are full of surprises.

But then, there are people who say I am, too.

I plunked down on the step next to . . . er . . . Ben.

"So you're a guy with a great imagination. You must be, or you wouldn't be getting your graduate degree in film. So what do you think of it all?"

"You mean Noreen's murder?" He lit another cigarette but, thank goodness, he had the good sense to exhale in the other direction. "If the cops ever figure out what happened, I'm gonna turn it into a screenplay."

I hoped I looked impressed. "Not just that. What about the whole paranormal investigation show? Jacklyn told me she fakes her way through it."

"Jacklyn." When he snorted, a stream of smoke shot out his nose. "Not my favorite subject."

"I thought Noreen was the one nobody liked."

"True." He tapped ash into the flowers, and I found myself hoping that cigarette ash contained magical properties that could keep cats away. "It's not everybody who doesn't like talking about Jacklyn. That would be just me."

A brief picture flashed through my mind: gorgeous, musky Jacklyn and this scarecrow of a camera guy. "You and Jacklyn . . . ?"

"Yup." He tipped back his head and it didn't take an ounce of imagination to know he was picturing what I'd just been picturing. Only in Technicolor and with surround sound. "She's something, huh? Way better in bed than Noreen ever was."

I nearly choked. "You're telling me that you and Noreen . . . ?"

"Come off it! Just because you live on an island in the middle of nowhere doesn't mean you're some prude. Not a cute chick like you!" He gave me a smile. "Yeah, Noreen and I, we'd hook up once in a while."

"But it didn't last. Who broke it off?"

He shrugged. "Her? Me? I honestly can't say. I can say that Noreen was demanding. She wanted to be the boss. And it's one thing, you know, when you're in front of the camera or you're leading a ghost hunt. Then somebody's got to be in charge. I get that. But in real life, it's not supposed to operate like that. There's supposed to be give and take."

"And Noreen wanted to take but not give."

"You got that right." Done with that cigarette, he added the butt to the one on his shoe top.

"But Jacklyn was different?"

"More girly, you know?" There was that look again. Dreamy, drunken, besotted. It might not have been true love, but I had no doubt there was a whole lot of true lust going on.

"That's why Noreen didn't like her."

"Noreen didn't like anyone."

I thought about the snippet of video I'd seen back at the police station and what Noreen had said to the person off camera about how that person shouldn't be angry anymore. "Was there anyone Noreen didn't like more than anyone else lately?" I asked him. "Someone she'd been fighting with?"

Eddie . . . er . . . Ben barked out a laugh. "Who wasn't she fighting with? Every minute of every day, Noreen found someone, somewhere to get into it with. She didn't like the way we stood when we shot video. She didn't agree with the sound tech when she listened to his recordings.

She didn't like the way Dimitri did the intro on one of our spots or the research Rick and David found out about a site we were investigating. I'll tell you what, I've never met a person anywhere who was as miserable as Noreen. And she let the world know it."

"Who was the latest person?"

He shot me a look. "You mean before she died? If you ask me, it's a toss-up. Dimitri was steaming mad at her."

"Because of the magazine article she published that used all his research."

"You know about that?" I can't say for sure, but I think he was impressed. "Then you know David went looking for him Wednesday night and Dimitri wasn't around."

"David mentioned it."

"And you know about Thursday morning, too, right?" He rubbed a finger under his nose. "Maybe you don't know. You weren't around Thursday morning."

"I left breakfast for all of you."

"Yeah, well, obviously Noreen didn't make it to the table."

"Obviously."

"But you know, Dimitri didn't, either."

This was news, and I guess the sudden gleam in my eye told Ben . . . er . . . never mind! I guess the gleam in my eye told the cameraman as much. "I bet David didn't mention it because the way I remember it, he came down late," he said. "He couldn't say who was there before him and who wasn't. But I was the first one down, see. I'm usually an early riser. I never saw hide nor hair of Dimitri that morning."

"He wasn't in his room Wednesday night, and he wasn't back Thursday morning." I thought back to when I'd run into him at the park. He'd been walking back from the ferry dock with Jacklyn and I'd just assumed he'd gone to meet her. But what if—

"Do you know where he went?" I asked the cameraman.

"Not a clue. I do know he was plenty mad at Noreen on account of that magazine article. What do they call that on the cop shows on TV? Motive? Dimitri, he had plenty of motive."

And opportunity, it sounded like.

But then, maybe he wasn't the only one. "And Jacklyn— she didn't like Noreen, either."

"Believe me, the feeling was mutual," the cameraman said. No big news there. "Jacklyn and Noreen were like oil and water. All crazy, all the time."

"That's why Noreen tossed Jacklyn out of EGG."

"And that's why Noreen started spreading dirt about her and Dimitri."

"Noreen and Dimitri?" Even my imagination wasn't good enough to picture that.

Apparently, the cameraman knew it, because a grin split his beard. "It wasn't true," he said. "Not a word of it. But Noreen, she knew she could get Jacklyn's goat. Even after Jacklyn was gone, I heard Noreen would text her with Dimitri this and Dimitri that. You know, like the two of them were an item. I know Jacklyn called once or twice and the two of them went at it over the phone, and I hear they had some pretty epic text fights. Between that and the screaming that went on when Noreen gave Jacklyn the boot . . . Lordy, those girls were at each other twenty-four-seven."

"And still, Jacklyn says she came here to thank Noreen for giving her the opportunity to take the soap opera job."

He gave me a sharp look. "You think? The way I heard it, that job out in Hollywood wasn't all it was cracked up to be, and she showed up here to beg for her old job back.

And it worked, didn't it? Jacklyn got her old job back, all right."

"But only because Noreen is dead."

"Dead and gone." Ben . . . er . . . Eddie plucked the cigarette butts into one hand and stood and turned toward the house, and in an effort (a subtle one, I hope) to block his path, I got up, too, and climbed one step.

"So Noreen and Jacklyn hated each other." I stated the obvious. "But there's no way Jacklyn could have killed her. She wasn't on the island until after Noreen was dead."

"Well, it all depends who you hear the story from."

Electricity zinged through me. "Are you telling me Jacklyn was here on Wednesday?"

"I can't say. Not for sure. I can tell you that when we were coming back from the winery, we were driving through town, and there's this bar with the big windows that look out over the park."

I knew which bar he was talking about.

"And there was a woman sitting there, and a guy across the table from her. And this flare went up in my brain. That's the way it happens when I'm thinking about story and camera angles and things like that. In that one instant the whole scene flashed in front of my eyes and . . . Well, you won't get it. People who aren't involved with film never do."

"Try me," I suggested.

He drew in a breath. "The first thing I thought of was that the scene had great atmosphere. A couple talking in a bar. Soft light spilling from overhead. The trees outside and the way the wind blew them around and the way their reflection in the window swayed and made the whole thing look as if had been filmed underwater. And it happened in just a heartbeat. You know, the way these things sometimes do. I remember thinking how perfect it all was, because say what you will about her, but Jacklyn is a gorgeous woman, and I remember thinking it was perfect because she was in the scene." He shook himself as he must have done that night.

"And then we were already past the bar and I couldn't get another look and I told myself I was imagining things. The lady in the bar, maybe she just looked like Jacklyn."

"Maybe," I conceded. "But it could have been her."

The cameraman laughed. "Now you sound like you just stepped out of the script of one of those cop shows. Yeah, if I was under oath, I'd have to admit that it could have been her. But she says she wasn't on the island when Noreen was killed, and if that's what Jacklyn says . . ."

"Not a liar, huh?"

He slid me a look. "I didn't say that. Let's just say that I don't think she'd lie unless she had a real good reason to lie."

"A really good reason like murder?"

"Hey, I never said that, either. I only know that Noreen being dead and Jacklyn sleeping with Dimitri, it's all worked in her favor. It's getting her second billing on the show and plenty of time in front of the camera. But then, that's the thing about Jacklyn, see? Jacklyn gets what Jacklyn wants, and that girl, she wants to be a star."

◈ 17 ◈

It wasn't hard to find a photograph of Jacklyn online. Whoever was in charge of the EGG website was on the ball and had already added her to the team. Aside from announcing the first episode of *Ghost Getters*, the site featured pictures and bios of each team member.

Well, except for Fiona.

I printed out the picture and raced off to town, and just a little while after I left the B and B, I was standing in the bar that the cameraman had told me about.

"That's her, all right." The bartender was a crusty middle-aged guy named Barry whom I'd met at various and sundry Chamber of Commerce functions. He had a head like a bullet and a crop of silver hair. "Hard to forget a girl that pretty. She sat right over there." He poked his chin toward the windows that looked out over the park. "She was with some guy who wore sunglasses the whole time. Imagine that! The middle of the night, and the guy was wearing sunglasses. You'd think he was some kind of movie star or something. Had on one of those hats, too. You know, the kind with the brim all the way around. Like Indiana Jones."

"You didn't happen to catch his name?"

I knew it was too much to ask, so honestly, I shouldn't have been disappointed when Barry grunted. "I did hear him say something about the airport, though. Looks like he didn't come over on one of the ferries. Flew in, and said he was flying out, too, as soon as him and that good-looking babe . . ." He slid another look at Jacklyn's photo. "Said he was flying out as soon as they were done doing their business. And it's not like I was eavesdropping or anything. I just happened to be cleaning up the table next to where they were sitting, and I heard what he said, see, and that's when I told him there aren't any lights at our airport. No planes in or out at night."

"What did he think of that?"

Barry grabbed a toothpick from the bar and stuck it between his teeth. "Didn't seem to much care. Said he'd find someone to take him back to the mainland on a boat if that's what it took."

"Did he?"

"I sent him over to Pat Bakersfield. You know the guy."

I did.

"Pat isn't fussy when it comes to how he can make a few extra bucks. I knew he'd take the guy back to the mainland if that's what he wanted. And if he paid enough."

It's a no-brainer where I went next.

I found Pat Bakersfield touching up the blue stripes painted on the side of his boat at the private marina near the yacht club.

"I made quite a killing that night!" The sun brushed the western horizon, and when Pat grinned, the light gleamed against his teeth. "Got a call from Barry about the one guy who wanted to get to the mainland, and then I got another fare, too. What are the chances? Two guys who need to go to the mainland fast at the end of October! All told, I made a fast five hundred bucks. Charged each of them one-fifty, and the older guy, the guy with the hat, he gave me a two-hundred-dollar tip when we got to Sandusky." He leaned in and elbowed me in the ribs. "Five hundred. Cash. Tax-free."

"The guy Barry sent over, did he say what his name was?"

"I didn't ask." Pat dabbed his paintbrush to the stripe that outlined the railing of his sleek yellow and blue cigarette racing boat. "I mean, when a guy's wearing sunglasses in the middle of the night, seems to me the whole point is that he doesn't want people to know who he is."

"And the other guy?"

"Him? Oh, I seen him around. He was at the bar the other night. And that night it rained, he and a bunch of other dumbbells were walking around outside the hotel, like they were looking for something."

Something like ghosts?

I couldn't afford to make a mistake, so I tried not to lead Pat on in any way. "Describe him," I said.

"Good-looking guy. Dark. Young. But there must have been something wrong with him. I thought before we got to Sandusky, he was going to cough up a lung."

Two days before Halloween, and the day dawned in appropriate fashion. The blue skies over the island were polkadotted with fat gray clouds, and a chill breeze held the promise of colder days to come. Leaves danced through the air in a rainbow swirl, and when they landed, they raced each other down the road and piled in crispy mounds against rocks and tree trunks and my front steps.

In between making about a dozen phone calls, I'd been busy the night before putting what I hoped were the last touches on Marianne's manuscript. I should have been tired, but truth be told, I felt energized and, for the first time in nearly a week, encouraged.

I had two viable suspects in Noreen's murder. Neither of whom was Kate. And even more importantly, I knew how I was going to figure out which of them—Dimitri or Jacklyn— was the murderer.

The first expert who would help me put my plan into action was a young, savvy guy named Aaron, who arrived long before breakfast. I explained to him what I wanted to do, and Aaron, who came highly recommended, told me exactly what it was all going to cost. To my credit, I hyper- ventilated for only a couple minutes. When I finished catching my breath, we struck a deal that included me pay- ing all the expenses for him and his team, including lodg- ing and meals for the weekend. Aaron made the calls and arranged for technicians to come and go throughout the day, their presence (I hoped) explained away as merely vis- its from electricians and plumbers, a painter, and a guy who was there to check the foundation on the garage. By the time the ghost getters got to the breakfast table, Aaron was in my private suite taking care of the details, and I was ready with a platter of still-warm sweet rolls.

I set the rolls on the table, where I'd already put out a couple of carafes of coffee, as well as yogurt and fruit, and watched as, one by one, the members of EGG were capti- vated by the enticing aroma of cinnamon. Their eyes opened a little wider. They sat up a little straighter. David was the first one to reach for the rolls. He took two and passed the serving dish to Liam, who took three. I called into the kitchen to Meg to put another batch of rolls into the oven and made my move.

"Dimitri, I was wondering if I could talk to you."

He had just taken a bite of his cinnamon roll and he had gooey cream cheese and powdered sugar icing on his lips. "Go ahead," he said.

Was I a good enough actress to pull this off? I hesitated for what I hoped was an appropriate amount of time. "I feel a little silly," I admitted. For a woman who is a lot of things, but never silly, this was something of an effort. "I've never made a secret of the fact that I don't believe in ghosts or anything, but something happened here last night, and . . ."

Dimitri might still be working on his first cup of coffee, but I guess ghost hunters have an instinct about these sorts of things. He sat up like a shot, his dark eyes aglow. "Are you saying—?"

"I don't know what I'm saying, only that I saw something last night, and I can't explain it. Not rationally, anyway."

By now, I had everyone's attention. But then, that's pretty easy to do when you've got ghost getters gathered at your dining room table and you're suddenly talking about things that go bump in the night.

There was an empty seat between David and Liam, and I dropped into it, the better to look around the table and make sure I had all of EGG's attention. "I thought I heard something during the night, you see, like footsteps. And I figured it was one of you, and I got up to see what you needed, and . . ." Was the shiver too much? Apparently not, because, done shivering, I saw that all their gazes were glued to me. "There was something . . . someone . . . in the parlor. Not a person. Not a real person. I just saw a sort of . . ." This time, I tried a shrug. "It was a misty sort of—"

"An apparition!" Rick's eyes lit. David's hands grasped the table. Dimitri looked very much like one of those marble statues I'd thought of when I'd first seen him. Frozen in time.

Fiona's cheeks were bright with color, and I swear, both Ben and Eddie would have gotten up right then and there and gone for their cameras if they weren't afraid they'd miss something I had to say.

Jacklyn? Don't think I didn't notice that she simply sat back and gave me a squint-eyed look that made me think she was wondering what I was up to.

I ignored her.

"It walked out of the parlor and up the stairs and"—I wrapped my arms around myself—"when I went to follow it, it just . . . well, if I told anyone else this, I know they'd think I was crazy, but you all . . . you all believe me, don't you? When I went to follow it, it just disappeared. I don't believe in ghosts. At least I never have. And now I'm wondering . . . I mean, this is an old house, and after everything you've all said about limestone and flowing water and trapped energy . . . what I was wondering is that if you're not busy tonight and you're looking for a place to do an investigation . . ."

I didn't need to finish the sentence. Before I went to get the next batch of cinnamon rolls, they were already talking about where they'd set up cameras and tape recorders for the ghost hunt at Bea & Bees, and everything was moving forward.

Just the way I wanted it to.

I couldn't invite Chandra to join me because she would have been so darned excited about the very idea of ghosts at the B and B that she wouldn't sit still. Or keep quiet. Or believe me when I explained that everything that was about to happen was carefully choreographed, completely staged, and totally phony. Chandra, see, is a true believer, and besides, from what I'd been told, she was planning on spending the evening on her last-minute Halloween preparations. In Chandra's world, there are never too many jack-o'-lanterns, pumpkin-shaped cookies, or treat bags filled to the brim that she—resplendent in her witch garb—would hand out at the big party in the park in two nights.

Luella, too, was not available. According to the weather forecast, these were the last fine days of fall weather, and Luella had been out on the lake all day, fishing for walleye in the deepest waters near the Canadian border. I couldn't possibly ask her to sacrifice sleep in the name of my spooky scheme.

That left Kate, and since she was the one I most wanted with me that evening, it made as much sense inviting her as it did having Hank join us.

By seven o'clock, when I promised EGG that I would be gone and they'd have the B and B completely to themselves until the wee hours of the morning, the three of us had snuck into my garage via the back door. We joined Aaron and a phalanx of technicians and the equipment they'd tucked away in there during the day when I made sure the ghost getters were so busy planning their attack on my supposedly haunted digs that they couldn't pay any attention to what was going on outside.

Hank hovered behind Aaron, who was monitoring a bank of screens where feeds showed us each room of my house. "Are you sure this is going to work?" he asked. "Aren't they going to know we're watching?"

"No way!" Aaron shook his head. "We've got cameras in clocks, cameras in air vents, cameras in light fixtures. From what I saw when I was in there with Bea and pretending to be a painter"—he had loved playing along with the little game, and he gave me a smile—"those paranormal investigators might think they're hot stuff, but they don't have a clue or the cash to work with equipment nearly as sophisticated as what I have. It's surveillance equipment, just like the stuff the feds use. No way they're ever going to notice equipment that small."

"You arranged all this? For me?" Kate glanced from the video screens to another table where another technician wearing headphones was listening to—and recording—every word spoken by my resident ghost getters. "It must have cost a fortune."

She was right, but I waved away her concern. If I couldn't use my money to help my friends, what was it for?

Another technician, this one a soft-spoken Brit named Terry, hurried by. "We're set," he told me. "As soon as you say the word."

I stepped closer to the screens and watched as, inside, Dimitri gave his crew last-minute instructions.

"I don't think we want anything to happen too soon," I told my own crew. "That will look too fake."

"Like it isn't fake?" Kate rolled her eyes.

"Like we can't let them catch on," I told her.

And we didn't.

For the next few hours, snug in the garage, where earlier in the day one group of workers had covered the windows with dark paper and others had set up the equipment and a refreshment station for coffee and snacks, we watched EGG go through the motions.

Or at least we tried.

There were only so many times I could hear so many EGG-head duos ask the same questions—"What is your name?" "Why are you still here?" "What are you looking for?"—to the empty air in the silent house before I thought I'd lose my mind. I left the experts I'd paid so well to do their thing and motioned Hank and Kate over to a table and chairs in the far corner of the garage.

"I hope you're planning on doing something soon." Hank rubbed the back of his neck with one hand. "Watching ghost hunting is a lot like watching paint dry."

"You got that right!" I pushed a dish of mixed nuts in front of him, and he happily crunched away. "I'm thinking another ten minutes," I told Kate. "Are you ready?"

I'd warned her to dress for the chilly weather, and she tugged her gray scarf a little tighter around the collar of her black parka. "I don't know. What if it doesn't work? What if . . ." She dared a look at Hank, who was so busy picking out the peanuts so he could concentrate on finding the almonds and the cashews that he didn't pay any attention. "What if we're no closer to any answers by the end of the night than we are now?"

"Then we're no worse off."

"Hey, Bea!" Aaron waved me over. "That guy, Dimitri . . ." He pointed to one of the TV screens. "He's finally in your parlor and he's all alone. Want to start?"

I told him I did.

Kate, Hank, and I gathered behind Aaron and held our collective breaths, and Aaron signaled to the sound technician, and don't ask me exactly what they did or exactly how they did it, but these guys made magic happen.

Just as Dimitri finished asking, "Is anyone here with me?" a sound like a whisper on the wind drifted through my parlor.

"Sandusky," the soft voice said.

Dimitri's head came up. His shoulders shot back. He had a digital tape recorder in one hand, and he stuck it out a little farther into the darkness. "What did you say? Say it again so I know you're here. Can you repeat what you just said?"

This time, the voice was a little louder, a little clearer. Just as the sound tech and I had agreed it would be.

"Sandusky."

"Sandusky?" Something told me Dimitri was expecting a message with a little more unearthly oomph. "Is that what you said? Did you say 'Sandusky'?"

"Sandusky."

Dimitri spoke into the tape recorder. "Just so we double-check this when we listen to the evidence, guys, I'm in the parlor and I'm getting a disembodied voice. I clearly heard it say 'Sandusky,' and Sandusky is a city over on the mainland. Did you live in Sandusky?" he said, this time to the blackness around him.

"You went to Sandusky."

I swear, even on the TV screen, I saw every ounce of blood drain from Dimitri's face when he froze right there next to my fireplace.

I figured that would be the reaction we'd get. Just like I figured that Dimitri might be shocked enough to call in one of the other investigators. Or walk out of the room.

Before that could happen, I signaled that it was time for the *pièce de résistance,* and once again, the technicians did their hocus-pocus.

There on the screen and right before Dimitri's eyes, a ghostly light shimmered in the darkness.

"Look at that!" Even Hank, who'd been briefed about what was going to happen and what we hoped to accomplish, couldn't contain his excitement. He darted closer to the screen and pointed. "What the heck? What the heck is going on? Bea, you're not telling me—"

"It's all smoke and mirrors, Hank," I reminded him, because honestly, he looked so amazed, I thought the poor guy was going to keel over. "It's done with cameras and computers. Like the special effects in a movie or in a stage performance. Just watch, Hank. If I know Dimitri, he's not going to pass up an opportunity like this to communicate with the Other Side."

Kate grabbed my arm and squeezed so tight I was pretty sure she was going to cut off my blood supply. "And he's going to admit that he killed Noreen?"

"That's what we're hoping for," I told her. "We know he left the house after they all got back from the winery. We know he wasn't in his room that night. We know he went to the mainland. Hank and I . . ." I looked his way. "We wondered if maybe Dimitri was trying to establish some kind of crazy alibi."

"Or to ditch evidence," Hank added. "Like the plastic we figure he moved the body in."

The hazy image on the screen came into sharper focus, and I have to admit, even though I knew it was as phony baloney as it gets, my heart beat a little faster. I couldn't help myself—I thought of poor Ichabod Crane and mean ol' Brom Bones. If he'd had today's technology, Brom wouldn't have had to dress up like the Headless Horseman to scare the bejeebers out of Ichabod.

I could only imagine how Dimitri felt seeing the holographic image take shape right before his very eyes. Especially when it raised a not-quite-solid arm and pointed right at him.

"Sandusky."

Even though I'd come up with the plan and the script the technicians were using in our little ruse, the single, whispered word shot chills up my back.

Dimitri nodded. "I . . . I was there. Last week. But why—"

"Noreen's dead!" I had asked the technicians to arrange a ghostly voice that sounded convincing, but I had never expected one that could crawl through my bloodstream and leave ice in its wake. When Kate clung to my arm even tighter, I was actually grateful. "Noreen's dead and you"—there was the pointed hand again, and the image wavered—"you were not here."

Dimitri gulped so hard, I saw his Adam's apple bob. The light was poor, but I swear, tears glistened on his cheeks.

For a second, I actually felt guilty about manipulating his emotions like this.

Until I reminded myself that we were out to catch a killer.

"I . . . I had to leave," Dimitri stammered. "I couldn't stay."

"Because of . . . Noreen. Noreen's murder." The last word trailed away like the final keen of a banshee's call.

"No." Dimitri stepped forward, and since we couldn't let him get too close to the apparition, the technicians made the ghost fade away.

For a second, Dimitri stared at the empty air in front of him in stunned silence.

Then the ghost appeared again, this time over near the ceiling in the far corner of the room.

Just like we did, Dimitri watched in amazement as streams of light twirled and coalesced into a person-shaped mass. "You ran away," the eerie voice crooned. "You killed her and ran away."

Dimitri shook his head. "Did Noreen tell you that? It's true."

My heart skipped a beat.

"It's true I wasn't here at the house," Dimitri continued, and that heartbeat of mine settled right back down. "But not because of her. Not because of Noreen. It was because of my allergy. A mold allergy. I had an attack at the winery, and it was a bad one. I had to go to the mainland to an ER to get treatment." He brushed his hands over his cheeks. "Don't you see?" he asked what he thought was a genuine entity. "I can't tell anyone. If the rest of the crew finds out . . . if the viewing public hears that I have a mold allergy. Ghosts . . . I mean you . . . I mean some of you . . . some of you hang out in some pretty nasty places. If anybody finds out I have a mold allergy, I'll be the laughingstock of the paranormal community."

"Sounds like he has an alibi."

Hank didn't need to tell me. It wasn't what I wanted to hear, and I kicked the leg of the closest chair and Aaron turned off the ghost. Together, we watched the image fade, along with the excited expression on Dimitri's face.

"It didn't work." Kate was crying, too. For all different reasons than Dimitri had been. She buried her face in my shoulder. "I thought this was going to clear me, and it didn't work."

"We've still got Jacklyn," I reminded her, and made her stand up so she could watch the screens. "Look. She and Rick are in suite one upstairs."

We watched them do a quick turn around the room. While Rick took what he called "base readings" to search for spikes in the room's electromagnetic energy, Jacklyn perched on the side of the bed.

"How long did Dimitri say we had to do this?" she asked.

Rick checked his meter. "I dunno. A couple more hours. I'm not getting anything in here."

"You could be," Jacklyn cooed and patted the bed beside her.

"Oh my gosh!" Kate and I screeched at the same time. "She's not—?"

She was. Rick joined her on the bed, and Jacklyn giggled. It was a deep, throaty sound.

"Hey, keep it down," Rick said. "We don't want Dimitri to hear."

"Dimitri doesn't have a clue." She wrapped her arms around his neck. "It will be just like the other night after that producer left, the one who wants me to be in that movie of his. You and me, Rickie, all night long."

They kissed, and I swear, I couldn't signal to Aaron fast enough. "Turn off that camera!"

He did, and we all let out a collective breath of relief.

"So . . ." Hank hooked his thumbs in his belt. "Somebody want to tell me we didn't just learn what I think we all just learned?"

He wasn't talking about Jacklyn and Rick.

And I knew I was the somebody who was responsible for this whole thing, so I was the somebody with my heart in my throat and my hopes dashed who had no choice but to say, "What we just learned is that both Dimitri and Jacklyn have alibis for the time Noreen was killed. Neither one of them is our murderer."

❄ 18 ❄

So Dimitri didn't meet Jacklyn at the ferry the day we found Noreen's body. Jacklyn met Dimitri at the ferry.

I knew this for a fact, because as unethical, underhanded, and so against the unwritten innkeeper rules as it was, I went through both Dimitri's and Jacklyn's rooms the next morning when they were down at breakfast. I found the paperwork from Dimitri's ER visit in Sandusky. It said he'd checked out of there at ten in the morning. I also found Jacklyn's ferry receipt that showed she was, indeed, on the island the night of the murder. I would have done the happy dance if her time weren't accounted for, first at Barry's Bar, then at the hotel downtown. I found a receipt for that, too. No, it didn't specifically say she'd been there with Rick, but it gave a room number and said there were two occupants. After what I'd seen (and nearly seen—yikes!) on-screen the night before, I had no doubt who she'd been with or what they'd been up to.

I will admit, this was the most miserable day-before-Halloween morning ever.

My plan was a major bust.

One of my best friends was still a murder suspect.

Thanks to the hours and hours I'd spent filling in the blanks of Marianne's manuscript, I now had only a couple small things to check. But even that didn't cheer me, I told myself, tapping the pages into a neat pile—I suspected Marianne would see through my attempted smoke screen the moment she read it.

I was doomed.

Kate was doomed.

I had failed.

I went through the motions, stacking Marianne's manuscript atop the big mailing envelope she'd originally brought it over in and getting the house settled for the day. It was almost noon when the phone rang.

"Bea." Kate's voice vibrated with something more than excitement, and in response, a shiver crawled up my spine and snaked over my shoulders. "You need to get over here to the winery. I think . . ." I wasn't sure if the gurgle I heard was one of terror, delight, or heartbreak. "I think I've caught the murderer."

I confess, she caught me flat-footed.

I stammered something about how she should call Hank instead of me, but Kate would have none of it.

"You've got to get here, Bea. Now."

When Kate has that kind of mettle in her voice, it's impossible to argue.

I got in my car and got over to the winery as quickly as I could.

Kate met me at the front door. "I was in my office," she said, without even bothering to say hello, "and I just happened to glance up at the security camera monitors. Bea, I can't even . . ." She gulped, and her eyes filled with tears. "What are we going to do?" she asked.

"Well, the first thing you're going to do is explain."

She shook her head and grabbed my arm. "You're going to have to see it for yourself to believe it. Hank told me about that camera the cops found. He told me how it was found in the room where you found Noreen's body. That's got to be . . ." She gulped. "That's got to be what the murderer is looking for."

Without another word, she hauled me through the tasting room to the fermentation room and beyond. When we got to the warehouse, she announced to the workers in there that, as of that moment, they were officially on break. Once they had cleared out and she had shut the warehouse door behind them, she closed in on the door that led into the old storeroom where I'd found Noreen's body.

"There's no other explanation, is there?" she asked, and since she must have known I didn't have a clue what she was talking about, I guess she was talking to herself. "Only a guilty person would come back to look for the camera, right?" Like she'd just remembered I was there, her gaze snapped to mine. "Right?"

"I don't know," I admitted. "I'm confused. If you'd just tell me—"

"No." She pointed to the storeroom door, and I saw that it was open the tiniest bit. Of course, that made sense if the person inside knew that the storeroom door only opened from inside the warehouse.

"In there," Kate whispered and motioned. "The killer's in there."

I neared the door and bent an ear. There was someone in there, all right—I could hear footsteps and see that the someone in question hadn't turned on the lights. Even as I watched, the beam of a flashlight arced over the far wall. I reminded myself how the room was laid out, what was in there and what it all looked like, and before I could talk myself out of what I shouldn't have talked myself into in the first place, I threw open the door and turned on the lights.

The person on the other side of the room froze and stared at me.

I stared right back.

That is, before I found my voice and stammered out, "Chandra!"

By the time we got to Kate's office, Kate was in tears, Chandra was sobbing so hard she could barely breathe, and I was so completely befuddled, I was sure my head was going to explode.

"Sit." I deposited Kate in one chair and Chandra in another, then hurried over to the mini fridge near Kate's desk and grabbed two bottles of water. "Drink," I said, handing out the water and waiting until both my friends finished. It was only then that I cast an eagle eye in Chandra's direction and demanded, "Explain."

"I . . . I . . ." Chandra pulled in breath after unsteady breath. "I came to the winery and I told the people up front that I had to see Kate and they know me and . . . and . . ."

"And instead of going to Kate's office, you ducked into that back storeroom." I finished the thought for Chandra, and who could blame me. If I waited for her to stop stammering and start making sense, I was going to grow old sitting there.

Chandra's head bobbed. "I had to get back there and I couldn't tell anybody and—"

"I was right. You were looking for the camera you left behind." Kate's hand flew to her throat. "You killed Noreen."

The tears started again. From both of them.

Before I drowned, I demanded that everybody keep quiet. "Deep breaths, Chandra," I advised her. "Start from the beginning."

"The beginning. Sure." I swear, Chandra's cheeks were the same color as the grinning ghost on her black sweatshirt. "I came because I had to, you see, because somebody was going to find it and when they did, they were going to know I was here and then Hank would find out and then—"

Chandra's voice got louder and more panicked by the syllable, and there was no use trying to talk above it. I held up a hand to stop her.

"Somebody was going to find what?" I asked her. "Are you talking about the camera?"

She drew in a long breath and let it out slowly, then reached into her pocket. She came out holding one of the dangling beaded witch hat earrings I'd seen her wear just a week earlier. "I lost it," she said, her voice wooden. "In the storeroom. The night of the murder."

My heart stopped. I swear it did. When it started up again with a bang, I flinched. "Chandra, are you saying what I think you're saying? You . . . you were there?"

Chandra looked down at the floor, and when she looked up again, her cheeks were wet with tears. "I don't know anything about the camera you're talking about, but I knew I lost my earring. I knew if Hank found it he was going to figure out I was there. I couldn't let that happen."

"But Hank didn't find it," I said. Chandra still held the earring. The way her hands shook, the beads caught the light and winked at me when I asked, "It was in the storeroom?"

"In a sort of crevice. It must have gotten kicked there when—"

"When you killed Noreen." Kate gasped. "Oh my goodness, what are we going to do? Don't worry, Chandra. I'll call my attorney. We'll raise the bail money. We won't let you go to prison." She listened to her own words and gulped. "But you have to, don't you? You deserve to go to prison. You killed Noreen!"

Chandra's mouth twisted. "I did not!" She leapt out of her chair and paced to the window, and I couldn't help but notice that the oil lamp was there. Chandra stomped her way back in the other direction. "How can you say that?" she asked Kate. "How can you even think I'm the killer!"

"But you were there." Kate popped out of her chair, too, and stood toe to toe with Chandra. "You were looking to recover evidence. You said you lost the earring the night of the murder, and—"

I stepped between them, nudging them farther apart. "And something tells me there's more to this story than Chandra's telling us. Go ahead." I motioned her back into her chair. "And this time, start from the real beginning."

Chandra settled herself, and while she was at it, I got Kate to sit back down, too.

"Chandra." I took my own chair. "What were you doing in the storeroom the night of the murder?"

"I was supposed to be . . ." Chandra heaved a breath. "Noreen thought . . ." She pulled at her hair. "Noreen wanted me to pose as Sleepy Harlow. You know, so she could get a video of the ghost."

I wasn't surprised by the subterfuge. After all, I knew Noreen was planning something. The bit of video Hank found proved that. What did amaze me was Noreen's choice of a coconspirator. "Why?" I asked Chandra.

She spent a few seconds breathing hard, steeling herself to tell us the story. "It started last year," she finally admitted. "When the ghost hunters were here on the island. Noreen approached me. She said she wanted me to do something for her. Something that would help her establish herself as a leader in the paranormal community."

"You were the ghost in that video?" I stared at Chandra in stunned amazement. "Why?"

She shrugged. "I thought . . . Okay, I admit it, it wasn't the smartest thing to do, but Noreen, she told me that if she could just get some kind of evidence, then she'd get her TV show, and once she had her TV show, she'd have more money to investigate and more equipment and more backup. And she said once that happened, then she could find the real Sleepy because she said she believed Sleepy's ghost really is on the island, just like I believe. And she convinced me that's what she was really looking for, and if only I'd help . . . just that one time . . . if only I'd help, then she'd get all the resources she needed and then she'd really be able to find Sleepy's ghost."

I thought back to that snippet of video. "Then this year when she came back, she asked you to do it again." Chandra's fresh tears told me all I needed to know. "You refused. That's what you two were fighting about."

Chandra's jaw dropped. I promised myself I'd explain it all to her later. For now, there were more important things to worry about. "When you told her no—"

"I realized she never really wanted to find Sleepy. Not the real Sleepy. All Noreen wanted was to get famous.

That's why I said no, Bea. I met her in the storeroom, just like I said I would, and that's when I told her I wasn't going to do it. That's when I lost my earring, too." Chandra tucked the little witch hat in her pocket. "I thought for sure if Hank found it, he'd figure out I was there and he'd think I was the killer. I was so worried, I didn't know what to do. He'd ask me if I was angry at Noreen, and I'd have to admit I was. She lied to her investigation team. She lied to the public. But I . . . I swear I didn't kill her."

"No, but someone else sure did." Again, I thought about that video. "She convinced someone else to play Sleepy that night," I told both Chandra and Kate. "And that someone is the murderer."

"Well, it wasn't me." Chandra's shoulders shot back.

"And it wasn't me." Kate sat up a little straighter.

"And it wasn't Jacklyn or Dimitri," I grumbled.

That left me right back where I started from.

"Watch out for snakes!"

I was about to hop off the *Miss Luella*, and I froze, one hand on the railing, the other one flying automatically to my heart. Yeah, like that might actually stop the sudden, loud clattering from inside my chest.

"Snakes." As if I hadn't heard her—believe me, I had, which would explain why my knees were knocking together like maracas—Luella came up beside me and pointed toward the shoreline. "They like to hide in the rocks," she said. "There. There. There." Her finger arced over the rocky outcropping where I was determined to go ashore. Now that she'd pointed them out, they were easy to see, Lake Erie water snakes (*lews*, some of the islanders call them), sunning their fat gray bodies in what little warmth the afternoon sun provided. "You'll probably run into a whole bunch of 'em. Not to worry." Luella clapped a hand to my shoulder. "They bite, but they're not poisonous."

A wave licked the side of the *Miss Luella*, pitching it toward the spit of land where I intended to disembark, and the resulting ripples splashed the rocks. The water swished perilously close to one of the snakes, and it raised its head, opened its beady eyes and gave us what I could only call an indignant look before it slithered away.

"You're sure you want to do this?" Luella asked.

I was.

Or at least I had been.

Before I saw the snakes.

Though I tried not to, it was impossible to keep my gaze off the remaining two reptiles. They were maybe three feet long and plenty plump, and the one closest to the boat—closest to where I'd have to step ashore—had a fat white belly.

I swallowed hard. "I need to do this."

Luella knew better than to argue, but she was, after all, a woman of a certain age, and if experience had taught me nothing else, it was that women of that certain age feel free to speak their minds. It was one of the things I admired about them. Except when I was the one on the other end of what they had to say.

"You could have asked Levi to come along. You know, for backup. I know, I know . . . you can take care of yourself. So can I. But if there's one thing I've learned in the seventy-some years I've been around, it's that it never hurts to have a guy around when it comes to things like snakes."

"I could have asked him." Though I wasn't anywhere near that certain age, I was never shy about speaking my mind, either. "But I don't want him here."

"He might not be afraid of snakes."

"I might not be, either," I said, because it was kinder than pointing out that no matter his assets (and there were many), Levi was, in fact, afraid of birds. Could snakes be far behind?

Along with jeans, a sweatshirt, and a thick jacket, I'd worn a pair of sturdy hiking boots, and I pointed down at them. "I'll be fine," I assured Luella. "With any luck, I'll be all the way over to Wilder's in just a few minutes."

"Uh huh." I pretended not to hear the skepticism in Luella's voice. She swiveled her head to the right and squinted. As a lifelong islander she knew what I knew— Wilder's was a little more than a mile away. Even on flat land, it would take me more than a few minutes to get there. "Why?" she asked.

I knew she would ask, and she had every right. After all, I had begged this favor of Luella: a few minutes on the *Miss Luella* to get to the beach close to where island natives claimed there were hidden caves. She had a group of fishermen waiting for her back at the dock, and I had no business wasting her time.

"Marianne consulted the harbor master's records pertaining to one of the trips Sleepy took to Middle Island. According to what she found, it took him two hours to get back here from there."

She turned to peer north. "Impossible. Unless he rowed across the lake! It's only seven miles."

"Exactly. I just wonder what else he might have been up to."

One of Luella's silvery brows slid up. "And that matters because it's important to that book you're trying to rewrite."

Luella had, after all, been at the B and B the morning

Jerry Garcia paid a visit and ruined the manuscript. She knew exactly what I was up to.

"I guess I'm just curious," I admitted.

She pursed her lips. "Sleepy might have stopped at Middle Bass or North Bass," she said, indicating the two nearby smaller and less-developed islands we could see not far offshore of South Bass.

"He might." I'd already thought of that, too. "But if there's any truth to the story, he might have had a secret spot where he offloaded his liquor."

Luella waved a hand. "And you think it might be around here somewhere."

"I looked over maps of the island last night. Lots and lots of maps. I talked to the old-timers who hang out at the café. This spot makes the most sense. Sleepy could have come from Middle Island, stowed the liquor, then gone to the harbor and docked his boat there. That would explain the missing two hours."

"But what happened in those missing two hours more than eighty years ago doesn't really matter, does it? You don't care about this just because of Sleepy."

I wasn't surprised that Luella saw right through me. Chandra never would have. Chandra takes everyone and everything at face value and believes people are, at heart, good and honest. Kate, of course, wouldn't have waited this long to ask me what I was really up to. But then, Kate's as no-nonsense as anyone I've ever met. These days, she was also worried, silent, and disconnected from the friends who desperately wanted to help her.

Luella was more subtle. But no less practical.

I laid it on the line. "Kate was at the winery waiting for Noreen the night Noreen was killed. But Kate didn't see her come in on any of the cameras. That means Noreen found another way in, and I wondered if it was through the series of caves that are supposed to be around here. Chandra confirmed it. She and Noreen got in through the caves."

"You think that's how the killer got in, too."

"Either they were together, or the killer followed Noreen. Noreen knew the killer was coming. She was waiting for him so they could film that phony ghost scene together."

"And that person wasn't Kate."

I puffed out a long breath of frustration. I'd told Luella all about what had happened with Chandra at the winery earlier in the day, so I didn't need to catch her up on that part of my thinking. "You know it wasn't Kate, Luella. And you know it wasn't Chandra. So do I. I thought if I could go in through the caves the way Noreen and Chandra did—the way Noreen and her killer might have—I thought maybe I'll see something or find something or . . ." I squeezed my hands into fists and grumbled with frustration. "Or I don't know what! But I know I have to do something."

"And what if you run into ol' Sleepy down there?"

"You think I should be more afraid of the ghost than I am of the snakes?" I asked Luella.

"I think you should be careful."

I assured her I would be, and that I'd be perfectly safe, too. I had experience as a caver, if only a casual one, and I wasn't dumb. I had a personal GPS tracking device on me, as well as a lantern, flashlight, and a first aid kit in the backpack slung over my shoulder. Before she could convince me that it wasn't the best idea in the world and that maybe I should reconsider, I hauled myself over the side of the *Miss Luella* and hopped onto the nearest large, flat rock. The snake that had been basking there in the sun did not appreciate the interruption. It reared, hissed, and—thank goodness—decided I wasn't worth the effort. The last I saw of it, it was slithering over to another, smaller rock where there was just as much sun and less human interference.

One snake down, and who knew how many hundreds more to go.

Before the heebie-jeebies got the better of me, I turned to signal to Luella that it was all right for her to leave. I watched the boat head west toward the harbor and felt suddenly like a shipwrecked sailor marooned in the middle of nowhere.

"Ridiculous!" I reminded myself in a voice loud enough to annoy that third snake lounging nearby. It gave me a snaky little glare, settled down, and went right back to sleep. I was as ready as I'd ever be, and besides, I had no choice but to move forward. Now that the *Miss Luella* was long gone, I could stay exactly where I was and accomplish nothing at all, or start out along the beach. I was twenty yards from where I'd hopped off Luella's boat when I finally found a dark, damp entrance tucked into the hillside.

"Like you expected a cave to be anything else?" I reminded myself.

I got out the flashlight and the battery-operated lantern and, thus armed, I edged into the cave. I'd gone no more than ten feet when I met a solid stone wall. So not what I'd been hoping for! I arced the beam of the flashlight left and right and relief washed over me. There was another opening not far away.

I splashed my way through nasty-smelling puddles and stood in openmouthed awe in a cavern with a high ceiling where stalagmites (or were they stalactites?) hung in suspended animation like stone icicles.

A noise from the coal-black darkness behind me sent me spinning around.

A footstep. I swear it was a footstep.

I glided the beam of my flashlight around the cavern, fighting to block out the noise of my own suddenly frantically beating heart.

Silence pressed on my ears, disturbed only now and again by the *ping* of dripping water.

Nothing else. No footsteps.

I told myself to get a grip and kept right on walking, and was rewarded for it when I finally saw a crude wooden door positioned in the rock wall in front of me.

I set down my lantern so I could use both hands to give the doorknob a tug. That's when I heard another noise from the darkness behind: the sharp slap of a footfall against stone.

"Hey! Another cave explorer! I've got lanterns and flashlights," I called out, forcing myself to sound like discovering someone else down there in the dark was actually a good thing. "Come on and join me and let's see where this passage leads."

Brave words.

Or at least they would have been if the dull echo of my own voice didn't fall dead in the musty silence.

Like it or not, my mind flashed to Crown Hill Cemetery and that disturbing bit of shadow that had played hide-and-seek with us.

That is, right before it flashed to that long-unused storage room where I'd found Noreen's body.

Panic manifested itself in my suddenly damp palms. I grabbed the doorknob in shaky fingers, but the wood around it was wet and rotted. When I pulled, the knob came off in my hand. I tossed the old knob on the ground, stuck a hand through the opening left by the missing doorknob, braced my fingers against the far side of the door, and pulled.

The door whooshed open and a sickening, rotted smell filled my nose. I found myself in a room walled with bricks laid in a basket-weave pattern, just like the room in which I'd found Noreen and the battered plasmometer, and I forced myself to visualize what these rooms had been like back in the day when both Grandma Carrie and Sleepy Harlow had lived on the island. The winery had used this room and others like it for storage, but I could also see why they had been eventually abandoned. This close to the shoreline, mold stained the walls in long black streaks, and water pooled on the floor. If I bent an ear and listened very carefully, I could hear the sound of the lake just on the other side of the wall. There were rotted wooden shelves here, too, just like there were in the room where I'd found Noreen, and there was something on one of those shelves.

I froze, the beam of my flashlight trained on an old wooden box.

"Treasure chest?"

Even to my own ears, the words sounded ridiculous. But the siren call of them was impossible to resist. I carefully stepped around a wide, deep hole that must somehow have been directly connected to the lake; the water in it swished back and forth.

Like there was some primordial creature breathing in there.

I slapped the thought aside, grabbed on to the box, and flipped open the top.

There was a layer of fabric inside, and I carefully

unwrapped it and found a stack of letters wrapped with ribbon, along with something else—something that winked and flashed in the beam of my flashlight.

I was so busy reaching inside to see what it might be, I didn't realize that I felt a change in the air and by the time I did, it was already too late. A cold gust of musty air crawled over my neck and down the back of my jacket, and I spun around.

I barely had time to react before something hard whacked me in the side of my head.

My arms flew out to my sides and my knees locked. Right before stars burst behind my eyes and I crumbled onto the wet stone floor, my flashlight beam arced across the room, and for one terrifying moment, I caught sight of my attacker.

There was no mistaking the black, gaping hole where his head should have been.

❖ 19 ❖

Cold water tickled my nose.

Somewhere inside my thumping head, I knew this was a bad thing, and automatically, I lifted a hand that felt as if it were made of cast iron to brush the water away.

Just as I had hoped, the slimy water retreated. For like half a second. Then it washed back at me. I gasped, and it rushed into my mouth.

I choked, and spit and gagged. I sat up like a shot, and when my eyes flew open, I found myself in total, impenetrable darkness.

My heart raced, and panic didn't just lick at the edges of my composure—it tore it away completely with sharp-edged teeth. My jeans were soaked. My hair was wet. My head felt like a split coconut.

For I don't know how long, it was all I could do to keep from falling back down onto the wet floor and curling into a fetal position. That is, until consciousness rose like the quickly climbing water. Or maybe it was that chilly, foul-smelling water itself that made me shake myself back to reality. With what felt like a kick from a mule, I remembered that I'd been attacked, and the quick glimpse I'd had of the man without the head.

At least his didn't hurt like hell.

Not funny, I told myself.

This was no time to be funny.

The water inched up to my ankles and I remembered the hole I'd seen in the floor, the one I'd guessed was directly connected to the lake. Looks like I was right. There are no tides on the Great Lakes, not like there are in oceans, but there are what are called *seiches*.

"Saysh." Slowly and carefully, my tongue too thick and my throat too dry, I pronounced the word the way I'd heard islanders say it, and thought about how they'd explained it: When wind pushes down on one part of a lake, water in other parts automatically rises. It made sense. Even to a physics-challenged person like me. Those waves undulate back and forth, back and forth, like water in a bathtub. Seiches can affect the lake for days after the kinds of strong storms we'd had earlier in the week. I'm no scientist, never have been, but I knew the seiche was making the water rise out of that hole and fill the cavern where I'd been lying unconscious since being attacked.

"You've got to get out of here, Bea," I told myself. Good plan. Too bad the voice that echoed back at me from the darkness didn't sound anywhere near as brave as I'd hoped it would.

Hanging on to the wooden shelves I'd seen when I arrived at the storage room, I managed to get to my feet, and I kicked through the water, hoping to make contact with my flashlight or my lantern.

No luck, and no way I was going to search with my hands. I wasn't so out of it that I'd forgotten the lews.

My hands slick and unsteady, I got my phone out of my pocket and turned on the flashlight app.

When I confirmed that I was alone in the storeroom, I let go a shaky breath.

No headless ghost.

I shined the light in the direction of the watery hole I'd discovered earlier and saw that now, it looked more like a pond than simply a puddle. Water slapped my shins.

I needed to find a way out of the old storeroom.

And fast.

I'd already started to feel my way along the wall, the wooden shelves as my guide, when I remembered the box I'd been looking through when I was bushwhacked. Step by careful step, I made my way back to the other side of the room, aiming my light at the shelves and grumbling a curse when I saw that the box was gone.

"You fell, it fell." I wasn't sure how good the theory was, but at least it gave me hope. If nothing else, there in that lightless room with the cold water inching higher every moment, hope was what I needed.

I shined my light under the shelves, and the first thing I saw was a fat lews, looking decidedly unhappy at being disturbed.

"Not going to panic," I told myself, backing away. "Not going to panic."

I knew the mantra would calm me only so long.

My heart in my throat, my stomach tied in painful knots that tightened by the second, I ignored the reptile and kept on looking.

When the light landed on the wooden box, I admit it, I hummed a bit of the "Hallelujah Chorus."

Water had already starting licking at the stack of letters inside the box, and I couldn't take the chance that they'd get even wetter. I closed my eyes (yeah, like that was going to help if there was a snake hiding under the fabric that lined the box), grabbed the letters, and felt around for the shiny object I'd seen in the instant before I got conked. My fingers closed over something cold and metallic, and I stuffed that in the inside pocket of my jacket along with the letters, made sure there was nothing else in the box, and knew it was time to get out of Dodge.

There was less chance that the headless ghost went toward the winery than there was that he was hiding out in the caverns through which I'd already come, so I focused on finding the door that would lead me to the next old storeroom. Thank goodness, it wasn't far away.

The moment I stepped into it, drippy, smelly, and grateful, I knew where I was.

It was the storeroom where I'd found Noreen's body.

One shower didn't seem like enough, so when I got home, I took two: one to get rid of the stench of mold, and the other to soothe my aching muscles and calm my still-shattered nerves.

The way I figured it, a glass of really good Chilean Carménère wouldn't hurt, either.

With EGG gone for the evening, I had the house to myself, and I put on my favorite jammies (the ones with the pink flamingoes on them), built a fire in the parlor, and poked and prodded it until the blaze was bright and the heat of the flames seeped through me and warmed me inside and out.

It was only then and with half the glass of wine gone that I allowed myself to think about what had happened earlier that day.

Of course I knew that headless assailant who conked me in the cavern wasn't really Sleepy Harlow. I mean, not the real Sleepy Harlow, the dead Sleepy Harlow. It was someone who was playing our local ghost; maybe the same someone Noreen had arranged to take Chandra's place. Someone who didn't want me poking around in his business.

A shiver skittered over my shoulders, and I grabbed for the knitted afghan I kept on the back of the couch and tugged it over my shoulders.

Between headless mobsters, dark caverns, and snakes— I couldn't help it, I shivered again—I was pretty sure I'd never calm my jumpy stomach.

I needed a distraction, and I found it in the form of the letters I'd brought out of the cavern with me. With the flames cracking and throwing a soft orange glow, I untied the ribbon bound around the letters and started looking them over.

Two hours later, I was no closer to discovering who killed Noreen.

But I had learned some pretty amazing things.

It was almost enough to make me forget my headache.

The ghost getters got in very late, and by then, I was totally wiped. From the place where I'd fallen asleep on the parlor couch, I listened to them spill into the house and climb up the stairs, promising myself I'd waylay them one by one in the morning.

I was as good as my word, and when breakfast was done, I made my move.

"Hey, Liam." He was about to disappear back upstairs to listen for recorded EVPs, or look for spooky evidence on video, or take a nap—whatever it was ghost getters did when they weren't getting ghosts. Lucky for me, Liam was too polite to plow right through me. And I was too smart to move away from the bottom of the stairway so he could get around me.

I glanced toward the parlor. "I was wondering if you could help me."

Liam was a muscular guy with short arms, thick hands, and cheeks like a bulldog's. He yelled up the stairs to tell Dimitri he'd be up in a couple of minutes, and when I waved my hand, Vanna-like, toward the parlor, he stepped inside.

He breathed in deep. "You made a fire last night."

"It was chilly."

He shifted from foot to foot. "So . . . you saw another entity?"

I couldn't stand the thought of stringing him along. "Nothing like that. It's just that . . . I heard you and Dimitri talking the other day and you said you could really use your plasmometer. I thought—"

"You're going to talk to the cops for us?" A smile washed over his doughy face. "That's great!"

I didn't make any promises. That much is to my credit. I also didn't tell him he was dead wrong. I guess that pretty much canceled out the credit.

"I thought you could tell me more about it," I said.

"The plasmometer? Oh yeah, sure. So you can explain it to the cops, make them realize that we really need it. I figured they didn't have the slightest idea what the thing is or why it's such an important piece of equipment."

Not exactly the way I'd heard it from Noreen's lips on that video she made right before she died. For now, I was keeping that bit of info under wraps.

"Noreen designed the plasmometer, right? And you built it according to her specifications."

"That's right. I can't take credit for anything other than following the plans. Noreen, she was the genius. She was the one who was brilliant."

There was that word again. Just like last time I'd spoken to Liam.

"So how does something like the plasmometer happen?" I asked, and I didn't have to pretend to be interested. I was as curious about the machine as I was about the death of the "genius" who'd invented it. "I mean, you don't just wake up one day and say you're going to invent a device that will make it possible for ghosts to manifest, do you?"

"If you're dedicated to your profession, you do," Liam told me.

Call me crazy, but I thought a woman who staged a ghostly apparition just so she could film it was anything but dedicated.

"I get that," I said, even though I really didn't. "I mean, when you're really into something like paranormal investigations, it's all you think about. You want to spend every day improving your craft."

"Exactly." Liam perched himself on the arm of the couch, then thought better of it. I was grateful. He was a beefy guy, and it was an expensive couch. "We tried some other things back in the day. You know, some other equipment that we bought. Then we built a few pieces of our own. But none of it worked. I mean, not like the Turner Plasmometer. Genius. That thing is nothing but pure genius."

"And you're going to build another one."

"If we can't get ours back. Or if we can't repair ours." Liam darted toward the doorway. "You want to see the plans?"

He didn't have to ask me twice.

Within five minutes we were in the kitchen, where Liam unrolled the plans for the plasmometer on the counter. With a dramatic gesture, he stepped back so I could get a better look.

I forgave him the drama. After all, he was on television, or he would be soon. And apparently, an invention of this magnitude deserved something of a drumroll.

The plans were on sixteen by twenty paper, and they reminded me of a blueprint.

Well, a blueprint drawn by a Jack Russell. On a caffeine high. And taking steroids.

There at the center of the paper was a rough sketch of the plasmometer, and around it lines and zigzags and arrows pointed to various parts of the machine and labeled what each was. That made sense to me.

What didn't was the rest of the mess.

Coffee stains.

Words crossed out.

Erasures.

Some parts of the plan were drawn with even, careful lines and inked in to be easily readable. Other parts of it were filled in with orange crayon.

Some portions of the drawing were so detailed and meticulous, I could see how Liam would have had an easy time following them. Others were smudged and caked with something brown.

I bent closer and sniffed.

Peanut butter.

"Didn't any of this make you suspicious?" I asked Liam.

"Any of . . ." He glanced down at the plans. "Oh, you mean the smudges and stuff? Why would it? Hey, I might not have a great scientific mind. I mean, not like Noreen. But that doesn't mean I don't appreciate brilliance. You know, creative energy and all that."

"But Noreen was . . ." I didn't think I needed to soften my words. Not for Liam. After all, he'd worked with Noreen.

"She stacked the equipment alphabetically," I reminded him, even though I shouldn't have had to. "She arranged and rearranged and cataloged and made lists. Do you really think—"

"That doesn't mean she wasn't a great inventor."

"No, it doesn't, but—"

"And it doesn't mean the plasmometer is any less valuable to us in our work."

"Of course not, but—"

"Hey, who cares how the chick did it!" Liam grabbed the plans, rolled them up, and tucked them back in the heavy cardboard tube they'd come out of. "All that matters is that the thing works. And that you're going to talk to the cops for us about getting it back." Grinning, he walked out of the kitchen. "Wait until I tell the rest of 'em. They're going to be freakin' stoked!"

I left him to his return-of-the-plasmometer fantasies. I had my own work to take care of, so I shut myself in my private suite and got to work on the Internet.

"Turner Plasmometer," I said to myself as I keyed in the words.

Up popped a few dozen sites.

One was EGG's own website, and just as I expected, they spent an entire page singing the praises of the piece of equipment Noreen had so clearly thought was junk. Other sites I visited belonged to other paranormal investigation groups. A few congratulated EGG on the plasmometer and the advances they'd made in the field of searching for spooks because of it. A few others were decidedly jealous. If only they'd thought of it first! If only they'd put two and two together and made the connections the wonderful and fabulous and genius Noreen Turner did. They, too, could have had their own reality TV shows.

I guess there's a purpose for everything, even carping. By the time I found my way to the blog of someone named Ted Fywell, I was so used to hearing "if only" that I didn't pay much attention.

Until I read further.

I sat up, propped my elbows on my desk and stared at the computer screen. This Fywell guy lived in New Mexico, and according to a website filled with misspelled words and questionable grammar, he said that he was an engineer who specialized in making equipment for paranormal investigators.

He had the testimonials to prove it.

"Awesome dude," one investigator was quoted as saying.

"Far-out spectacular!" another commented.

But what really caught my eye was a long, ranting post where Fywell claimed he, not Noreen Turner, was the one who'd actually invented the plasmometer.

I checked the clock, did some quick calculations to figure out the time in New Mexico, did some more research on the Internet, and made a few calls.

"Fywell? Ted Fywell?" Turns out Ted's day job was as a

professor of Engineering Design and Technology at Eastern New Mexico University in Roswell. Didn't it figure.
The man on the other end of the phone sounded confused
when I asked for Ted.

"You can't exactly talk to him," he said.

"I could leave a message. Or if he's not there, you could
give me his home number. It's important."

"Not to Ted. Ted Fywell, he's been dead for going on a
year now."

❖ 20 ❖

After a few more phone calls and a couple more hours of Internet research, I had pieced together the story of Ted Fywell's untimely demise.

Suicide.

His coworkers said they weren't surprised. Ted had always been something of an odd duck, they told me. A genius of the old-school, crazy-in-the-head, eccentric variety who was focused to the point of obsession with paranormal research. Once he heard about the Turner Plasmometer, his always-erratic mind latched on to the story of its unqualified success and Ted claimed the plasmometer as his own.

From then on, there was no going back. Ted's behavior became more erratic. He missed classes. He grew more isolated. He had paranoid delusions about a break-in at his home and the resulting fire that, the fire chief out in

Roswell told me, looked plenty suspicious. The chief had been circumspect, and though I was disappointed by his lack of candor, I couldn't blame him for not coming right out and saying Fywell had started the fire himself.

How did all this tie into Noreen Turner's murder?

As far as I could see, it didn't.

At least, not until I dug a little further.

Halloween morning dawned clear and chilly, and by ten o'clock, I had a theory. And a plan.

As long as I was paying expenses for Aaron and his team of technical wonder workers who'd created the ghost in my parlor, I figured I might as well get my money's worth.

Fortunately, Aaron agreed. To him, each new special effects challenge was an opportunity to hone his skills. And besides, he confessed, it sounded like a heck of a lot of fun, even if this time, the challenge wasn't so much spooky ghosts and eerie voices as it was just plain, old-fashioned theatrical illusion.

By noon, I'd talked to Chandra and Luella and, yes, even to Levi, and they agreed to help in any way they could.

At one, I met the ferry so I could personally welcome Marianne and Alvin home, and while I was at it, I threw myself at Marianne's mercy. And after all that time of worrying and wondering what Marianne would think when I told her the story of Jerry the Destroyer? Well, maybe having a scary medical problem and serious surgery changes your outlook on life and your appreciation of even the small things. Marianne listened—and burst into laughter. That is, right before she apologized left and right for causing me so much trouble and so much work.

She couldn't wait to read my version of Charlie Harlow's

story, she told me, even after I warned her that after what I had planned for that night, she might have a little extra work to do on the book. Though I remained mysterious about the details, she and Alvin played along. They said they'd be at the Halloween party I was planning, even though their costumes—Lucy and Charlie Brown—didn't quite fit in with my theme.

I convinced Kate to join us, too, though I have to say, that was the most difficult part of my day. She was sure that she wasn't long for the non-prison world and, because of that, more depressed than ever. It is a tribute to her faith in me and her friendship that she agreed at all.

By six, with the sun hanging over Lake Erie like one of the dozens of pumpkins lit in the park for the huge costume party going on over there, everything was ready. Even I—who had, after all, given Aaron instructions as well as carte blanche when it came to expenses—was impressed when I walked to what used to be the Orient Express restaurant.

"So? Huh? What do you think?" Aaron was dressed as a bartender with a white apron looped around his neck, and he was justly proud of what he'd accomplished. He held out his arms and spun around. "Some transformation, huh?"

That was putting it mildly.

When last I'd been there, the Orient Express was a typical walk-in Chinese restaurant with a counter against the wall opposite the door and a few tables out front where folks could wait for their to-go meals or eat in if they wanted.

Now . . .

I looked around in openmouthed wonder.

Now, I swear, I was standing in a Prohibition-era speakeasy.

The front counter had been turned into a bar, where Aaron had been drying beer mugs when I walked in. The few white café tables Peter Chan, the Orient Express's murdered proprietor, had had out front had been replaced by a dozen wooden tables. Each one had a flickering candle on it that added to the ambiance of the ceiling fans that swirled overhead and the spotlights that shone on potted palms in the corners. There wasn't room for a live band (thank goodness—I wouldn't have wanted to pay for one!), but Aaron had music piped in: Louis Armstrong and Bessie Smith and Al Jolson. Two women stood ready to serve drinks and there was a guy in a pin-striped suit stationed at the front door whose job it was to demand that each person he let in knew the password I'd included in the email invitations I'd sent out that morning: "Bea sent me."

"Bea sent me."

Three cheers for Levi for following my instructions. When he walked in, he looked as amazed as I felt.

"Incredible." It took me a moment to realize he wasn't looking around at the speakeasy, but checking out the gold-colored flapper dress I wore. "How'd you ever come up with a costume like that at such short notice?"

There was no use explaining the frantic call to the costume shop in Cleveland, the special messenger delivery, the cost. I was flattered, and smiled. For his part, Levi was dressed just as I asked him to, in dark work pants and a white shirt. He'd rolled the sleeves above his elbows and added a jaunty tweed walking cap. I hadn't requested the hat, but I approved. It gave him a certain roguish look that was perfect for the part I had asked him to play.

"You had it easy," I told him, because that seemed a better option than pointing out that he looked delectable. "Guys usually do when it comes to costumes."

As if to prove it, Hank showed up in a black suit and a fedora. He had a cigar clenched between his teeth. He had a woman on each arm. The moll on his right—complete with a red strapless dress and a feathered headband—was none other than Chandra. For the record, she looks better in red than she does in green. The woman on his left, resplendent in a blue beaded gown that wasn't at all true to the period but was beautiful nonetheless, was Luella. I realized I'd never seen her in a dress—or dangling earrings, for that matter.

Over the next twenty minutes, my guests drifted in, including all of the ghost getters. They weren't sure what I had planned, but they made it clear that whatever it was, they were eager to get it over with so they could get out and start hunting on this, what they called the one night of the year when the veil between the physical world and the spiritual one was the thinnest. Ben and Eddie each wore T-shirts that said *This Is My Costume.* Liam, Rick, and David looked no different than ever and informed me that they were dressed as members of EGG. Jacklyn wore her pink kimono, and Dimitri had on a makeshift toga that seemed appropriate considering his Mediterranean good looks. At least until I realized the toga was made out of one of the bedsheets from the B and B.

I recognized Fiona's costume at once; it was one of Chandra's caftans, this one a swirl of purples and blues that set off that spectacular howlite necklace of hers just right.

Kate didn't bother with a costume, and I didn't criticize. I was so grateful to see her that the moment she arrived, I sat her at the table closest to the bar, ordered her a classic speakeasy drink—the gin rickey—and told her to get comfortable.

Lucy and Charlie Brown, it should be noted, arrived right on time, Alvin in his yellow t-shirt with a black zig-zag and Marianne in a blue dress and saddle shoes. Okay, so they weren't exactly Prohibition-era anything, but that didn't keep them from looking as cute as can be.

"We're ready," I said to Levi when I zipped past him to make sure Marianne was comfortable. "Everybody's here."

"Go for it," he said.

And I did.

"Ladies and gentlemen!" I stepped to the center of the room. "Thank you for joining us this evening to celebrate Halloween. My name is Carrie Wilder."

Kate sat up.

"We're here tonight," I continued, "to tell you all a story. A story about me and this man." I held out a hand and Levi joined me. "This is somebody you all know: Charlie Sleepy Harlow."

The ghost getters applauded. Marianne looked pleased as punch. Hank knew what I was up to, but Chandra and Luella had only been given the bare bones of the plan. They were sitting with Kate, and like her, they sat up and took notice.

Once I had everyone's attention, I signaled to Aaron, who brought an oil lamp out from behind the bar. I lit it and left it there.

"A lamp," I said. "And Kate, though this one isn't yours, you'll recognize it. It's just like the one Carrie Wilder . . ." I pointed to myself, just to remind them which role I was playing. "Carrie Wilder put this lamp on her windowsill at the winery every day. Sometimes she lit it and sometimes she didn't, and some people"—I glanced at Levi—"some people thought I was crazy to think that the lamp was a signal, but I've recently found out that I was right. You see,

I recently found a number of old letters. Written to Carrie Wilder from Charlie Harlow. And from Charlie Harlow to Carrie Wilder."

Marianne's mouth dropped open. "Is that the surprise you said you had for me? Carrie and Sleepy, they were friends?"

"They were more than friends. Kate, you should be the first to know, and I'm sorry I'm not going tell you in private, but you'll understand when I'm done. You see, Sleepy Harlow, he was your great-grandfather."

"No!" I couldn't tell if she was happy or outraged or just so gobsmacked that she couldn't think what else to say. "The family story is that Carrie's husband died before my grandfather was born."

"Well, that's sort of true," I told her. "Your grandfather's father died, all right, but he wasn't Carrie's husband. Oh, they planned to get married, but they never had the chance. Carrie's father was furious, both about who she intended to marry and the fact that she was pregnant before the *I do's* were said."

"Which is why . . ." Levi stepped forward. "It's why he obliterated the oil lamp Carrie had added to Sleepy's tombstone. She put it there as a tribute to her love."

"But your great-great grandfather," I told Kate, "didn't want the world to know that his daughter was having the child of a gangster. Because we all know that's what Sleepy was, right?"

I saw a couple nods and heard a couple, "You bets!" I figured that's the reaction we'd get, and that was Hank's cue to step forward.

"Sleepy worked with gangsters." I motioned toward Hank. "He supplied them with Canadian liquor. And eventually, he got on the wrong side of those gangsters. We've all talked about it, haven't we? Sleepy did something to make the mob bosses really mad. They killed him and cut off his head. Nasty!" I didn't have to pretend to shiver, because every time I thought about it, I had the same reaction. "And awfully violent, even for those years filled with gangland shootings and revenge killings. But thanks to those letters, we finally know why he suffered such a vicious death."

Just as I'd instructed him, Levi turned toward the bar while I was saying all this, and now, he turned back again. He'd taken the time to pin something to his white shirt, and it winked in the light of the nearest candle.

As much as I wanted to make the announcement, I knew it wasn't my place. I waited for Kate to figure it out. Her jaw dropped, and when she finally snapped it shut, she stammered, "Sleepy was a cop!"

"He was a G-man, working undercover to infiltrate the gangs of bootleggers," I said.

"But why"—Kate got up and closed in on Levi so she could examine the badge he'd pinned on his chest—"why didn't anyone ever say anything?"

I would explain to Kate in detail when we had the time. For now, it was simpler to say, "From what I've been able to find out, he was working under the direction of a man in Chicago. The day before Sleepy was killed, that federal agent had a heart attack. He was in the hospital for weeks, and he ended up dying. The secret of Sleepy's undercover status died with him."

"Then he wasn't a gangster?" Marianne's suddenly pale face looked terrible against her blue dress. "Then everything in my book, it's all . . . wrong?"

"It's all facts," I reminded her. "And you have a new chapter to write. Thanks to the letters, you've got information that no one else has ever known, not since Carrie Wilder bundled up their love letters and Sleepy's badge and hid them in one of the old storage rooms at the winery." I glanced around at the small crowd. "See, Sleepy really did leave a treasure. The letters and his badge. That was his treasure."

"Letters?" David's mouth puckered. "Not exactly the stuff great stories are made of."

"That's where you're wrong, young man," Luella told him. "I'll tell you what, Bea, that's the most wonderful and romantic story I've ever heard. Imagine, Sleepy and Carrie Wilder. Congratulations, Kate." She put a hand on Kate's arm. "You've not only got a new ancestor—you've got one who's a hero!"

Jacklyn didn't even bother to stifle a yawn. "Terrific little story, but really, we've got a lot to do tonight." She scraped her chair back from the table. "So if this doesn't have anything to do with us—"

"But it does," I told her. "You see, Sleepy has everything to do with Noreen's murder."

What's the old saying about being able to hear a pin drop? I don't know about that, exactly, but I can say that in the silence that descended, I could clearly hear the whoosh of the ceiling fan above my head and the clink of glasses when Aaron poured a couple more beers for the ghost getters and the waitresses delivered them to the tables. I let the silence settle.

"Noreen Turner," I told them all, "was a complete and total phony."

"There's a big surprise," Jacklyn grumbled.

"Not fair." Big points for Liam for defending Noreen's honor. "Okay, so the chick could be annoying—"

"And obnoxious," David added.

"And high-and-mighty," Rick said.

"And as crazy as all get-out," Dimitri said. "But what does that have to do with Sleepy?"

"It has to do with Sleepy because a leopard—or, in this case, a camouflaged ghost getter—doesn't change its spots. Dimitri, you remember how Noreen stole your research for her magazine article—"

"I'll say." Dimitri slugged down the rest of his beer and chinked the empty glass against the table.

"Well, that's the whole point," I told him. "You see, Noreen was exactly what so many of you told me she was. She wanted to make a name for herself in the paranormal world. And she was willing to do anything to do it. Even if it meant stealing the plans for a new piece of equipment and then naming it after herself: the Turner Plasmometer."

"No, no, no!" Liam sat back and crossed his arms over his chest. "That's not possible. I showed you the plans. I told you, they were Noreen's."

"Actually, they were Ted Fywell's." I pivoted just a bit to my right. "Isn't that right, Fiona?"

The kid clutched her hands together on the table in front of her. "I . . . I don't know what you're talking about."

"Sure you do." I glided closer. "Because you know the story of Ted Fywell. The fire at his home a couple years ago . . . You knew about that, right? In that fire, Ted thought he lost the plans for a new invention of his, the Fywell Plasmometer."

Fiona frowned. "Why would somebody lie about a thing like that?"

"There's been a lot of lying going on," I said. "First from Noreen. I think she's the one who stole those plans.

And she set the fire, didn't she, Fiona? So that Ted would think the plans had burned up. Then when word got out that Noreen had produced the Turner Plasmometer . . ."

Fiona dropped her face in her hands, and when she looked up again, her cheeks were stained with tears. "He thought the plans were gone. He didn't think they'd be stolen. Then Noreen took credit and"—she sobbed—"it broke his heart."

"Wait a minute!" Dimitri popped out of his chair. "You mean Noreen didn't invent the plasmometer?"

"The plans should have been your first clue," I told him. "The erasures? The crayon? The spilled coffee? Honestly, do you think Noreen would have let any of that get by her?"

Dimitri's dark brows veed over his eyes. "We just thought—"

"That she was a genius," Liam squeaked. "That's how geniuses work."

"That's how Ted Fywell worked," I told him. "And you knew that, didn't you, Fiona? Just like you knew that Ted committed suicide and it was all Noreen's fault."

"That doesn't mean anything." Her hands flat against the tabletop, Fiona stood. "It's just something I read about. Just something that told me what kind of person Noreen really was. It doesn't mean I did anything. I never even knew Ted Fywell."

I didn't think she'd make this easy.

I reached over to the bar and picked up the picture of Ted Fywell I'd printed from a story about him on the Internet.

"Then explain this." I showed the picture to Fiona, and the ghost getters gathered around to see what I was talking about.

David pointed. "He's wearing Fiona's stone necklace."

"No," I corrected him. "She's wearing his. Because Ted

Fywell . . ." I had other photos, and I passed them around. "In every photo Ted Fywell's taken in the last few years, he's been wearing that gorgeous howlite necklace you have on now, Fiona. That's why you wore it in the first place, am I right? So Noreen would see it. So she would know why you joined the group."

Fiona's shoulders dropped. "She never even noticed."

Dimitri took the photo of Ted out of Fiona's hands. "So what's the story?" he asked. "Fywell and Fiona—there's no connection."

"Do you want to tell them, Fiona?" She clamped her lips shut, so I told them instead. "Fiona kept her original last name, but she was Ted Fywell's stepdaughter. When she realized what Noreen had done, she joined the group and tried to get Noreen to admit that she stole the plasmometer plans. She wanted Ted to get the credit he deserved for the plasmometer. Right, Fiona?"

She nodded, and tears streamed down her cheeks. "I didn't come here to kill her," she sobbed. "But then Noreen . . . Noreen asked me to dress up as Sleepy Harlow and meet her at the winery so we could shoot a phony video. And then Noreen . . ." Her words were nearly lost beneath the sound of her tears. "When we got ready to shoot the video, Noreen said the plasmometer was junk. Junk! It was Ted's dream. He killed himself because she stole the plans and the credit. And Noreen said it was junk. I couldn't help myself. I was so mad. All I could think was that Noreen had ruined Ted's life. And my mother's life. And my life, too. I loved Ted like he was my real dad. And I got so mad, I just picked up that plasmometer and . . ."

She didn't have to finish. I remembered that flash of video I'd seen and the look on Noreen's face right before the plasmometer came down on her head.

Hank moved forward, and I knew he was going to put handcuffs on Fiona. I stopped him with a look. "One more thing," I said. "You had the Sleepy costume. You're the one who we've seen on the island. The headless ghost."

She nodded. "I heard about the legend and the treasure. I thought it was a real treasure, you know. Not just some stupid letters. I thought I could find it, and I figured if people thought there was a ghost, they wouldn't come looking for me."

Levi moved over to stand at my side. "That's why you were on Middle Island that day. That's why you couldn't let us see it was you."

"Yeah," Fiona grumbled.

"But wait!" Chandra had been deep in thought, and now she got up and walked over to where we stood. "Fiona couldn't have done it. She was at my house at the time of the murder. She was playing a CD of chanting and burning incense and—"

When Hank put Fiona's hands behind her back and slapped the cuffs on her, the kid shot Chandra a look that was acid. "Just because the music was playing didn't mean I didn't start the music and light the incense, then leave," she said. "Some people!" She snorted. "Some people believe anything!"

By the time Hank took Fiona away and the ghost getters cleared out to do their Halloween thing, it was late. I promised Marianne I'd bring copies of Sleepy's and Carrie's letters over to her the next morning, and she and Alvin left. Chandra couldn't pass up the opportunity to celebrate her favorite day of the year in proper fashion. She'd brought her witch outfit with her, and her makeup, too, and, gloriously green, she headed to the park for the party and took Kate and Luella with her. I told them I'd catch up to them later and, one by one, blew out the candles on the tables in the speakeasy and told Aaron and his crew they could close up and go to the party, too.

"Good work!" Levi told me when we got outside. "If you hadn't made the Fywell connection, the truth never would have come out."

"I'm glad it did." It was chilly, and I hadn't brought a coat. I chafed my hands up and down my bare arms. "I'm going to go home and change."

"And then come back to the park?"

I would have liked to tell Levi no, but there was a little thread of hope that ran through his words that made the unspoken invitation impossible to resist.

"I'll drive you," he said.

We were quiet all the way home.

"So?" He stopped his Jeep in my driveway and turned to me. "You're lost in thought. Sorry that our Sleepy is as big a phony as the Headless Horseman?"

"Kind of," I admitted. "Not that I ever believed in him or anything. It's just that"—I got out of the car and started for the house, and Levi walked at my side—"it was a great story, wasn't it? And now . . ." The candle in my glowering pumpkin guttered in a cool, sharp breeze. "Well, it's kind of fun to believe in fairy tales, isn't it?"

We climbed the steps. "You can come in," I told Levi. "I'll get a coat and a hat and—"

My attention was caught by movement on the other side of the street, and I stopped and hurried to the porch railing for a better look.

"Do you see what I see?" I asked Levi.

And I knew he did, because he couldn't manage to say a word.

Instead, he slipped a hand in mine, and together, we watched a shadow outlined by the moonlight glinting against the water. It was a man. And he didn't have a head.

"It's just our imagination," I told Levi.

"Absolutely."

"And it can't be real."

"No, it can't," he said.

A moment later, the wind blew and the trees rustled, and the shadow was gone.

Still, we didn't move. We stood there staring at the lake and wondering what we'd just seen.

And Levi kept hold of my hand.

If you enjoyed this book, try a taste of

CHILI CON CARNAGE

The first book in Kylie Logan's
Chili Cook-off Mysteries

*Available in paperback
from Berkley Prime Crime*

❖ 1 ❖

"Who died and left you boss?"

It was one of those what-do-you-call-its, a rhetorical question, so really, Sylvia shouldn't have given me that know-it-all look of hers. Eyes scrunched, head tilted slightly forward, she looked me up and down, and her top lip curled when she said, "Since when does the giant chili pepper get to ask the questions?"

Okay, so I hadn't picked the best of all possible moments to confront her, I mean, what with her wearing crisp khakis and a jalapeño-colored polo shirt with the Texas Jack logo over her heart and me in a giant red chili pepper costume that covered my head and body all the way down past my hips.

She looked neat and professional—as always—with her honey-colored hair pulled back in a ponytail, and far cooler than I was feeling with the sun of a New Mexico

September beating down on me. But hey, Sylvia might be a neatnik and taller than me by a head, but no way was she ever going to look as good as I do in fishnet stockings and stilettos.

Just so she wouldn't forget it, I shuffled said stilettos against the blacktop of the parking lot behind where we'd set up Texas Jack Pierce's Hot-Cha Chili Seasoning Palace. It was the day before the opening of the Taos Chili Showdown and though technically I didn't need the practice, I did need an excuse not to have to help Sylvia stick labels on spice jars. Rehearsing the routine I'd use to attract the crowds that would begin arriving the next morning was as good an excuse as any. While I was showing off my dancing talents (not as artistic as they were enthusiastic), I gave Sylvia the I-have-better-legs-than-you grin. Too bad she couldn't see it, what with my face being covered and all.

"The Chili Chick gets to ask the questions," I reminded her, stopping to catch my breath, "because the Chili Chick is equal partners with you in this little venture. Which means the Chili Chick has equal say. Which means my original question stands. Who died and left you boss?"

Sylvia rolled those sky-blue eyes of hers like she always does when I get the best of her and she refuses to admit it. Which is all the time. "All I did was change the prices on a couple of our most popular products," she said. "All-Purpose Chili Cha-Cha, Global Warming, and—"

"Thermal Conversion. Yeah, I know. You changed the prices. And I didn't know anything about it until I showed up this morning and started setting up the stand. You have an awful short memory, Sylvia. When we took over, we agreed—"

"To make all decisions jointly. Yes, I remember." I

guess that didn't mean she had to like it, because those perfectly bowed lips of hers puckered. "I decided to make the change last night because I was going through the books and realized we were missing out on a gold mine. Those are our biggest-selling items, and by jacking the price up just a tad, we can increase our profit margin by—"

Since she couldn't see me yawn, I made enough noise to let her know what was going on inside my Chili Chick costume.

"See?" She tossed her head. "I knew you wouldn't be interested. Which is exactly why I didn't bother to tell you. Besides, you weren't even here last night." Her lips thinned. "You knew there were seasonings to mix last night, Maxie. Tomorrow's the first day of the cook-off and we always do our best business in the first few hours. But instead of helping, you ran off. With that loser Roberto, right? You left me high and dry and I had to stay up well past midnight. I had to do everything. All by myself."

She was right. I'd bailed. And truth be told, Roberto hadn't been worth it. Not that he wasn't cute. And marginally sexy. It's just that any guy who thinks drinking über-quantities of tequila is the way to a girl's heart isn't exactly my type.

I was actually all set to apologize until Sylvia added a little singsong, "And you didn't come in until what was it, three this morning?"

Apology forgotten, I propped my fists on my hips. Well, not exactly on my hips since my hips were camouflaged by the red chili. "So in addition to being the one who makes the decisions and doesn't tell me, now you're my mother?"

Oh, that stung her. Just like I hoped it would. I knew it for sure because Sylvia's slim shoulders shot back a fraction of an inch and her chin came up. The word *mother* always does that to Sylvia. But then, talking about mothers makes her think of my mother. And thinking about my mother makes her think about how my mother stole her father from her mother.

Got that?

Sylvia and I, see, are half sisters. We share the same father, the aforementioned Texas Jack Pierce, and we have mothers who are as different as . . . well, as Sylvia and I are.

"Not that it's any of your business," I reminded her, "but I happened to have a date last night."

"With Roberto." No one could do a tongue click quite like Sylvia. But then, she had a lot of practice. "I told you when he signed on, that roadie's up to no good. Honestly, I thought you'd be smarter about men. I mean, after All You've Been Through."

The capital letters are my addition, though I swear, if it was humanly possible to speak in upper case, Sylvia would have mastered the skill by now. Like she didn't like talk of mothers in general and mine in particular, I was not exactly thrilled when she dropped the whole All You've Been Through thing.

Which is, of course, exactly why she mentioned it.

"We were talking about you raising prices," I said, and since my teeth were clenched, I hoped she could hear me from behind the red mesh that covered my face so I could see out of the chili and customers couldn't easily see in. "We weren't talking about Edik and what happened back in Chicago."

"No, but maybe we should."

Uh-oh. There it was. That sympathetic look. The tender, understanding voice. Before I could back away, Sylvia grabbed my hand and dragged me closer. She liked to do this when she was playing big sister. Well, big half sister. I liked to resist because, let's face it, she didn't really care. All Sylvia wanted to do was remind me what a mess I'd made of my life back in Chicago. That, and the fact that she'd never in a million years be stupid enough to make the same mistakes I had.

"You've got to work through this problem of yours, Maxie," she insisted, and then before I could point out the obvious fact that there was no problem and, therefore, no chance of working through it, she went right on. "You keep getting involved with guys who are all wrong for you. Obviously Edik—"

"Was hotter than a habanero and great in bed." I knew she'd get all pinch-faced on me when I said this.

Which is exactly why I did.

Sylvia is an attractive woman. When she's not as puckered as a prune. "He also stole how much from you? Fifty thousand dollars? And left your credit rating a shambles. Honestly, Maxie, if you can't see that Roberto's going to do the same thing—"

"He's not. Because I'm not going to give him a chance." This much was true. Rather than admit I'd already decided I was never going out with Roberto again, I added, "Roberto's good for a few laughs. Nothing else."

"Like the nothing else you were doing until three o'clock this morning?"

"Like I said, a few laughs." It was easier than explaining about the tequila and the bar and the fight and the cops. It was also easier than even trying to begin to explain what I knew in my heart: With Edik, I'd learned my lesson. Oh yeah, he was firecracker hot, and as drop-dead delicious as any rock band lead guitarist in the western hemisphere. But Edik was a creep who thought of Edik first, last, and always. I'd caught on a little too late, but believe me, I wasn't going to let it happen again. Because there was no way, no how, I was ever going to let myself fall in love again. Not madly, completely, and totally in love. Not like I'd been with Edik.

"Listen . . ." If I wasn't wearing the Chili Chick costume, I would have scraped a hand through my dark, spiky hair. The way it was, all I could do was pat the side of the giant chili pepper. Something told me it didn't have the same effect, and no way did it express the sort of frustration I always felt when Sylvia pretended that she was the loving big sister (okay, half sister) and I needed her guidance to find my way through the minefield that is my love life. "I can take care of myself," I reminded her.

Her smile was so brittle, I waited to hear the crack. "Yes, and you proved that back in Chicago, didn't you?"

I bit the inside of my mouth. It was that or the long line of vendors around us who were getting their booths ready for the next day's opening festivities would hear a string of profanity hotter than any chili mix in the great state of New Mexico.

"What happened in Chicago was a mistake," I said.

"You admit it?"

"Of course I admit it." My arms stuck out the side of the costume (the better to wave folks toward Texas Jack's stand), and I threw my hands in the air. "What, you want me to say it wasn't? That I liked being taken to the cleaners by the man I loved?"

Sylvia's golden eyebrows dipped over her eyes. "Did you? Love him?" There was that annoying note of compassion again. Like Sylvia might actually know what it's like to get her heart broken. Thirty-two years old and honest, I was pretty sure she was still a virgin. It was the only thing that could possibly explain how tightly wound she was. "I'm sorry, Maxie. I never thought—"

"Whatever." The perfect all-purpose response, and delivered at the right moment, too. The PA system that had been set up in the parking lot of the fairgrounds hosting the cook-off buzzed and crackled, and Bob Tumbleweed Ballew, our organizer and emcee, announced that there would be a vendor meeting that evening precisely at six o'clock. Since there was a vendor meeting precisely at six o'clock the night before every Showdown, it pretty much went without saying, but hey, there wasn't one of us among the couple dozen vendors following the chili circuit who would ever mention it. Tumbleweed liked making announcements, and listening to him was way better than listening to Sylvia. I guess she knew it. She huffed into the Palace.

I decide to practice a little more.

Arms waving, hands beckoning, feet moving to the only routine I remembered from a long-ago tap class that thankfully proved to my mother once and for all that I was not made for the stage, I dance-stepped my way to the front of our booth just the way I would do the next day when the Showdown opened.

"Lookin' good, Chili Chick!" This from Tumbleweed, who came out of the trailer where he and his wife, Ruth Ann, handled all the admin work that went into the Showdown. He stopped long enough to beam a smile at me. "Just you wait until tomorrow. There's not a cowboy in New Mexico who will be able to resist you, sweetheart!"

I didn't take offense. After all, Tumbleweed was at least seventy and I'd known him since back when I was a kid and I spent my summers traveling the chili circuit with Jack (and, unfortunately, with Sylvia, too). In fact, Tumbleweed was Jack's best friend, the one who'd called me when—

Even inside the clumsy costume and standing in the blazing sun, I shivered.

"Hey, not losing heart, are you?" Like I said, Tumbleweed and I had been friends a long time; he knew exactly what I was thinking. He pressed my hand. "We're going to find him, honey."

"I know." I did. Deep down in my heart I knew we were going to locate Jack, who'd been missing for nearly six weeks now. Tell that to the lump of emotion that blocked my throat and made it impossible for me to swallow. "But no one's seen him, Tumbleweed, and—"

He chuckled and waved away my worries as if they were nothing more annoying than the brown ambush bug that flew out of the flowering shrubs near where we were standing and did a flyby between us. "I know Texas Jack and you know Texas Jack." He grinned and winked. "We both know he's got an eye for the ladies and a taste for adventure. He'll be back, honey. And when he is, he's gonna be as happy as a hornet in honey to see what you two girls have done to keep the business going." Tumbleweed slid a look over to the stand where Sylvia was putting the last-minute touches on the catering trailer we hauled around behind our RV.

Not that there was a whole lot to do. The Palace was only seven by fourteen—smaller than a lot of the trailers the other vendors and chili cook-off contestants used. It had a wide concession window at one end and inside, a stove, fridge, worktable, and shelves where we displayed our wares. Jack being Jack, he didn't allow the trailer's small size to stymie business. The Palace was painted chili pepper red and the sign above it—the one that featured Jack's smiling face—was impossible-to-miss yellow with alligator-green lettering. The Palace was flashy. Some people said it was trashy. I thought it was beautiful, and I loved it like no other thing on Earth.

It looked like mind reading went both ways, because as I watched Tumbleweed look over the Palace and Sylvia working away like a busy little beaver inside it, I knew what was on his mind. When I shook my head, the chili costume swayed from side to side. "I just don't get it, Tumbleweed. I know why I'm here."

"Yup." He nodded. "To look for that wandering daddy of yours. And to help forget All You've Been Through, of course."

Did everyone on the cook-off circuit know the pitiful story of my love life?

Tumbleweed ignored my groan. "Hey, I get it. I've fallen in love with the wrong sort a couple times myself." Another chuckle jiggled his ample belly inside the blue Taos T-shirt he was wearing. "Nothing like Texas Jack, of course! It sounds cruel to say he's the type to love 'em and leave 'em, 'cept he really is. When Jack falls in love with a woman . . ." Tumbleweed sighed. "Well, I suppose you've heard it from your mama. When Jack falls in love, that woman becomes his whole entire world. He really does devote himself to her, body and soul."

"Until the next woman comes along." I was long past judging, so I was just reporting facts.

Another laugh out of Tumbleweed. "Your mama never held it against him, though, did she?" He didn't wait for me to answer. He didn't need to. Tumbleweed spit a long stream of tobacco juice on the ground. "Nope, none of them ever did except maybe Norma." He glanced toward where Sylvia was setting out a pile of shopping bags with Texas Jack's face on them. "Always thought Sylvia's mama was too high-strung to be the Chili Chick. After all,

Chick . . ." He gave me a friendly pat on the . . . er . . . chili. "The Chili Chick is a legend on the cook-off circuit. Has been since your daddy thought of her as a way to attract attention and bring in customers. Sylvia's mom . . . the way I remember it, Norma was a last-minute fill-in when the Chick before her found out she was pregnant. Oh, Norma, she could dance passably well. But she never had that right spark. Then when your mama came along . . ." Tumbleweed whistled low under his breath, and I understood why.

In many ways, my mom and I are a lot alike. Except that instead of being cute (oh, how I hate that word!) like me, Pam is drop-dead gorgeous. The story says that Jack took one look at her in those fishnet stockings and lost his heart right on the spot. Too bad he was married to Norma at the time, who was back home in Seattle and heard the news long-distance that he wanted out.

My mom and dad have been divorced going on twenty years, but I thought about the way my mom still looked when Jack's name came up in conversation. Wistful. And about the way Sylvia's mom had looked the one time Jack and I showed up at her door to pick up Sylvia and take her on the road.

To say hell hath no fury was putting it mildly.

I turned to Tumbleweed. "You don't think Norma's still so angry that she might have—"

"Stop that right this instant." He tried for a stern look, but with Tumbleweed, that's always a long shot. I blame his flapping jowls, his too-big ears, and that mile-wide grin that erupts at the most inconvenient times. "You remember what the cops in Abilene said, honey, when I first realized Jack was gone. No sign of foul play. And nothing missing from the stand, so they didn't figure on a robbery. And Jack's things weren't left behind. Wherever he went, he went willingly."

It was what I'd told myself a thousand times since I got the call. Years before, Jack had given Tumbleweed an order: If anything ever happened to him, he was to get in contact with Sylvia and me so we could take over the business.

Take over, we did. Me, because I was convinced if I stayed on the circuit long enough, I'd find out what had happened to Jack. And besides, it didn't hurt that the call came right at the time I needed to get far, far away from Chicago, my broken heart, and the debt collectors who were calling at all hours.

Sylvia . . .

From inside the Chili Chick, I slid her another look and, even though I was sure she couldn't hear me, I leaned closer to Tumbleweed, my voice lowered to a conspiratorial whisper. "Why do you suppose she's really here?"

He sucked on his bottom lip. "I'd like to say it's because she's just as interested in finding Jack as you are."

"Except you know that's not true."

Tumbleweed rocked back on his heels. "Well, she did mention something the other day. Told me she was thinking of writing a cookbook."

This is not as odd as it sounds, since before she got the call about Jack and how we needed to take over the Palace until he returned, Sylvia was a writer for a foodie magazine back in Seattle. "I thought she only ate tofu and weeds."

"And chili, apparently." When he looked Sylvia's way, Tumbleweed's eyes were beady. "Said she's even preparing a special recipe. You know, so that she can enter the contests."

Suddenly, Sylvia mixing up spices the night before

made more sense. "Well, that explains why she was mixing up a batch of chili to bring to the meeting tonight. She's going to use us as guinea pigs, perfect a couple recipes, then when she gets a few wins under her belt, I bet a publisher would pay more attention to her cookbook. Opportunistic little b—"

"Now, now, Chili Chick." Tumbleweed wagged a finger at me. "Don't you go and let that famous temper of yours get out of control. You ain't gonna find Jack if you're so busy fightin' with your sister—"

"Half sister."

He didn't dignify this with a response. In fact, all Tumbleweed did was pull one corner of his mouth into a humorless smile. "Ain't gonna get you nowhere if you two kill each other first."

Murder? One look at Sylvia behind the counter all cool and composed and not sweating from standing in the sun, and I considered the suggestion. But honestly, only for a second. Then again, I saw that she had a case of spice jars to unload, so I got my own little bit of revenge by pretending to be busy practicing my little heart out.

I wonder if I would have kept right on dancing if I'd known that within twenty-four hours, talk of murder would be as impossible to escape as a dose of heartburn after a great big bowl of Texas Red.

M769T0910

M1322AS0514

P.O. 0003490625